The Sight of Her Was Almost Keir's Undoing.

Yes, he told himself, it was her all right. His woman. No, she wasn't his. Not anymore.

The years had wrought no change. Oh, maybe she was somewhat thinner, and there were dark smudges under her eyes that he hadn't remembered. They made her seem more fragile than ever. But her hair was the same. Its fine, silvery strands had always reminded him of trapped moonlight and still did. And the graceful lines of her slender body were unmistakable.

Oh, God, why now? he groaned silently. Why did she have to show up now, just when he had managed to glue himself together and put his life back on track?

Dear Reader:

There is an electricity between two people in love that makes everything they do magic, larger than life. This is what we bring you in SILHOUETTE INTIMATE MOMENTS.

SILHOUETTE INTIMATE MOMENTS are longer, more sensuous romance novels filled with adventure, suspense, glamor or melodrama. These books have an element no one else has tapped: excitement.

We are proud to present the very best romance has to offer from the very best romance writers. In the coming months look for some of your favorite authors such as Elizabeth Lowell, Nora Roberts, Erin St. Claire and Brooke Hastings.

SILHOUETTE INTIMATE MOMENTS are for the woman who wants more than she has ever had before. These books are for you.

Karen Solem
Editor-in-Chief
Silhouette Books

Everything But Time

Mary Lynn Baxter

Silhouette Intimate Moments

Published by Silhouette Books New York

America's Publisher of Contemporary Romance

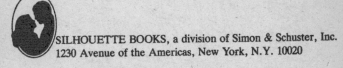SILHOUETTE BOOKS, a division of Simon & Schuster, Inc.
1230 Avenue of the Americas, New York, N.Y. 10020

Distributed by Pocket Books

ISBN: 0-671-52312-0

First Silhouette Books printing November, 1984

10 9 8 7 6 5 4 3 2 1

America's Publisher of Contemporary Romance

Printed in the U.S.A.

Books by Mary Lynn Baxter

Silhouette Special Edition

All Our Tomorrows #9
Tears of Yesterday #31
Autumn Awakening #96

Silhouette Desire

Shared Moments #24

Silhouette Intimate Moments

Another Kind of Love #19
Memories That Linger #52
Everything but Time #74

This book is dedicated
with love
to the faithful customers of D & B Book Store

Chapter 1

The door chimes pealed loudly and insistently.

"Damn," Danielle Davis muttered under her breath, her blue eyes darting from the image in the mirror downward to the gold watch circling her slender wrist. Seven o'clock. It was much too early in the morning for a casual visitor and much too early for bookstore customers, she thought, fighting back the twinge of fear that twisted through her like a dull knife.

The hairbrush slipped from her clammy grasp. It was the clatter of it hitting the glass cosmetic tray that forced Danielle to move. Shaking her head in disgust for letting her imagination run wild, she pivoted on her heels and rushed out of the room, suddenly afraid that the continuing sound of the doorbell would wake up Ann.

She had just stepped on the top step of the carpeted staircase when a chirpy voice called up to her.

"I'm up, I'll see to the door."

Thank goodness for Jusie, Danielle thought as she turned away from the stairs and made her way down a short hall where she paused and poked her head around the door on the right. If it weren't for Justine Evans, who was both friend and housekeeper and at times guardian angel all rolled into one, she would not be able to survive much less work in her bookstore full time or teach night classes at the university.

Danielle tiptoed across the room, coming to stand beside the twin bed and peered down at her two-and-a-half-year-old daughter, Ann, who was sleeping dead to the world.

Looking at her, Danielle marveled anew at how fortunate she was to have been blessed with such a miracle. Tears burned the back of her eyes as she took in the tiny, delicate features: the rose-flushed, heart-shaped face; long, thick eyelashes which fanned over deep green eyes, complementing a perfectly shaped nose and a silky mop of black curls.

Automatically Danielle's finger reached out and captured an errant curl dangling across the tiny forehead and moved it aside. If only she weren't her father made over. . . . No! Don't think like that, she berated herself. Don't think about *him!*

Ann stirred, burying her teddy bear up under her chin. This action brought Danielle out of her wandering thoughts. Sighing deeply, she leaned over and grazed Ann's cheek with her lips before hurriedly exiting the room.

She met Jusie at the head of the stairs.

Her housekeeper's almond-shaped brown eyes were pensive and a frown wrinkled her forehead. "There's a man to see you. If I didn't know better, I'd say he looks like he's one of those FBI agents or Internal Revenue dudes," she whispered conspiratorially, although it was impossible for him to hear their conversation.

Seeing Danielle's face suddenly lose its color, Jusie's frown deepened. "Want me to tell him to get lost?"

Before Danielle had a chance to speak, however, Jusie went on, bobbing her gray curls up and down, "Huh, the way I see it, seven o'clock isn't the time to conduct any business."

Danielle shook her head, making an effort to swallow the lump in her throat. "It's . . . it's all right, Jusie, I'll talk to him. If you'll show him to the office and then get us some coffee, I'd appreciate it." She tried to smile, but it was impossible; her lips were too stiff.

Jusie looked as though she would like to have argued, but seeing the stubborn set of Danielle's shoulders, she thought better of it. Instead she spun around and took her more than ample frame back down the stairs.

Danielle stood for a moment chewing the delicate lining of her lower lip, trying to ease her churning insides. *Cool it, for heaven's sakes! You're making a mountain out of a molehill.* It was probably just a salesman making an early call. Oh, hell, who was she trying to kid? She knew it was no salesman. It was trouble spelled out with a capital T. She might as well go downstairs and face the music. But why now? After all this time.

For the past three years, Danielle's life had settled into a pattern. She loved her work, owning and managing a small but lucrative bookstore across the street from the university campus in the quaint East Texas town of Nacogdoches, Texas. Adding to her pleasure was the convenience of having her business in the same building as her home. By being frugal she had saved enough money to buy an old two-story house and remodel it, making the upstairs into an apartment and the downstairs into a bookstore. It was an ideal setup, allowing her to be close to Ann while she worked.

It was the first time in Danielle's life that she had ever had a home and family. Or had roots. To Danielle, creating a home filled with love and security for her daughter and herself was the most important thing in life. Having been reared in an orphanage with no knowledge of her parentage, she'd had a hard life. She had learned at an early age that she could count on no one but herself. As a result she was fiercely independent and maintained an aloof shell around her which few could penetrate. Now that she had finally attained a happy home atmosphere, she was resentful of anyone or anything that tried to interfere with it.

Smoothing her hands down her corduroy skirt, she breathed deeply and began a slow but determined descent down the stairs. Without hesitation, she twisted the knob and opened the door that screened the stairs leading up to her private apartment. For once she did not pause to glance at the racks of paperback and hardcover books that graced the numerous racks in multicolored splendor. She marched through the maze as though someone had a gun pointed to her head and was threatening to pull the trigger at any given moment.

The door to her office was open. She paused long enough on the threshold to view the tall stranger standing in front of the bookshelves decorating one complete wall of her office. She judged him to be in his late fifties, and he still appeared to be in excellent physical condition. Although he was dressed immaculately, dapper was not the right word because he was too tall and thickset. His hair was slightly gray, but his skin was tanned and healthy as though he kept in shape through rigorous exercising. He was casually thumbing through the pages of a book when he looked up and saw her standing in the door. He seemed to tense, although his ready smile belied this.

"Good morning, Ms. Davis. I'm Tony Welch from the U.S. Marshal Service." In two long strides he was standing in front of Danielle with his hand extended.

Danielle had to squelch the urge to turn and run. But somehow she managed to stand reed straight as his thick fingers made contact with her long slender ones.

Although she tried, she could not disguise the way her nerves were jumping chaotically throughout her system. Her trembling hand spoke for itself. The moment he uttered the words, U.S. Marshal, it was only by a supreme effort of self-discipline that she was able to rigidly brace her sagging body.

She quickly withdrew her hand and linked it tightly with her other one and gave him a plastic smile. "What can I do for you, Mr. Welch?" she asked, knowing that she was being impolite by not asking him to have a seat. But she was not interested in exchanging pleasantries with this stranger. She just wanted him to state his business and get out of her house and out of her life as quickly as he had come into them.

Tony Welch's dark eyes narrowed slightly at her frozen tone, but he smiled, showing uneven teeth through his thin lips. "First of all let me apologize for disturbing you at this ungodly hour of the morning, but when you hear what I have to say, perhaps you'll understand."

Danielle had her doubts, but she kept her face expressionless and moved not one muscle as she waited him out.

He suddenly shifted his gaze away from hers. Danielle followed his eyes as they rested on the gaily striped couch in the corner of the room. He turned back to face her. This time his voice had an exasperated edge to it. "Do you mind if we sit down? What I have to say will take a while."

Danielle felt a heat brush her cheeks at being caught red-handed with her rudeness. Yet she could not bring herself to apologize. "Of course, I don't mind," she said, gesturing toward the comfortable couch. "My housekeeper will be in shortly with coffee." That was as close to an apology as he was going to get, she told herself defiantly.

He smiled. "Thanks. A cup of coffee sure sounds good, especially on such a cold damp morning." He lowered his frame easily onto the couch while unbuttoning his coat, allowing him the freedom to stretch his arm across the back of the cushion. "Does it always get this cold in East Texas?" He smiled again, obviously trying to put Danielle at ease. "It's a helluva lot colder here than it is in D.C."

Danielle worked at making her voice sound normal, but she was afraid that her words came out sounding strained and unnatural. "This . . . this is the first January since I've been here that the weather has been this cold," she murmured tersely.

A silence followed her words.

"The minute I stepped off the plane, the chill cut clear through to my bones," he added, continuing to indulge in meaningless small talk in spite of the edge to her voice.

She nodded stiffly before turning her back and covering the short distance to stand in front of the ceiling-to-floor window behind her desk. For a moment, she watched the barren oak tree limbs bobbing up and down in the blustery wind. The weather was a duplicate of how she felt, she thought, dreary and extremely unsettled.

Suddenly she could not wait another second to find out why this man had intruded upon her life. She was tired of inane chatter; she wanted action.

Twisting around, she began coldly, "Mr. Welch, I'm sure you didn't come all this way just to discuss the weather. So if you don't mind—" She halted in midsentence when she noticed Jusie standing inside the door balancing a tray laden with a coffeepot and two cups and a plate of steaming doughnuts. Although she knew that Jusie's homemade delicacies were delicious, food of any kind was the furthest thing from her mind. Her stomach revolted at the idea.

She flashed Jusie a weak but reassuring smile before quickly introducing Tony Welch. He stood up as Jusie set the tray in the middle of Danielle's desk and smiled at her politely. Jusie then turned to leave, but not before bestowing upon Danielle a questioning look.

"Thanks, Jusie," was all Danielle said to her housekeeper's retreating back before focusing her attention once again on Tony Welch. "How do you like your coffee?" she inquired, stifling the urge to sling the hot liquid in his calm face, only to be suddenly appalled at her vicious thoughts.

Tony Welch sat back, crossing one leg over the other, and watched Danielle. He had not missed the play of disruptive emotions that flickered across her delicate features, but it did nothing to take away from the pleasure of looking at her. He appreciated gentle beauty when he saw it, and Danielle Davis was exceptionally attractive.

She had soft blue eyes; they were a stunning combination with her blond hair and fair skin. In spite of her past and the difficulties she had overcome, they were expressive, very open. The eyes of a woman who had endured the trials of life, yet had not gained much knowledge of it. He could see himself reflected in them as she held the cup of coffee out to him. Suddenly he hated himself and his job for having to bring more pain down on those fragile shoulders. But he had to do it. If not him, someone else . . .

As he reached for the cup, wide blue eyes collided with his. "You're right," he said gruffly, turning away. "I didn't come here to talk about the weather."

"Exactly why did you come?" Danielle demanded quietly while lowering herself into her desk chair where she could keep her gaze pinned to this man who she knew was about to bring fear and uncertainty back into her life.

"You're needed in Washington, immediately," he said without preamble. He tried to ignore the way she flinched as though he'd struck her.

"Go on."

"I'm here to take you back with me, if possible,

today. If not today, then first thing tomorrow morning."

"Why?" The simple word was barely audible.

"The Russian agent that has so effectively and easily escaped the FBI's clutches for the last three years is finally in custody." He paused and eyed her closely. "Or at least we think he is. And that's where you come in. As you well know, you're the only one who can identify the gentleman." The way he sneered the word "gentleman" was not lost on Danielle. "You remain the only link that can tie up this entire nasty mess."

Although her legs felt as though they were made of jelly, Danielle got up out of the chair and stood glowering down at him. Suddenly this nice, soft-spoken man had become her enemy. He was here to pull the rug out from under her well-ordered life, a life that she had paid dearly to obtain. And she had no intention of giving up without a fight.

Dots of color stained each cheek as her eyes bore into his. "Mr. Welch, I . . ."

He held up his hand, aborting her flow of words. "Before you say anything else, I want to assure you that within the next forty-eight hours you will be on a plane on your way back home. And I also want to stress that neither you nor your daughter will be in any danger. You have my word on that."

Danielle did not believe him. Sheer terror had replaced the fear inside her, causing her stomach to churn violently. He had no idea what he was asking. She felt herself begin to slowly unravel on the inside, a feeling she had hoped never to experience again. But this time she would fight them to the bitter end.

Ignoring the silent plea in Tony Welch's eyes, she said coldly, "I'm sorry, but there's no way I can comply with your ultimatum. My daughter is ill with a cold, and I have no one other than myself to operate the bookstore. Plus, I've just begun teaching a class two nights a week at the university." She paused, nervously sweeping a wisp of silky hair off her cheek. "Surely there is another way this can be handled without me having to go to Washington." This time her eyes were pleading with him to understand. And she knew that her voice was heavy with panic, but she could not help it.

"There's no other way. I assure you."

"But couldn't . . . couldn't an artist do a drawing of his face or take a picture of him and let me identify him that way?" She was grasping at straws; she realized that, but she was desperate. She would also do anything to keep from having to take one step away from home.

He shook his head, a regretful look on his face. "I'm afraid not. My orders were to escort you in person and that's what I have to do."

Danielle remained silent, her soft, rounded eyes imploring him to back down even though she was in reality butting her head against a brick wall. When the government had taken over her life three years ago, it had done so with a swift precision. But then they had disappeared, leaving her to live a normal life. Fool that she was, she had begun to think that she would never hear from them again. . . .

"Ms. Davis, surely you want this man behind bars, so you'll be truly free. The last remaining shadow will have then disappeared from your life, and your past will finally be laid to rest." His voice was soft, soothing, yet persuasive. Spoken like a cool professional, she thought, using psychology to get her to do exactly as he wanted her to do.

Danielle swallowed the panic that was threatening to choke her. "All right, Mr. Welch. You win. I'll accompany you to Washington, but I expect you and the rest of your cronies to live up to your end of the bargain."

Tony Welch rose and buttoned his jacket, signaling that the interview was over. "Again you have my word on that, Ms. Davis." He sealed the promise with a tentative smile.

Danielle folded her arms and began rubbing them, trying to circulate the blood through her suddenly stiff limbs. "I'm going to hold you to that promise," she said soberly; yet there was an edge of hostility in her voice that could not be ignored.

"Don't worry, everything will be fine." He paused for a moment. "Just to prove I'm not your enemy, why don't we plan to leave early in the morning instead of today. That should give you ample time to make arrangements regarding your work and your daughter."

She couldn't quite bring herself to thank him, but she did manage to flex her lips into a small smile. "I'll be ready."

He inclined his head before making his way toward the door. He then stopped and turned around. Danielle had not moved. She just stood there staring at him with those haunted blue eyes, looking tragically alone and defeated. He had to squelch the urge to tell her to forget the whole damned mess, that he'd never bother her again. He cursed inwardly before he spoke. "Don't bother to see me out," he said brusquely. "I know the way."

The moment Danielle heard the front door of the bookstore slam, she covered the short distance to the couch and collapsed onto it. Immediately the tears began to flow. She could have stopped breathing more easily than she could have stopped the liquid pain from saturating her cheeks. How could she possibly endure returning to the place that had brought her so much heartache? But then she bitterly reminded herself that she had no say in the matter. The die had been cast a long time ago.

The East Texas day dawned clear and crisp. The moment Danielle opened her eyes to the insistent clamor of the alarm clock, the events of yesterday and the nightmares of today came tumbling down, threaten-

ing to crush the breath from her. Finding the courage to
get up, she flung aside the covers while thrusting to
the back of her mind the heavy sense of dread and
impending doom. Swiftly, she padded to the bathroom.

Thirty minutes later, she was dressed in a milk
chocolate lightweight wool suit with a multicolored
blouse giving the outfit a warm splash of color. But
nothing could overcome the drawn look or the dark
circles that played havoc with her fragile beauty. Danielle eyed her flight bag sitting by the door draped with
her caramel-colored all-weather coat as though it were
an evil object to be shunned. She shivered unconsciously as she walked out of the room, switching off the light
behind her.

She went straight to Ann's room. Thank goodness
her daughter was now sleeping soundly. It had been
after two o'clock before she had gotten Ann to sleep.
She had rocked the fretful child until she was exhausted, both mentally and physically. As she leaned
over now and laid the back of her hand against the
chubby cheek, Danielle was relieved to see that Ann's
fever had broken and that her breathing was almost
back to normal.

She felt Jusie's presence behind her as she laid her
lips against Ann's cool cheek, fighting to keep the tears
at bay.

Jusie laid a comforting hand on Danielle's shoulder.
"She'll be fine."

Danielle turned around and into the arms of her
friend. "I . . . I know," she gulped, wallowing in the
strength of Jusie's hold. "It's . . . it's just that I've
never left her before." She pulled away and blinked
back the tears. "I can hardly stand the thought of doing
so now."

"Don't you worry your pretty head about this child.
You just take care of your urgent business and come
home. You know I love you and Ann more than

anything, that I'd die before I'd let anything happen to either of you."

"I know, and I love you dearly for it too."

Jusie smiled. "Well, let's just say we're both lucky and let it go at that." Then her smile suddenly faded. "That man is downstairs waiting."

They hugged each other again before Danielle turned and walked out of the room without a backward glance, having learned the hard way that it never pays to look back.

It was a solemn-faced Danielle that boarded the plane two hours later at Houston's Intercontinental airport. Tony Welch had opted to rent a car and drive the hundred and eighteen miles to Houston rather than take a small plane out of the local airport. They had made the entire trip in silence. Danielle had been in no mood to talk and had not encouraged him to do so either.

Now as the Boeing 727 sped through the sky, she stared out the window at the white clouds that reminded her of white cotton balls landscaping the heavens. From time to time she was aware of Tony Welch's eyes boring into the back of her head, but she continued to ignore him, fighting to overcome the misery that had a stranglehold on her heart.

"Ms. Davis, would you care for a drink?" The sound of his calm voice forced her to turn around. Both he and a smiling flight attendant were eyeing her intently. The marshal had a canned Coke sitting on the tray in front of him.

Danielle hesitated before answering. "No . . . no, I don't think so. Not now, but thanks anyway." She smiled at the attractive attendant. "Maybe later," she added.

"Are you sure?" Welch asked softly. "Nothing like a caffeine fix to revive the sagging spirits." He grinned, obviously hoping to tease her out of her pensive mood.

But Danielle wasn't buying. She knew that if she accepted a drink, she would be forced to make polite conversation with him, and she did not want to. She wanted to be left alone, to try and stamp out the terrible sensation of impending disaster she felt; to try and make sense of the changes that were taking place.

"I'm sure," she answered at last, feeling his eyes heavy upon her. She turned away.

As if sensing that she was in no mood to talk, Welch shifted in his seat and said, "Maybe a little shut-eye will do us both good, help pass the time."

"Maybe so," she said, fitting her head snugly against the cushioned seat and the wall of the plane and closing her eyes. However, sleep refused to come. Even the steady hum of the plane's engines failed to quiet her jumbled thoughts. Why did her past have to resurface now? she asked herself in silent anguish. Hadn't she suffered enough?

She had worked long and hard to overcome the crippling liability of having been reared in an orphanage. She had been left on the doorstep of the home when she was only a few days old, or so she had been told. Her parents had never been traced. Even though the home had met her physical needs, her mental and emotional needs had suffered.

When she had reached eighteen, she walked out and began working night and day, sometimes doing three jobs to work her way through college. When she graduated, she obtained a job in one of the most prestigious law firms in the D.C. area. A firm which handled top secret government contracts. But after two years with the firm her happiness had skidded to a screeching halt, plunging her into a living nightmare. . . .

"Ms. Davis, wake up, we're getting ready to land."

Suddenly her eyes flew open, and for a moment she searched the cabin of the plane while she groped to get her bearings. Then she heard the low timbre of her companion's voice and her whereabouts came toppling down upon her with a vengeance.

"Are you all right?" he asked soberly, though his brows knitted together showing concern.

Danielle struggled to sit upright, straightening the folds of her pleated skirt as she did so. A fleeting, but reassuring smile briefly flexed her lips.

"Yes, I'm fine. It's been a long time since I slept this soundly." She paused, pushing the silken weight of her hair away from her face in a nervous gesture. "Staying up half the night with my daughter must have taken more of my energy than I realized," she added.

But that was only partly the truth. It was the dread of what she would face today that had kept her eyes wide open after she had put Ann to bed. Just the thought of having to look at the Russian agent again, even through a screening room, made her blood run cold. However, she did not want this stranger to know how she felt. She had already lowered her guard and let him see how frightened and uneasy she was. She did not want or need his pity. She was perfectly capable of handling it alone. That was one aspect of her life that had not changed, would never change. Loneliness remained her silent companion.

"Ms. Davis, isn't that great." Again Tony Welch's voice pulled her out of her gloomy thoughts just as the giant plane made rough contact with the runway and ground to a halt.

With clammy hands, Danielle unfastened her seatbelt. "I'm . . . I'm sorry, I wasn't paying attention."

Tony Welch smiled. "The pilot just announced the sun is shining brightly. Maybe that's a good omen." He paused slightly before adding, "For both of us."

"I hope you're right," she said softly, but the tension in her voice mocked her words.

It was time to go. She could not postpone it any longer. Slowly she rose, and stepping in front of Tony

Welch, she began her slow descent down the crowded aisle.

With each step she took, however, her nervousness increased. Oh, God, she thought frantically, could she muster the courage to set foot on Washington soil? It had been so long. There were so many memories.

Suddenly she stopped, unable to go on. She gripped the handle on her overnight bag until she felt the leather cut into the soft flesh of her hand.

"It won't be long now and it'll all be over." Tony Welch's reassuring voice prodded her into instant action.

Somehow she managed to regain her composure to get out of the plane into the waiting government car. Neither spoke as the driver sped away from National Airport and merged into the traffic. The sounds and smells of the city permeated her senses as they sat in silence while the driver maneuvered the nondescript vehicle the fifteen miles from the National Airport, across the bridge and into the downtown area. Nothing had changed, she noticed as they eased past the impressive Lincoln Memorial and the enduring Washington Monument before turning onto Constitution Avenue.

There was a time when she truly loved the multi-cultured city with its beehive of activities, all centered around the hustle bustle of making this country function as a united nation.

But the only emotion she felt now was one of emptiness. All the glamor and hype meant nothing. Instead her mind was filled with getting this ordeal behind her as quickly as possible and returning to the quiet sanity of her uncomplicated lifestyle.

Why, then, she wondered, was she plagued with the nagging doubt that her life was about to make another ninety degree turn?

Marshal Luke Cassidy's office was on the fourth floor of the district court building. Two entire floors were occupied by the U.S. Marshal Service, for which he was totally responsible.

Cassidy's desk was facing the window so that the panorama of the great city moved constantly before him. He found the scene below him powerful food for thought: Aesthetically he loved it for its typical mixture of beauty and ugliness. The city, reflecting the harsh bright sky above, its outer boundary cut by jagged horizons of tall buildings, the glimpse of trees, was part of the reason he loved this job, accepted so readily the tremendous burdens that rested on his thin shoulders.

But today he wasn't feeling so proud. For a little of nothing, he'd chuck the whole thing and walk out without a backward glance. He had spent an hour studying the file on Danielle Davis, refreshing his memory about this woman who in the last three years had been left alone to continue her life in a normal fashion.

The only significant change during that time was the birth of her daughter, born seven months after she came under that their protection. She had refused to answer questions concerning the birth. And they had not pressed her to do so. As long as circumstances, whatever they were, posed no threat to her safety, his office did not interfere.

It was unfortunate for her that things had to change.

With a sigh, Cassidy closed the file before glancing sideways at another file lying inches away. Just looking at the words "Confidential—Top Secret" stamped on the front caused his blood to boil. "God-damned incompetence," he mumbled aloud, looking down at his watch. It was one-thirty; she should be there any moment.

Suddenly the buzzer on his desk announced both Welch and Ms. Davis.

Cassidy buzzed back. "Send them in."

When she entered his office, he hastily circled the desk, his hand held out to her, a tall, neat man, with a thin Irish face and dark brown eyes, a mop of curly hair clipped short and combed back from his face, the air of authority prevalent.

"Good afternoon, Tony. Ms. Davis. Have a seat, won't you?"

He hadn't remembered her being so pretty. Had she always had that stunning silver blond hair and those beautiful blue eyes? They pierced his heart when she looked at him.

"Do you smoke?" he asked, reaching in his left suit pocket for a pack of cigarettes.

"No, thank you," she said politely.

He noticed that her hands were shaking.

"Tony, I know you've got things to do. I want to speak to Ms. Davis alone. I'll send for you later."

"All right, sir," Tony Welch said, speaking for the first time. Then he turned to Danielle. "I wish we could have met under happier circumstances." A sad smile touched his lips. "If I don't see you again, good luck."

Danielle watched him go, suddenly wishing that she could follow him. There was something about this room, this man . . .

"Ms. Davis, I've never been one to beat around the bush or take up one's valuable time with senseless babbling, so I'll speak bluntly." He sat down and then leaned forward, looking at her, a hard glint reflected in his eyes. "Unfortunately there's been a change in plans."

For a moment Danielle's eyes brightened. "I'm . . . I'm afraid I don't understand." Dare she hope that this ordeal would be over before it had even begun?

He made a savage gesture. "Of course, you don't. And the hell of it, I don't either. But due to circumstances beyond my control, the Russian agent is no longer in the FBI's custody." His mouth had tightened into a bitter line.

"In that case," Danielle said, staring at him," . . . in that case, Mr. Cassidy, what am I doing here?"

"I wasn't informed of this until you and Welch were boarding the plane. Shortly before you came in, I was going over the details of what happened yesterday," he added tersely.

She lifted a hand to her throat. "Where . . . where does this leave me?"

"Here, I'm afraid."

For a moment there was a long silence.

"No!" She shrank back a little, away from him. She didn't want to listen to him anymore. Staying was an impossibility; there was no point in discussing it.

"There's more," he continued bluntly.

"Please don't." Danielle made a movement as if she were going to leave.

"Ms. Davis." The firm tone of his voice stopped her cold. "We have strong reason to believe that your cover has been blown, that the agent and his counterpart can identify you."

Danielle's bag clattered to the floor. She turned so white that Cassidy bounded out of his chair, afraid for a moment that she might collapse. He bent down and gave her back her purse before placing a hand on her shoulder.

"I'm sorry," he said. "I know how you must feel. It's a damned mess."

"It can't be true," she whispered. "It just can't be true."

"I've got the proof right here—in this folder." He picked up the manila envelope and slapped it against his leg before pitching it back on his desk. "But we know that Letsukov is still in the D.C. area. Our security has been so tight, there's no way out. We've tied up all the mass transportation routes as well as launching a full-scale manhunt for him and his partner, a man by the name of Zoya." His eyes glistened dangerously. "It's only a matter of time before we have them both under wraps."

"Oh, my God," Danielle whispered, sinking forward, as the blinding tears came with a rush. "What about . . . my daughter? Is—is she in danger, too?"

"No, absolutely not. But to alleviate any concern on your part, we're sending a deputy marshal to stay with your child and housekeeper until this mess is cleared up."

In spite of Danielle's effort to hold her chin steady, it began to wobble again uncontrollably. "Please . . . can't I just go home?" Her face was whiter than tissue paper.

Cassidy did not move. He waited, letting her cry. If she didn't, he was positive that she would have fainted.

After she had composed herself somewhat, Cassidy went on, "I understand how you feel, but it's imperative that you remain under tight security until the Russians are apprehended."

"No!" She shivered, trying to pull her coat closer. She felt cold, as if all the windows in the room were open.

Cassidy acted as though she hadn't spoken. "Our top man is on his way up now. You'll be under his protective custody in a retreat in the mountains of Virginia while the FBI is combing the area." He paused significantly. "Will you cooperate?"

Danielle looked directly at him; her eyes were swollen, her makeup smudged. She looked ill. "Do I have a choice?" she demanded bitterly, before getting up and walking dejectedly to stand in front of a window.

"No," Cassidy said to her back. "I'm afraid you don't. But I can promise you we'll—" He paused, the insistent knock on the door claiming his attention.

"Come in," he bellowed.

Danielle heard the door open but didn't turn around.

"Dammit Cassidy, I told you to get someone else for this assignment!"

Suddenly every muscle in Danielle's body froze. She felt as though her whole body had been immersed in freezing water.

She would recognize that voice anywhere, even though it had been over three years since she'd last heard it. Oh, God, no! It couldn't be. Surely it wasn't Keir McBride, the only man she'd ever loved.

For a split second, she did not think she could move. Then on legs barely supporting her, she turned around, positive that her exhausted mind had failed her. . . . But it hadn't. Eyes that were the exact replica of her daughter's stared back at her.

He stood tall and stiff, disturbingly unfamiliar, yet achingly familiar.

Then his harsh words effectively sliced the silence. "Dammit to hell, Cassidy, what kind of game are you playing? This woman's not Danielle Davis, she's Erin Richards!"

Chapter 2

KEIR MCBRIDE MADE IT HIS BUSINESS ALWAYS TO BE IN control of any and every situation. Vietnam had taught him that—the hard way. He could break a man's neck with his bare hands; he could walk for miles with almost no water and no food; he could adjust to scorching heat and bitter cold. He was an expert with weapons. He was a natural marksman.

In Washington, he was known to be a silent man, too silent, one who rarely smiled. He was widely envied and respected but not well liked. His skill with a rifle and his accuracy with a pistol had earned him a top-seated position in the agency.

When a job reeked of danger, he was their man. His rise in the ranks of the U.S. Marshal Service had been swift and sure. He had gained the reputation as being tough as nails and always in charge. There was nothing he couldn't handle.

But the office staff and field investigators would be astonished if they could see him now. The sight of this woman was almost his undoing.

29

Although he continued to stand as if cast in concrete, his green eyes narrowed into tiny pinpoints of steel as they categorized everything about her.

Yes, he told himself, *it's Erin all right. His Erin. No, goddammit, she's not your Erin. Not anymore. She's your past. Natalie's your future. Remember that!*

The years had wrought no change. Oh, maybe she was somewhat thinner, and there were dark smudges under her eyes that he hadn't remembered. They made her seem more fragile than ever. But her hair was the same. Its fine silvery strands had always reminded him of trapped moonlight and still did. And the graceful lines of her slender body were unmistakable, the way her blouse outlined the gentle curves of her breasts . . .

Oh, God, why now? he groaned silently. Why did she have to show up now just when he had managed to glue himself back together and put his life back on track?

When he had discovered that she was missing, he had reacted like a madman. He'd hired the best private detective in the area to track her down. Nothing. She had vanished as though the earth had opened up and swallowed her, leaving a dead silence and a hole in his heart as big as the Grand Canyon.

And now here she was standing before him in the flesh, looking cool and composed and lovely as ever, even in the face of danger. Damn her to hell! Suddenly, a new surge of anger tore through his jagged nerves, sending his temper to the explosive point.

"McBride, sit down," Luke Cassidy barked, effectively slicing into the heavy silence. "If you'd read her god-damned file, you'd know what was going on." Then his eyes narrowed shrewdly, not missing a second of the scene being acted out before him. "I won't take the time to find out how you two knew each other. That's not important now. But what *is* important is getting Ms. Davis out of the Washington area."

By sheer force of will Keir removed his eyes from Danielle's face whose composure was no longer intact; her mouth was slightly open now and her eyes were glazed with shock. He turned toward his boss, his eyes like cold chips of ice. "Who the hell had a chance to look at a file? I was told to report immediately to take a top priority assignment. I was given the bare facts and nothing more. If you'll remember correctly, you promised me two weeks off." He paused. "And if you'll also remember, I was to have gotten married this week."

Another profound silence settled over the room, leaving each occupant stranded to cope with tangled thoughts and emotions. It was almost as if they were puppets dangling from a string, only to have the string suddenly break, leaving their thoughts scattered in different directions.

Cassidy actually looked disconcerted. "Er . . . sorry about that, my boy, but I needed you to handle this case. I promise I'll make it up to you and Natalie when we have that Russian bastard back in our clutches." He almost smiled. "I'll even throw in the champagne. How's that for a bonus?"

Danielle could not head off the horrified moan that escaped through her trembling lips. She clawed at the air for her next breath.

The shock of learning that her life was in danger on top of having Keir walk through the door after three years, only to brutally announce his wedding plans, was too much. Questions with no answers began swirling around in her head, making her feel dizzy and disoriented. Surely Keir McBride, the rich playboy and the only son of a renowned senator could not be a U.S. Marshal? It was ludicrous! Unbelievable!

She had reconciled long ago that she would never lay eyes on this man again. After all, wasn't she a totally new person with a new name, a new life, a new identity? Chances of their paths crossing were one in a million. How could fate play such a dirty trick on her after all she had been through?

While she was still reeling from the possible repercussions of those unanswered questions, the vision of Ann's tiny face leapt in front of her face. *Oh, God,* she whimpered in silent agony, *the baby. Their baby!*

Suddenly the room began to spin as the floor raced up to meet her. "Oh, God . . ." she said again, fighting the black void that was closing in around her.

"Dammit, man, she's fainted!" Cassidy's voice thundered through the room just as Danielle's body made contact with the carpet.

Although Keir was the first to reach her, it was Luke Cassidy who lifted her slight frame into his arms and carried her to a small couch in the corner of the room.

Keir stood transfixed, his eyes locked on Danielle's lifeless form, his own breathing coming in short gasps while his heart was pounding violently. What the hell was the matter with him? Suddenly out of the blue the truth reached out and slapped him in the face. *You're afraid to touch her, you bloody fool!*

Gut-wrenching fear surging through him kept him immobile. Suddenly he saw the entire situation slipping beyond his control. The thought of being cooped up with her for days, maybe weeks . . . Oh, God, it didn't bear thinking about. Luke would just have to replace him, that's all. Sweat popped out on his face as he looked down at her still form, her hair spread like silver thread over the cushion.

"McBride, for chrissakes, buzz Amy and tell her to get in here pronto with coffee and a brandy. And tell her no calls. I don't want us disturbed."

Cassidy's order yanked Keir out of his stupor. Glad to have something constructive to do, he jammed a finger down on the buzzer and in a clear authoritative tone gave the secretary the message. It seemed only a matter of minutes before she was coming through the door.

Danielle was beginning to come around when she felt someone touch her shoulder. It was a light hand, not the heavy hand of Cassidy, nor Keir's gentle one. She would have known Keir's touch anywhere, anytime. . . . She shivered and raised her glazed eyes upward. A girl was beside her, holding a glass in one hand. She had a pleasant face, with curly brown hair and a calm voice.

"Drink this," the voice suggested. "It'll make you feel better." Danielle did as she was told, feeling the fiery liquid scald her stomach. Gradually the tension began to ease. She noticed with relief that she had been left in peace. Immediately she began pulling herself back together, soothing her tumbled curls back into order and adjusting her skirt. Cassidy was sitting at his desk shuffling through papers, and Keir was standing with his back to her, staring out the window.

Her eyes flickered to Keir. She could see the display of muscles as he held himself stiff and straight as an arrow. God, what an impossible situation. He hated her, she knew that. And she didn't blame him. But then she wasn't without her own bitter memories, either.

Why then did she have the sudden urge to dart across the room and fling herself in his arms and beg him to hold her, to tell her everything was going to be all right? Of course, that was impossible. It was over between them. However, she did not regret it. Could not regret it. Because of Ann. The only good that had come out of their affair was the perfect child they had created. Again she was blinded by sheer mindless terror. What would Keir do if he ever found out about Ann? He must never know. . . .

"Ms. Davis, are you feeling better now?"

Cassidy's level voice claimed her attention, drawing her up with a start. "Yes . . . yes, I'm fine now, thank you."

"Are you up to traveling?" he asked.

Taking his gaze off Danielle, Keir swung around on his heels, his eyes zeroing in on his superior. "Replace me, Luke," he clipped savagely. "Get someone else to take care of . . . Er . . . I mean . . . "

"Dammit, man," Cassidy growled, "her name's Danielle. Danielle Davis. Don't forget that again. Surely I don't have to remind you how dangerous a slip like that could be?" Luke Cassidy had a way of spitting out words as though they were bullets.

Keir's tanned skin turned a shade paler, indicating his superior's words had hit their mark; but again his gaze returned to Danielle.

Luke Cassidy's eyes narrowed as they bounced back and forth between Danielle's pale figure and Keir's grim, unyielding one. "As I said before, I don't know what the hell's going on with you two. And furthermore I don't give a damn. But what I do give a damn about is Ms. Davis's safety." His eyes shifted to Keir. "You're the best man for the job. It's that simple. And I have to think I can depend on you to put personal feelings aside and do what you've been trained to do." He paused. "And haven't I already promised that when this is all over, I'll personally guarantee you get your time off?"

Keir felt himself drowning, but he was determined not to go under without a fight. "What about Tanner?" There was desperation underlying his words.

"Tanner's out of the question." Although Cassidy's voice had not risen one iota, it was nevertheless encased in steel. His mind was made up.

"Don't I have anything to say about this?" Danielle chimed in softly, turning troubled eyes squarely on Luke Cassidy's face. "After all, it's my life that's in danger."

Cassidy frowned, but his eyes softened considerably. "I'm afraid not, Ms. Davis. Believe me, I have your best interest at heart. And Marshal McBride is the best we have. I'm afraid you two are stuck with each other for the time being anyway." This time his voice brooked no argument. The subject was closed.

If it would have done any good or accomplished anything, Danielle would have simply sat there and cried for the injustice of it all. But tears no longer came easily to her, not those kinds of tears. Self-indulgent antics were for the weak. She had never been able to afford that luxury; it was too late to start now.

So instead of crying, she stood up and squared her shoulders as though the weight of the world rested on them. "If . . . if you don't mind, I'd like to go someplace private and make a telephone call."

"By all means," Cassidy said. "I'll have my secretary take care of it."

With each step she took toward the door, Danielle could feel Keir's eyes boring into the back of her head. In her mind's eye she could see his fierce eyebrows clamped together at a savage angle and his lips thinned to an almost invisible line. The total picture bore the distinct stamp of cold hostility.

She just prayed that she would make it to the door and out before her legs caved in beneath her. . . .

The snowflakes were spiraling downward from the azure sky, their different sizes and shapes giving the early afternoon an ethereal quality that no artist, no matter how talented, could capture on canvas. But Danielle was oblivious to the haunting beauty of the winter day. She was too caught up in her own misery.

She was sitting beside Keir in a blue unmarked Chevrolet on their way to the undisclosed destination in the mountains of Virginia. She had noticed vaguely that Keir had taken Route 7 out of the city; beyond that she knew nothing.

They had gotten off later than planned, but they'd had to wait for Cassidy's secretary to go shopping and buy Danielle several more articles of clothing. Also Keir had had to make arrangements for the heat to be

turned on in the cabin and food to be delivered. She
was aware of him with every fiber of her being. His
physical presence was too positive to ignore. His massive body filled the seat to suffocation; he smelled of
the strong brand of cigarettes he smoked. His hand on
the steering wheel was veined and powerful. Hands
that had transported her to the heights of passion and
beyond time after time. Her eyes fluttered shut against
the blinding pain of those memories. She sat carefully
so as not to touch him.

She shuddered just thinking about the moment in
Cassidy's office when Keir had walked into the room.
How she had managed to hold herself together was
beyond her. Even now she could still hear the violent
curses that had followed her out the door and into the
adjacent room where she had phoned Jusie and explained her change of plans.

Jusie had been upset, but had assured Danielle that
everything would be fine, that Ann was fine but missed
her mommie. Having to explain the presence of a U.S.
Marshal invading their home had been a different
matter altogether. Finally, however, she had convinced
Jusie that it was just a precaution and nothing more.
And she had prayed that it was true.

But convincing Jusie had in no way equaled the
contempt that had oozed from Keir's eyes when he had
come upon her and had demanded in a terse voice,
"Finish your call and come on. It's time to get the hell
out of here."

Those had been the only words he had spoken to her,
and they had been traveling now for about fifteen
minutes.

With a sigh, she sat forward and began pulling off her
coat. It was stifling in the small car. Suddenly a hand
shot out behind her and latched onto the collar of her
coat while she struggled out of it. She kept her gaze
averted, but she felt rather than saw him flinch as his
arm grazed her breast.

After that he moved very little. Her imagination might be running away from her, but it seemed as if he'd rather be uncomfortable than shift his body against hers.

She had a ridiculous impulse to burst into tears; it was like a nightmare. It couldn't be happening to her. For she had known the minute she saw him, even after three long years, that she had never gotten him out of her system. He had left a mark on her, a mark that had dulled, but never quite been erased over the years. But she must never allow him to know this. She must keep her guard up at all times. Because nothing had changed —their being together was still an impossible dream.

A brittle silence had settled between them, stretching her nerves to the breaking point. She knew that it would take only one word and the quiet would explode in their faces.

Against her better judgment, she ventured another look in his direction. Time had definitely wrought a change in his physical appearance, she thought. He had aged; gone was the flippant, happy-go-lucky charm that had amused her so easily—an emotion that up until she had met him was a rarity for her. Amusement was an underused commodity at the orphanage.

But now it seemed as though *his* face would break if he smiled. The grooves around his mouth were deeply carved, meant to endure. But the craggy imprint of his face that had been written on her brain with indelible ink was no different: the strong defiant chin, square jaw, the black unruly hair now interwoven with silver threads were unchanged. And those same startling green eyes still had the power to drive through her, straight to her soul.

If one were to consider his features separately, he wouldn't even fall in the category of nice looking, much less handsome, but the combination made him potently attractive. And with his tall, ruggedly built body, he radiated a male grace that few men could boast.

Yes, three years had changed him physically, but everything else was the same, she reminded herself bitterly. He was still the wandering nomad, flitting from one dangerous job to another, placing his life on the line daily. But then she remembered that at least in one respect he had changed—he was planning to get married. She couldn't help but wonder if his fiancée had the power to change him, to make him settle down where she had not.

"Why didn't you come and ask me for help?"

Danielle was shocked by his unexpected and startling question. She answered before she thought.

"Hah! How could I when I didn't even know where you were?" she choked. "If you'll think back a moment, you'll remember that you were off on another of your jaunts, taking care of, and I quote, 'important business.'" She made no effort to mask the sarcasm that punctuated each word she flung at him. Nor could she ward off the stinging sensation behind her eyes. Damn him! *This is an impossible situation,* she told herself frantically, *and getting worse with each twist and turn of the mountain road.*

Keir sighed deeply, seeing the rage in her face and the way she was trembling. Suddenly he had the urge to pull the car off the road and haul her into his arms and whisper in the delicate folds of her ear that everything was going to be all right, that he'd take care of her, that nothing or no one would ever hurt her again.

Damn, he was sweating. And in the dead of winter, too. He gripped the steering wheel until his knuckles began to turn white and he began to lose the circulation in his hands. *You ass, McBride! Where's your god-damned pride? Stop thinking about the way her mouth tasted when it hungrily searched for yours or the way her breasts filled your hand . . .*

She was not for him. She hadn't wanted him the first time around, so what made him think she'd want him now? It was over. Finished. He must think about Natalie. Damn, why couldn't he get his head on straight before something happened that he would regret for the rest of his life?

But before he could do that, he knew that he had to hear her side of the story from her own lips. He'd force her to tell him if he had to.

Keir rubbed his hand wearily across the back of his head. "Would you mind giving me the details?" he asked soberly. "I only know what Tanner told me when he summoned me to Cassidy's office this morning, and that wasn't much, just the hard cold facts and he showed me pictures of the Russian agents. It was enough to allow me to do my job and nothing more. Of course, he assumed I'd either read or would read your file."

Danielle was aware of what it had cost him to bury the hatchet for a moment and talk civilly to her. Even some of the inner tension seemed to have drained from him, she thought. His jaw was less rigid and his eyes were no longer shooting sparks at her.

"Oh, Keir, I don't know," she said, experiencing another jolt of raw panic. "I'm not sure I can even talk about it."

"Please try," he encouraged lightly.

"I . . . I still have terrible dreams, awful nightmares about that horrible day." She twisted her hands together. "I . . . I just don't think I can talk about it. . . ."

He stared at her broodingly, remembering his own trauma, how he had nearly gone berserk when he found out she was missing. "Please," he said simply.

A deep sigh shook her slender frame. "Why are you making me do this?" She looked down at her fingernails and then up at his face, noticing for the first time a tiny scar at the corner of his right eye. Even at a distance she could see the way the flesh was roughly drawn together. Just another battle scar, she thought harshly. "It . . . it won't change things, my explaining, that is."

"I know," he answered bleakly, "but at least it will clear a few things up in my own mind." A muscle in his jaw began to jump, and suddenly she knew that he had reverted to his old hostile self.

Although her tongue felt weighted with lead, she decided that she had nothing to lose by telling him the whole terrifying story, except maybe make her night-mares more real, more intimidating. "I . . . I had decided to stay and work late," she began, her voice low and shaky, "the night after you . . . you stormed out of my apartment."

She kept her head averted, not wanting to see the dark cloud that she knew would have settled over his face at the mention of that night. "I . . . I didn't know it at the time, of course, but no one knew I had planned to stay after hours. Anyway, I was on my way to the office of my boss, John Elsworth, to get a file. I had just turned the corner and was getting my file key out of my pocket when I heard muffled voices. I looked up and saw that Elsworth's door was open." She paused and closed her eyes fully for a moment, her long lashes throwing a veil over her cheekbones.

"Go on," he prodded, afraid that she wasn't going to continue.

Her eyes opened gently, though she still did not look at him. "I took a couple of hesitant steps up to the door and was about to knock and let my presence be known when I . . . I heard Mr. Elsworth say and I quote: 'This highly classified information was just sent over this morning. It's hot stuff and your government had better be willing to pay through the nose for it.' End of quote. As you can well imagine, I was horrified. I couldn't have moved even if I'd had a block of dynamite planted under my feet. But I must have gasped aloud, because both men whirled around and saw me staring at them, a terrified expression on my face. The . . . the last thing I remember before turning and tearing back down the hall was the murderous glint in both their eyes.''

She paused again, this time to try and control the violent tremor that was raking her body. For a moment, she thought she might be sick. How humiliating if she had to ask Keir to pull off the road.

But her instant pallor was not lost on him. Suddenly he hated himself for putting her through this, making her dredge up the past. Damn, but she must think him an inhuman bastard, or worse, he thought angrily. And in this instance, she wouldn't be far from wrong.

Danielle suddenly pressed her hands against her stomach and sucked her breath deep into her lungs. Cold sweat doused her body. She forced herself to concentrate on the steady hum of the engine, hoping it would lull her stomach back to normal. But luck was not with her. Keir began to glide the Chevrolet around a hairpin curve and by the time the road had straightened out, it was too late. Her insides were churning upside down. "Keir . . . I'm . . ."

Glancing up and into the rearview mirror to check the traffic, he nosed the car across the highway and onto the shoulder, bringing it to a dead stop, loose gravel flying under the wheel. Then as quick as lightning, Keir's arm shot across her and yanked open the door.

The cold mountain air slapping Danielle in the face did nothing to stop her from losing the contents of her stomach. A short time later she sat up and lobbed her head back against the seat in silent agony, unable to gather her scattered wits together. Too many things had happened in too brief a period, and she was exhausted.

Although he never said a word, Danielle felt him slide across the seat and suddenly stop within a hair's breadth of her. Instantly her heightened senses were aware of him. She could feel his warm breath misting

her face as the elusive smell of his cologne wafted by
her nostrils. If she so much as moved at all, their thighs
would have adhered to one another.

For a breathless moment, there was a stifling, agoniz-
ing silence.

Danielle did not move, did not breathe.

"God, I'm sorry," he groaned, taking in the chalky
white skin and the way her thick lashes clumped
together into wet little spikes. He held his body as tight
as a guitar string, crushing the desire that threatened to
erupt within him. It was happening all over again. She
was bewitching him. But he couldn't move, no matter
how much he wanted to. He was drowning in the
sensations of her.

The awareness seemed to stretch between them like
a silent scream.

As though pulled by a force beyond her control, she
glanced up at him, her eyes round and shadowed, her
lips so stiff she could barely speak. She ran her tongue
over them and said, "I'm sorry . . . if I disgusted you."
Her voice was just above a whisper.

His eyes were dark and probing. "Disgusted me? I
don't think anything you could do would disgust me."

Danielle's eyes widened further. Had she heard him
correctly? Suddenly another surge of panic rushed
through her. She was insane to allow her emotions to
get out of control. There was too much at stake. But
oh, God, every bone in her body ached for his touch. It
had been so long . . .

Unconsciously she moved. She would shrink away
from it all, just as some blossoms fold and close at
darkness. It was the only way she could cope. . . .

He sensed her withdrawal. He could not control the
harsh breath that ripped through his lungs. "Don't be
alarmed," he ground out harshly. "I wasn't going to
touch you." He was surprised to find that he was
trembling, and cursed himself for allowing her to get
under his skin.

Danielle shook her head. "I'm not alarmed," she murmured softly, but the moment was shattered, never to be recaptured.

There was another long silence as Keir abruptly returned to his side of the seat and flipped the ignition switch, gunning the engine into full power. His face once again looked as though it were hacked out of stone.

Danielle did not know how long they traveled before his cool voice penetrated her numbed senses. "Are you up to finishing your story?" he asked without looking in her direction.

"Yes," she replied dully, breathing deeply, wanting to put this horror show behind her as quickly as possible. "I don't remember ever having been so frightened in my life"—*except when I was having your child all alone,* a hyper little voice inside her head whispered—"as I was when I grabbed my purse and raced out of the building only minutes ahead of Elsworth. I jumped in the nearest taxi and told him to take me to an out-of-the-way motel. There I registered under a fake name and bolted myself in the room. I never stopped pacing the floor the entire night. I was terrified."

She paused a brief second and worried her bottom lip with her teeth. "Every time I heard the slightest noise, I just knew it was Elsworth coming after me. The next morning I went straight to the FBI's office without returning to my apartment. I knew if I didn't, my life wouldn't be worth a nickle."

"Did you have any trouble getting them to believe you?"

"I couldn't believe my luck. As you well know, Elsworth was a powerful man. It was a known fact he had several senators in his hip pocket. But after spilling my story, they informed me that Elsworth had been under surveillance for months on suspicion of espionage for selling high technology secrets and endangering the security of the United States and that my secret testimony to the grand jury would put both him and the Russian agent, Letsukov, behind bars for life.

"However, the Russian managed to elude the FBI and suddenly my life was in immediate danger. After that, it was a living hell." For a moment her voice faltered. She pressed her knees together to stop their shaking. But it made the shaking worse. "I decided to cooperate with the FBI and the U.S. Marshal's office, agreeing to disappear with a new identity: a new name, a new job and a new place to live."

Keir knew that he had pushed her to the limit. Pain and despair were written into the delicate lines of her face. "God, Erin . . ."

"Don't call me that," she hissed, swinging around to face him.

"Old habits die hard," he said harshly.

"Tell me about it," she countered.

"Why didn't you call me?"

She laughed without mirth. "I picked up the phone and was going to do just that when I remembered you were gone."

"Dammit, you could have at least gotten in touch with me later and told me what had happened."

"Why?"

"Goddammit, you know why!"

"It was over between us, remember? You had slammed out of my apartment the night before."

"Only because you all but kicked me out." His jaw was clenched to the breaking point. "God, you have no idea what my life was like when you disappeared without a trace. I was a raving lunatic when you couldn't be found. I couldn't imagine what had happened to you, where you'd gone. And your tracks were so damned well covered. I thought it was because of me. In spite of the hellacious row we'd had, I called you the moment I got back to the states." He ignored her whimpered cry and went on, "I was convinced we could work something out."

"Why are you telling me this now?" she cried, turning away from him, her shoulders shaking. "It's. . . too late." She paused, tugging painful fingers through her hair. "We. . . we can never go back," she added in a whisper.

Although their relationship had been doomed from the start, it was only during the times she spent locked in his arms that she experienced life at its finest. He had courted her, wooed her and, above all else, had taught her how to love. And when they parted, he had taken a portion of her heart with him.

After a short pause, Keir said, "When the detective I hired was unsuccessful in tracking you down, I chucked everything, and went to work full time for the government as a U.S. Marshal doing undercover work."

"What do you mean full time?" she asked, unable to mask her astonishment.

"The times I pulled my disappearing act, as you called it, I was on special assignment for the government. Of course, I wasn't allowed to tell you, but even if I could have, you wouldn't have understood. Would you?"

Oh, God, all that time he had been working for the government. That thought had never even crossed her mind. At times she had thought there might be another woman. And for one crazy moment, she had wondered if he was in trouble with the law. But a spy. Never.

"No," she said at last, "it wouldn't have made any difference. You were determined to do as you pleased no matter what I said. And you haven't changed. Chasing danger was always more important than I was, anyway." *And avoiding responsibility,* she added silently, thinking of the hours of pain and loneliness she had suffered in the hospital bearing his child.

When she had discovered that she was pregnant, she

almost went crazy. But never once did she consider doing anything about it. For the first time in her life, she would have someone who truly belonged to her. That was her only salvation during those lonely hours, weeks and months without Keir. Without that hope, she doubted if she could have survived.

"Goddammit, that was my job!"

She placed her hands over her ears. "Stop it!" she shouted. "What good is dredging up the past? All we're doing is making matters worse. I've about had all I can stand. Just leave me alone!"

She made an effort to tune out his fierce expletive, resting her head once more against the seat and closing her eyes, letting the numbness settle over her, feeling like her soul was withering and dying within her.

If only things could have been different, she agonized silently. If only she hadn't overheard that conversation that had changed her life so completely. If only she had known he had called her that fateful day. If only he wasn't getting married. If only she wasn't harboring the secret of having borne his child. If only . . . if only . . .

Chapter 3

THE SNOW WAS COMING DOWN THICKER AND FASTER NOW. It took all of Keir's concentration to keep the car on the slick road. The miles from D.C. to his cabin stretched interminably as his eyes swept across the Blue Ridge Mountains that seemed to hover around him like a brewing storm. This feeling merely added to his restlessness.

Not only were the close confines of the car hard to endure, but coupled with the presence of Er . . . no, goddammit, he reminded himself brutally, Danielle . . . His insides were crawling. Her perfume filled his nostrils; he could never have dreamed her scent.

He turned and looked at her. So soft and pale and lovely, he thought. Her soft curls caressed her shoulders like a silk scarf. Suddenly he flinched visibly at the dangerous path his thoughts were taking. His mouth drew into a thin, straight line, and once again his long fingers curled tightly around the steering wheel.

How was it possible to feel nothing but contempt for her on one hand and want her so badly on the other? he wondered. An irrational anger rose up into his throat.

Like a man possessed and hating himself for what he was feeling, he delved into his shirt pocket and jerked out a cigarette. He was trying hard to shake the nasty habit of smoking, but right now he needed something to occupy his hands. He reached out and ground his index finger against the interior lighter and, after a second, held the tip of it to the cigarette. He pulled on it deeply and hungrily. Clearly still not in control of his emotions, he glanced down at his watch, checked the rearview mirror and then looked back at her. She had not moved. Was she asleep? Or was she feigning sleep in order to mask her own chaotic emotions?

He forced his eyes back on the winding road before impatiently crushing the half-smoked cigarette into the ashtray. God, if he didn't get control of himself, he wouldn't make it through the rest of the day. He hoped that the FBI wouldn't bungle the job this time and those Russian bastards would soon be behind bars and this fiasco over. And what could be a highly volatile and dangerous situation would instead turn out to be boring and routine.

The thought of Danielle's life being threatened in any way made his blood run cold. But he wouldn't think like that. After all, it was his job to see that nothing happened to her. He had to keep a cool and level head and not allow his personal feelings to color his judgment, and remember that his life was no longer intertwined with hers.

But underneath all those reflections and emotions was a layer of fright unlike any he'd ever known before. He kept trying to avoid that fear. He had nothing to be afraid of, he insisted. But he knew better. He was afraid of the truth.

Every bone in his body suddenly felt strained to the

limit. Everything seemed to be failing him. His mind could dwell on nothing but her and his dilemma.

Not being able to stop himself, his eyes rested for another brief second on her pale features. Suddenly his mind became a wilderness of memories and impressions and he was frightened by an acute shortness of breath. God help him, but he still could not think of her as Danielle. When he had first met her she had been Erin. . . .

He remembered the party as though it had been yesterday. It had been a bore. It had been like dozens of others he'd attended: too many people crowded into several small rooms, the air stale and clogged with smoke and loud and unruly laughter, a constant ebb and flow of new arrivals, departing couples.

As a rule he didn't allow himself to be ramrodded into attending these affairs, but his father had been insistent. "You need the exposure, son," Raymond McBride had said, "especially if you plan on following in your old man's footsteps and becoming senator of Virginia when I retire. The law firm that's throwing the party handles the paperwork for some of the government's biggest contracts and there will be several important bigwigs present," he'd gone on to say.

At least the food wasn't bad, he thought as he helped himself to an indulgent portion from the buffet and wedged himself into a corner. He hated to admit it, but he was bored, bored listening to the uninspired dialogue and watching a cast that felt obliged to overact. He ate absently, his eyes moving over the faces—some overly animated, others empty—before coming to rest on a woman in the far corner of the room by the door. She stood listening to a tall, earnest-looking man who had her undivided attention, bending slightly toward her, as if for emphasis, as he spoke.

The words were lost to him, the music was far too

loud, but he stared, intrigued by the way the woman made a conscientious effort to pay attention. Every so often her eyes left the face of the man and searched space for an exit she might discreetly slip through.

She looked soft, Keir thought. She was of medium height, slim in a black cashmere sweater gown, with a string of pearls falling midway down her breasts. Her hair was a fine silvery color, swept away from her face, flattering and emphasizing her exquisite features. He was intrigued. He shifted closer to get a better look at her.

She could have been drinking any of several concoctions; the liquid in her glass clear. From time to time she took a sip from the glass in her right hand and regarded her companion over the rim. Keir settled more comfortably and continued to study her. On the middle finger of her right hand was a plain gold dome ring. She had on gold loop earrings that dangled when she moved her head. She was perfect, Keir decided, while he continued to eat, without tasting the food. He felt less isolated now, having someone to focus on.

The effects of his meeting with his father earlier in the day still clouded his mood and squeezed at his insides. In his mind he reran the scene with the same effect and disappointments. His father, glowering at him from under bushy gray eyebrows, his green eyes sparkling, but cold, saying, "Why don't you want to go into politics? Don't you think it's about time you settled down and quit hopping the globe and got a real job? Why *can't* you turn your flight service over to your partner and let him run it? Dammit, I want to retire and I want you to take my place in the senate chamber."

Keir's temper was still boiling on low simmer just thinking about that conversation. It made him furious to think that his father thought he never did an honest day's work in his life. His air-cargo business netted over two million dollars a year, yet that wasn't good enough. And he enjoyed every minute of it, being the free spirit that he was. Working on the inside at a desk or being at the beck and call of another person had never appealed to him. His job allowed him to travel all over the world. But more important, it served as a cover so that he could adequately perform his special assignments for the government. A fancy word for spying, he added with a grim twist to his lips. But he could not tell Raymond McBride about these top secret assignments. He could tell no one.

His thoughts shifting, the sweet, but determined lined face of his mother rose to haunt him. "I agree with your father—why don't you listen to him? Don't you think you've sown enough wild oats? You're thirty-five. It's time you thought seriously about marrying Natalie and settling down. She'd make a perfect politician's wife, don't you think?"

He shuddered, suddenly finding his thoughts terribly depressing. Why the hell had he given in and come to this party, anyway? But he knew. It was his mother's tears. They got to him every time, and she damn well knew it.

He carelessly thrust aside his empty plate, and when he shifted his gaze, the woman's eyes were on him. Even from a distance he could read the sadness that tinted their startling blue color. She appeared unhappy, out of place. Mildly flustered, he busied himself lighting a cigarette. When he next looked back, her companion had returned. She was holding a fresh glass of clear liquid, and her eyes were no longer turned in Keir's direction.

She had a magnificent body for a woman of such slight stature. It was impossible to determine her exact age, but he'd guess her to be anywhere from twenty-five to thirty years old. With that settled in his mind, he retrieved his drink from the top of the mantel where he'd left it and went on inspecting her. She had a graceful neck, slender hands, generously curved breasts, narrow waist and hips, lovely slender calves and ankles.

She fascinated him. Who was the man? Her husband? he wondered. She wore no wedding ring, but nowadays that didn't mean anything. His eyes refused to leave her. He'd rarely seen a woman so well put together, so appealingly sexual. Certainly different from Natalie, he thought with a slight twitch to his conscience. God, he knew Natalie loved him and was merely waiting for him to pop the question. But he couldn't do it, not yet. Commitments were not for him. At least not now.

Someone touched him on the arm. He swiveled with a start to see a long-time friend of his father's, Ed Watson, grinning up at him.

"How's it going, eh, Keir?" Watson asked, giving Keir's arm a squeeze.

"Couldn't be better." Keir smiled easily enough, though slightly put off by Watson, especially his political ambitions. He was always playing a role, tried too hard. Fear of becoming this type of person was one of the reasons he, Keir, kept resisting the pull into the political arena. He was too much his own person to be a yes man to anyone. Even to his own father.

"So how's business?" Ed was asking, his mouth stretched into a toothsome grin.

"Same old one and two," Keir answered coolly, waiting impatiently for Watson to move on, on to a more productive prey. To someone who could do him some good.

"How'd your old man manage to get you to this shindig? You look out of place as hell," Watson said, still grinning.

"I am. In fact, I was just thinking about leaving," Keir replied pointedly. And he was. He'd had enough.

Watson patted him on the arm. "Well, in that case, I guess I'll catch you later."

Keir watched in disgust as he crossed the room, bulldozing his way into a small group where he began talking with frenetic animation. Keir took it all in for a moment, then made his way through the crowd, spying the bar, suddenly needing a refill. And after that he planned to go home.

It was the perfume, a rich, heady scent, and then his arm inadvertently pressing into a woman's breasts that alerted him. Raising his eyes, he found he'd collided with the woman in black, who was now only inches away and was staring at him with rounded, suspicious eyes.

"Sorry," he said, trying in vain to put a safe distance between them. "I didn't spill anything on you, did I?"

"No . . . no, not as far as I can tell," she answered in a mellow tone before dipping her head to glance at the front of her dress. Then she looked up at him as though she still didn't trust him as far as she could throw him.

His pulse suddenly elevated. Her coolness struck a challenging chord within him. The touch-me-not expression in her clear blue eyes was saying "Get lost, Mister." But he was never one to back down from a challenge, especially where a beautiful woman was concerned.

"Good," he said disarmingly, then eased his lips into what he hoped was his most engaging grin. "I'm not always responsible for my actions at these affairs." His eyes were twinkling. "Sometimes a man will do most anything to break the boredom, even go as far as sloshing a drink on a lady's dress."

She lifted perfectly arched eyebrows. "And is that what you did?"

Keir laughed, both embarrassed and elated. "No, actually it was an accident, but I'm awfully glad it happened, nevertheless."

She wasn't smiling, yet. But there was a faint upturn at the corners of her mouth. A little more and she would have openly grinned. Keir held his breath, completely spellbound by her and by his sudden stroke of luck.

"Why is that?" she asked, lifting her glass to her mouth. She held it there, waiting for his answer.

Adrenaline pumped through his veins like liquid fire, giving him courage. "Truthfully?" he asked, the evening suddenly coming alive. He was beginning to enjoy himself.

"Oh, of course! Be truthful."

He was aware that she was mocking him in her own cool way, but that did not deter him. "Because it's given me the golden opportunity to talk to you," he said bluntly before pausing, trying to gauge her reaction to his bold statement.

For a moment, she looked disconcerted, then she gave him a begrudging smile. "At least you're honest."

Her smile dazzled him. "Would you like a refill?" he offered, determined to keep the conversation alive. He had watched her throat as she swallowed, emptying the contents of her glass. Her skin looked like cream-colored satin. He felt slightly dizzy from her perfume; it seemed to be in his mouth and at the back of his throat.

"Please," she said, giving him her glass. "I'm drinking Perrier with a twist of lime."

"Don't go away," he whispered, prepared to force his way through the crowd.

In a moment he pushed his way back through the crowd, drinks in hand, feeling an interior warmth spread pleasantly through his chest and belly. It was an anticipatory rush that had him smiling as he moved toward her, holding out her drink.

"Thank you," she said as she closed her hand around the glass, her eyes on his.

"By the way, I'm Keir McBride," he said, a boyish tilt to his lips.

She hesitated a moment as though weighing the consequences of telling him her name.

"I'm Erin Richards," she said.

"Glad to know you, Erin Richards." He smiled at her again. Her rounded breasts under the black dress drew his eyes.

"Are you with someone?" he asked.

She shook her head, lifting the glass to her mouth. "No, that was my boss I was talking to a moment ago."

So she'd been aware of him looking at her. That was a good sign, he told himself. "What brings you to this party?"

"Actually, I had no choice," she answered softly. "I work for the firm that's hosting this affair and I was told to be here." She appeared suddenly uncomfortable. "But I hate being closed in with all these people."

"My sentiments exactly. Would you like to leave?" he asked, glancing around.

"Yes," she said simply, although she avoided his eyes.

"Have you eaten?" he asked as they walked down the front path a short time later.

"I'm not hungry. How about you?"

"Me neither. A drink somewhere?" he pressed, hoping that the evening wasn't going to end so soon.

"No, I think not." She seemed uneasy as they reached his Mercedes and he opened the door for her. "I have an early appointment in the morning."

Disappointed, he opened the door on the driver's side and eased himself behind the wheel. Once again her perfume overwhelmed his senses.

"Where to?" he asked, trying to control his rising sense of frustration.

"If . . . if you'd like, we can go to my place," she began hesitantly. "I have a bottle of wine. . . . I can open that . . ."

"Great" he said and cranked up the ignition. He felt as if something had been settled. Without words, without the need for them, his future had just been decided.

"Your apartment is nice. It suits you," he said, looking at her poised just inside the doorway. Suddenly he longed to hold her and kiss her on the mouth. She had a perfectly shaped mouth, and he was intrigued by the way her lips moved when she spoke.

She smiled up at him as she slipped off her jacket and draped it across the back of the nearest chair.

Her every movement attracted him. She had a natural grace and moved well, long thighs shifting smoothly under the black fabric. He could almost feel the warm, sleek inner length of her thighs.

"Coffee?" she asked. "Or wine?"

"How about both?" He smiled and changed the subject. "This is really a super apartment."

"Thanks. I worked long and hard to get it exactly as I wanted it. Go ahead, look around while I get the coffee started."

He sank down on the beige sofa and gazed contentedly at the room, taking in the plants, the prints on the walls, the wicker furniture, the shelves filled with books.

She returned a few minutes later and sat down at the far end of the couch, crossed her legs and extended an arm along the back of the cushions.

"The . . . the coffee's perking," she said uneasily, as though she wasn't used to inviting strange men to her apartment.

He liked that about her. In fact he liked everything about her: the reserve she wore like a second skin that he was certain masked the shyness underneath and the underlying sensuality that had first charmed him, then aroused him. It was nothing overt, but all the more powerful because she was unaware of it. She was cut from a different bolt of cloth than the women he was used to.

"Tell me about yourself," he demanded softly, hoping to put her at ease.

She shrugged, turning her blue eyes on him. A man could lose himself in those eyes, he thought.

"There's not much to tell."

He smiled. "Let me be the judge of that."

She began fingering the strand of pearls around her neck. "Well . . . I grew up in an orphanage just outside the city." She paused as though to test his reaction to her confession. When he showed none, she went on. "After leaving the home, I worked my way through college, finally getting a degree in business law. The Elsworth law firm gave me my first job. That was four years ago; I've been there ever since." She smiled. "See, I told you my life was unexciting. I'm a homebody, but I'm happy."

"That's all that counts," he said, looking again at her eyes, and then her mouth.

"And you?"

He sighed, shifting his gaze. "My life's as different from yours as night and day."

She appeared surprised. "Oh, how's that?"

"I'm the controlling partner in an air-freight company, which means I travel a great deal." A grin spread slowly over his mouth. "It's in my blood. I can't seem to settle down for very long at a time."

She frowned. "I couldn't handle that. As I said before, I like my home."

"You sound like my mother. If she and my father had their way, I'd be married with two kids and campaigning for the U.S. Senate seat my father hopes to turn over to me in the near future."

Her frown deepened. "Is Raymond McBride your father?"

"The one and the same."

"I'm impressed. He's a powerful man."

Keir laughed. "He'd love to hear you say that."

Then suddenly Keir realized that the mood had

changed. She seemed distant, as though she had said too much, been too friendly.

"I'll get the coffee," she said, breaking the short silence.

"Sounds good."

He did not take his eyes off her as she rose and walked out of the room. She moved like liquid flowing from one point to the next. He reached to undo his jacket, again with a sense of matters having been settled. He wanted to spend time with her. He wanted to knock down that wall of reserve. He wanted to hold her slim soft body and listen, with his eyes closed, to her voice gently breaking the darkness. He wanted someone to relax with, to laugh with, to love.

She checked the coffeepot, then stood for a moment, leaning against the cabinet, trying to bring herself under control. She could not. She was too aware of everything about Keir McBride, almost of his very breathing. There was something incredibly magnetic about him.

God, what had possessed her to let him bring her home and then to ask him in for a drink? It was totally out of character for her. She had never done anything so rash in her life. Was it because he was so different from the stuffy lawyers she was used to dating?

Or was it because, when he'd brushed against her on his way out of the room, she'd felt a small shock, almost electric? Or was it simply that she liked the look of him, his craggy features, his boyish smile, the resonant depths of his voice, his probing eyes?

He had stared at her until she felt naked.

But she knew that she would be a fool to become involved with this man. She was no match for him. *You're out of your league, lady; he devours women like you. Keep that in mind!*

Anyway, after having learned who he was, who his father was, she knew that she could not allow him to stay. They were from two different worlds. After he drank his coffee she would ask him to leave. Yes, that would be the wisest move on her part, she reassured herself. She was just too lonely, too vulnerable to allow him to stay. . . .

Keir watched her closely as she returned to the room, once again robed with her cool composure.

"How do you take your coffee?" she asked, avoiding his eyes.

"Black, please."

A silence fell between them while she poured the brew into matching china cups and then handed him his, careful not to touch him.

Keir knew that the pleasant moments they had shared were gone. But there was always tomorrow, he thought as he took in the dark shadows coloring the tender skin beneath her eyes. It was time for him to go home. It was late, and hadn't she told him that she had to get up early?

He placed the cup on the table and looked at her softly. "It's time I went home. I didn't mean to keep you up so late."

"That's all right," she murmured, placing her half-full cup down beside his. Then she smiled. "Thank you for bringing me home."

He stood up and she followed suit.

"My pleasure," he said.

They walked to the front door, an awkward silence accenting their footsteps.

At the door he turned and looked down at her. He didn't want to leave. Instead he longed to close his hand gently over her rounded, cashmere-covered breast, to kiss her honeyed lips, to ease her into his arms and feel her breasts cushioning his chest while he tasted and explored the slick interior of her mouth.

She returned his burning gaze with wide, uncertain eyes. "Please . . . you'd better go."

"I can't," he groaned, "not until I do this."

At first, her lips trembled as he placed his mouth over hers. Then her arms slipped up and around his neck. Involuntarily.

His kiss deepened, easing her mouth open. His heart was pounding as his tongue slid into her mouth. She tasted so sweet, so good; he thought he'd explode from wanting her. But instinct held him in check.

He tore his mouth away, breathing hard. "When can I see you again?"

"Tomorrow," she whispered.

He eased himself away and kissed her once more on the side of the neck. "Until tomorrow."

Tomorrow was the first day of many days they spent together. They couldn't seem to get enough of one another. Somehow he had managed to persuade his partner to make his runs, thus freeing him to be with her. Keir was completely at her mercy. He wooed her with flowers, phone calls and long intimate dinners at her apartment and his.

But never once during those early days together did he take her to bed. Because she was different, he treated her as such. He wanted to gain her trust, to prove to her that he was not going to make love to her and then, having gotten what he wanted, walk out and leave her. She'd made him aware of feelings inside him that he never thought were there. Up until then a woman was a toy, a means of relief, something to show off, spend his money on. But this woman was different.

So for nearly two weeks, he kept a tight reign on his emotions. Then the night he planned to woo her into his bed, he received the dreaded phone call. He left that same day for South America.

The days dragged by, each seeming longer than the other. He thought that he would never get back to her, and when he finally did, he was unsure of his reception.

He was like an eager boy when he knocked on her door. His palms were sweaty and his heart was in his mouth.

The moment the door swung back, they devoured one another with their eyes.

"Darling . . ." he began huskily.

"Oh, Keir, I thought you'd never get back. I missed you so much," she whispered, tears darkening her eyes.

He crushed her to him, dizzy from relief at having her in his arms. It was pure magic.

"Please . . . promise me you won't ever leave me again."

He smoothed her silky curls. "Shhh, let's don't talk about that now. We have something much more important to take care of."

He took her hand in his and led her gently into the bedroom where he began slowly to undress her. She looked up at him, her eyes misty and trancelike; he thought he had never seen anything more beautiful.

As his hands sought and found the zipper on her dress, he paused, drawing her closer, and laid his lips against the throbbing sweetness of hers. He could feel her erect nipples through the sweater, the tips wonderful and hard.

"Oh, God . . ." he murmured hoarsely.

Her hand reached up and spanned his face. "I . . . I feel the same way," she whispered. "I feel as if my insides are on fire." She rubbed her cheek against his, all of her so remarkably soft and sweet-smelling.

It was almost more than he could bare. Her eyes, on his face, big and soft, sent his heart pounding, threatening to crack his rib cage.

With graceful precision, they undressed one another, fondling the clothing, the snaps, the buttons, as though everything were flesh.

When she was naked, Keir knelt, his hands everywhere on her.

"I . . . I hope I please you. . . ."

"Oh, my darling," he groaned, "you do please me. You're perfect."

With his tongue, he traced her curves, the spaces of her body, her breasts, the hollow below them, the line of her hips, her navel, the skin along the inside of her thighs before lowering his head to their parted sweetness.

A whimper, then a low cry escaped her. She felt as though she were lying back in water while constant dizzying waves washed over her again and again.

"Please . . ." she whimpered, drawing him up to lie beside her. . . .

"You're beautiful," he said, peering down at her. "And so is your body."

"Take it, it's yours."

Her soft plea filled his mouth as he bent to kiss her. He loved the feel of her lips, the shape and feel of her mouth, the impossible softness of her breasts, which were beautifully formed—small and round with full, pink nipples. He lowered his head to kiss her breast, easing a nipple between his lips, and she shivered, her fingers weaving through his hair.

She closed her eyes and examined the sensations, feeling herself starting to lose control. After a time, she pleaded, "Now . . . please . . . now."

Her body was small and tight around him. He whispered, "Easy, easy," as he felt her muscles relaxing in order to bring him in.

"I . . . think I'm falling in love with you," he murmured, feeling his carefully built defenses and control systems going haywire.

"I know I love you," she said clearly before moans of pleasure claimed them both, rendering them speechless.

He spilled deep inside her when it was time. He heard her answering cry as they rode the crest together.

* * *

The months thereafter were perfect. Again Keir postponed as many trips as he could in order to be with her. They spent their time loving, laughing and talking, learning about each other.

It was only after he began fulfilling his obligations to his company and to the government once again that their relationship began to deteriorate.

She could not understand why he was gone for long periods of time, and he could not tell her. She always stopped short of nagging him, though she showed her displeasure by retreating into her cold shell, closing him out. And there were other problems as well. She could not adjust to his family background. The fact that he had money and a father who was important gnawed at her. She wanted no part of the hoopla associated with politics. She was quite vocal about that.

Then things went from bad to worse. They began to try and change one another. She tried to mold him into the way she wanted him to be, to make him into something he was not. She wanted him to give up his air-freight business and get an eight-to-five job, come home to a tidy brick home with a white picket fence and dote on her. She assumed that his long absences were connected with his freight company. He, on the other hand, wanted her to trust him, to share his life with him the way it was.

Yet, he loved her and couldn't imagine life without her. Finally he was positive that he had her convinced that in spite of their problems, they could make it.

He walked into her apartment one evening after he had been gone for two weeks on a dangerous assignment. He was exhausted, yet hungry for the sight of her, hungry to hold her, to make love to her.

She was standing in front of the window, her back to him as the door closed behind him with a click.

"Darling . . ."

She swung around, her hair glistening like spun silver in the muted lamplight.

He knew the minute he saw the mutinous expression on her face that something was wrong. He fought off the fatigue along with the sinking feeling in the pit of his stomach.

"Keir . . . I don't want you to stay." She clamped down on her lip to still its trembling.

"What . . . what the hell does that mean?" he demanded harshly, taking a step forward. "Don't do this. . . . God, we only have tonight as it is." He paused, his breathing hoarse and uneven. "I have to leave again in the morning."

"No! I don't want to hear it." She wrapped her arms around herself like a shield. "And don't come near me. I . . . I can't take living like this any longer," she said, flushing deeply.

"What are you trying to say?" His voice was dangerously low.

"That . . . that it's over." Her eyes glistened with unshed tears. "I . . . can't, won't, take second place in your life a moment longer. I'm tired of sharing you with your work, of never knowing where you are, when you'll be home. I . . . I can't take it anymore. I need security, which is something you obviously know nothing about," she said bitterly.

"Are you telling me you don't love me?" His face changed as he looked at her, disbelief mirrored in his green eyes.

"No . . ." She hesitated for a moment, searching for the words that would once and for all end the barbed-wire tangle of their lives.

He closed his eyes, his jaw rigid as a spasm of pain flitted across his face. "Erin," he pleaded, his hand coming toward her. "Goddammit, don't do this to us!"

She shrank back against the wall, biting her lip.

"Can't you see? All we're doing is hurting one another." She paused and looked at him with her round, haunted eyes. "I'm . . . I'm sorry, it was a mistake," she whispered.

"A mistake!" Bitter fury made the word sting. "You selfish little bitch!"

She went deathly pale at the insult, but bent her head against the pain his words had inflicted.

"If it's my job . . ." He was all but begging now. "Maybe we could work something out."

She shook her head, her throat burning. "It's . . . it isn't just that. It's everything. We're so different . . . I'm afraid . . ." Her voice stopped in her throat.

Finally she said quietly. "Sometimes love just isn't enough."

He swore then; violence burned in his voice. "She doesn't want to get involved," he whispered menacingly. "Because it's disturbing. She might have to give up something, make a sacrifice, take a chance. You're a god-damned fake, Erin."

She turned away. "Please, just go. . . ."

"But then why should I waste any more of my life on someone who's afraid to love, to take a chance. May God help you," he said quietly, almost as if he were talking to himself.

He turned and walked out the door and out of her life without another word.

It was only through his work that he was able to push aside the pain and disillusionment which at times almost made him suicidal. After losing her, he chucked everything—his business, his political ambitions, and went to work full time for the government as a U.S. Marshal. At times he didn't care whether he lived or died.

But with the help of Natalie and pride in his work he was able to put the past behind him. He could almost believe he was truly happy. If not happy, then, at least, content. Until now . . .

Something alerted him, drew him sharply out of the chasm of his dark thoughts. He glanced quickly at Danielle, taking in the steady rise and fall of her chest.

Still his sharp wit told him that all was not right. He raised his eyes and peered through the rearview mirror. Lines of worry ruled his forehead as a seething oath flew from his lips.

Suddenly he ground down on the gears without mercy. The car lunged forward and around a curve at a daring rate of speed.

Danielle's eyes sprang open as she fought to maintain her balance. "Keir? . . ." The rest of her sentence was strangled in her throat as she was once more hurled against the door, the tires screeching and whining around another curve.

She stared at him, wild-eyed, fright pounding through her veins. "What's wrong?" she cried.

Ignoring her cry, Keir's arm reached over and frantically released the lock on the glove compartment. Danielle watched in shocked disbelief as he pulled out a gun.

She panicked. "Keir, for God's sake!"

"Be quiet and get down." His voice was as cold as steel and just as hard. "We're being followed."

Chapter 4

DANIELLE DID EXACTLY WHAT KEIR TOLD HER NOT TO DO. Danielle's head twirled around instantly and stared wild-eyed out the back window.

"Dammit," Keir hissed, "I told you to get down!"

"But . . . but . . . I don't see a car behind us," she stammered, relief beginning to replace the alarm his words had sent shooting through her. Obviously he was mistaken. They virtually had the highway to themselves. Now maybe he would pick up the piece of cold metal that rested like something evil on his thigh, she told herself. She tried not to stare at it, but her eyes were pulled toward it like a magnet. She shivered before slinking down lower in the seat.

"Take my word for it," Keir said tersely, "we haven't lost them. It's two men in a dark blue sedan, and they've been tailing us for no telling how long." And if he had kept his mind on his business, he would have spotted them earlier, an inner voice taunted.

He shifted his gaze back to the rearview mirror,

purposefully blocking from mind Danielle's chalky face and bloodless lips.

"Well, for the moment at least, it does appear that we have shaken them, or else they're lying low with something else up their sleeve." His voice held an ominous note, making her more aware than ever of the danger surrounding them.

He reminded her of an animal, sharp-witted and cunning, who seemed to spring to life when he scented danger. In his own way, Keir was as dangerous as the persons following them.

"Who do you think it is? Letsukov?"

"More than likely, or someone he's hired to do his dirty work."

The lump in her throat seemed to grow larger with each passing second. "What . . . what are we going to do?" she asked, though how she managed to push the words through her swollen throat was anybody's guess.

Keir did not answer for a moment, but she could feel the sudden tension in him.

Then he spoke grimly, "Try to lose them, if at all possible. I know this highway, and the roads that jut off from it, like the back of my hand. There's a short cut through to the other highway a few miles ahead, and if I can keep enough in front of them, I can take that cutoff. Between the approaching darkness and the thickening snow, we're certain to be invisible."

"Whatever you think best," she said, twisting her head to stare out the window. Keir was right, the snow seemed to be growing thicker, but thank goodness it wasn't sticking to the road—yet. That would have brought them to a virtual standstill. She watched as it swirled around the headlights like white rain. Keir was forced to slow down to a mere forty miles per hour, the road becoming slicker and more treacherous by the minute. But even forty was too fast for safety, she thought apprehensively.

The longer they traveled, the more her stomach curled with fear. Surely at this slow rate of speed, the blue car would catch up with them. Suddenly feeling claustrophobic, she cracked the window just enough to allow a stream of air to pass through. It was raw and cold.

There was a kind of unnatural hush over everything. There was no sound except the soft, steady purr of the engine. She was conscious of a strange sense of isolation, as though she and Keir were out of this world and drifting through space together. Time and distance seemed to have receded from them. She couldn't have said whether they had driven five, ten or fifteen miles.

"Keir," she said desperately.

"Yes."

She bit her lip nervously. "How . . . much farther before we turn off?"

"About another mile," he said, forcing a moderate tone to his voice while trying to ignore her frantic sigh that put a squeeze on his heart.

"Are they behind us now?" she asked, looking neither to the right or left.

"We picked them up again about a half mile back."

"Oh, God, Keir, I'm scared," she whimpered, biting down on her bottom lip to keep it from trembling.

"Tighten your seatbelt," he ordered crisply, slamming the gun under his leg with his right hand. Then suddenly he pushed down on the gears, doing an intricate dance between brake and accelerator. The car went into a violent skid turn. The world seemed to dip and move out of control as the Chevrolet started to slow and the tires completely lost their grip on the road's surface.

Then Keir felt a shudder as the wheels suddenly righted themselves and regained their hold on the highway. He shifted again, building speed, feeling confidence grow with every second.

He had made up his mind in a matter of seconds. He reasoned that it was now or never. He had to lose the car before he reached the cutoff or it would be too late. Damn the blasted snow, he cursed silently as the car slid along the wet, uneven track. But he held his speed, gripping the steering wheel so tightly that every bone in his body felt jammed.

But it paid off. When next he looked in the mirror, the twin beams of the chase car did not seem to have grown any larger.

"Thank God, we've lost them again," Keir said, keeping his eyes glued to the mirror. "Now if our luck will just hold for another five minutes, we'll ditch those bastards once and for all." There was an ugly underside to his tone.

Turning toward him, Danielle searched for his shadowed profile. She was amazed at how calm and composed he was. This was a side of Keir McBride she never knew existed. But then, she reminded herself, he had changed. There was a coldness, a hardness within him that had not been there before.

She had always heard the phrase "nerves of steel"—well, in this case, it fitted Keir to a T. Not once during that harrowing spin in the road when the car threatened to topple over on its side, did he so much as flinch. It appeared that Luke Cassidy was right, she thought. If you were flirting with danger, Keir was the man to have on your side. Why then was that thought so unsettling?

Suddenly Danielle was jarred out of her reverie as Keir made another sharp turn, the car lurching and bumping over potholes.

"Won't they finally figure out that we've turned off somewhere when they can no longer spot us in front of them?" she asked, trying to ignore the eerie darkness surrounding them while trying to control her rising fear, which refused to be suppressed.

Keir shifted down to a lower gear. "Probably, but there are other roads and cutoffs on both sides of the road. So by the time they turn around and come back to look for us, we'll be long gone."

"What do you think the chances are that they'll find the . . . cabin?" There was a feverish edge to her voice as she sought frantically for his reassurance.

"Slim," he said, bringing the car to a sudden halt. "And you'll see why when we get there. It's easier to get into Fort Knox than anywhere around the cabin." He turned his head around and began craning his neck, looking back toward the highway.

They sat silently listening for the sound of a passing car.

"What . . . what do we do now?" Danielle whispered, unable to stand the quiet another moment.

"Pray that the snow still isn't sticking so that we can get through here to the other highway. Hold tight."

He changed gears and nosed the car deeper onto the primitive mountain road. It was a nerve-wracking experience. The ground was painfully uneven, strewn with rocks and dotted with branches from fallen trees. It was impossible to see more than a yard or two beyond the headlights. The wheels lurched and slithered, tilting perilously on a frozen patch of snow, before threatening to stick altogether in a pool of mud and slush. Keir zigzagged this way and that, dodging obstacles before swinging the car around to face back toward the highway.

"Dammit to hell!" he whispered in a rage, slamming his fists into the steering wheel.

"What's . . . wrong now?" Danielle managed to eke out above the pounding of her heart.

"The god-damned road is closed. This is as far as we can go." He switched off the lights and the engine and added grimly, "And we'll be lucky if we can get out of here without a tow truck."

Her mouth was bone dry. She licked her lips several times before she could speak. "Why did you turn here if you knew—"

"Give me credit for having a little sense," he said savagely. "Of course, I didn't know it was impassable. It's been years since I used it, but I assumed it was still clear."

"As long as they don't find us. . . ." she said shakily. "Listen!"

"I don't hear anything."

"I do. Listen," he said again.

Then she heard it. She sat motionless and listened to the faint, steady purr of that other car, as it cruised slowly past them. She could feel the raw, cold air now like a heavy, smothering, icy weight pressing down on them, and cutting them off from the warm, real world of lights and firesides and warm, friendly people.

Danielle's ears were stretched to their limit. At the moment, she was aware that the snow, blanketing the sky, lent them their only protection. It blotted out the light. It provided a protective cloak over dark deeds.

She could feel Keir, taut and ready as a coiled spring beside her. He was close to her, yet disturbingly remote. She longed to slide her hand into his, but she knew that to him it would be a meaningless, irritating gesture. He wasn't conscious of the need for human contact. No matter how tightly her hand clung to his, he would still be alone. He wanted it that way.

He was shut away from her in his grim, silent fortress. She could not reach him. She could not tell what he was thinking or feeling.

Danielle could see the lights of the other car, like round, tawny eyes, looming through the falling snow. Her heart thudded, as though it were planning to stop beating at any given moment. The suspense was sapping all her endurance. She felt like a terrified animal, cowering in a thicket, watching the approach of hunters. Only it was a worse fear even than that because it was not for herself alone. She feared for Keir as well.

The lights were upon them. The hum of the engine

sounded abnormally loud in her overstrung ears. Then the car passed by . . . and she heard Keir draw a quick, deep, breath.

He said in an unnaturally light tone, "Well, it seems that for the moment, anyway, we've drawn a reprieve."

Terror struck anew within Danielle. "Do . . . do you think they will come back?" Visions of Ann's tiny face popped into focus. Suddenly she wondered if she would ever see her daughter again.

"They'll be back, no doubt about it. They'll search every road until they find us."

"What do you suggest we do now?" she asked, no longer attempting to mask the tremor in her voice. This could not be happening, could it? Surely she would wake up and find this was nothing but a bad dream. If someone had told her two days ago that she would be stranded on a lonely mountain road with Keir in the midst of a snowstorm playing chase with two "goons" in a blue car, she would have laughed. Things like that just didn't happen in the "real" world. Did they?

"This area used to be flooded with campers, myself included," he said at last. "This was my old stomping ground when I was a kid. And if I'm not mistaken, there used to be a hulled out place in the side of the mountain, sort of like a cave, not far from here." He paused again and she could almost see his mind clicking. "Even though they will spot the car, I'm hoping they'll decide against tracking us down in this kind of weather."

"Whatever . . . whatever you think best."

"Follow me, then!" he said abruptly, reaching across her once again to the glove compartment, his gun already secured in its holster. This time, he reached in and lifted out a small flashlight. "We'll use this where we can."

Danielle remained silent, fighting back the hysteria that was beginning to bubble just beneath the surface.

In an effort to keep from making a terrible situation worse, she made a big deal of slipping her arms into the sleeves of her all-weather coat and buckling the belt securely around her. She had just pushed her fingers into a pair of leather gloves when she felt rather than saw Keir's eyes on her.

"Do you have anything to put on your head?"

"No . . . but I'll be all right." Why this idiotic warmth? Because he had shown concern for her?

As though sensing she spoke the truth, he opened the door and slid out into the darkness. "Come on! It's scarcely the right time or season for hide-and-seek, but you might find the alternative even less enjoyable."

Danielle scooted out after him. He put his arm around her in a hard impersonal clasp. The darkness seemed to stalk them and engulf them. It was pitch black. She couldn't see anything. It was a terrible feeling; the soft wet flakes stung her face without her seeing them. She swallowed hard, fighting against a panic-stricken sense of being clawed at by something unknown, something evil.

"Scared?" Keir asked, close to her ears as he switched on the flashlight and she shivered.

"Me? Scared? Of course not, I'm just coming apart at the seams, that's all. But that's minor, wouldn't you say?"

A low throaty chuckle sounded close to her ear. "Oh, I'd say that's normal under the circumstances. When we get out of this mess, I'll disappear and let you have your nervous breakdown in peace." She had guts, he thought. He'd have to give her that.

If the entire situation weren't so bizarre, she would have been tempted to laugh. But his statement, she knew, did what it was intended to do and that was to ease the tension that encompassed them like an airtight bubble.

Then, impersonally, he nudged her forward. Heads bent against the driving flurries and the wind, they trudged over uneven ground, teeth chattering as the cold invaded their bones.

How long they continued on their nightmare journey through the darkness, Danielle could not have said. She was too intent on keeping her balance as they stumbled over unseen rocks and debris, trying to avoid being scratched and ripped by low overhanging branches while slithering through the crisp, stiff earth. Suddenly it all seemed to her painfully symbolic of what her future life would be. Barren, lonely, empty, no security, just endless suspense and struggles and misgivings. Certainly no love to brighten the darkness.

Keir said nothing to her, nor she to him. They were locked in a vacuum with one another seething with distrust, suspicion, derision and resentment. It was as though all the warmer, more endearing human emotions had been frozen in him. And in her.

The ground was even rougher than it had looked when the car had lurched and bounced over it. She stumbled again and again and would have fallen if Keir hadn't had his arm around her. There was nothing chivalrous or tender in his hold. His touch was fiercely impatient, as though he resented the entire undertaking, which of course he did and made no secret of it.

"Not much farther now," he said, his grip like a vise as he urged her steadily forward.

Her breath was coming in short, sharp, painful gasps by the time they collided with what felt like solid rock. Keir gave a stifled curse, and she winced at the pain which shot up her leg from the unexpected impact.

"Let's stop here," Keir said jerkily. "I think these rocks will provide us with enough cover."

"Are you sure we're far enough away?"

"Yes, as I said before, I don't think they'll venture too far from the road. And they know I'll have a gun."

"Would . . . would you use it?"

"You're damn right I'd use it." His voice was deadly calm and matter-of-fact.

Danielle shivered, falling against the rock, his words sending a barrage of chills through her that had nothing to do with the weather.

"It's like trying to eliminate bees," he went on, as if he were pursuing his own train of thought, completely oblivious of her. "One can kill them easily enough, but it seems pointless when there are so many of them. The most effective way of exterminating the hives is to kill the queen bee."

Another chill raked Danielle's body.

"Somehow I get the impression you're not referring to the Russians," she said faintly. "You actually hate and despise me, don't you?"

Keir moved away from her almost violently, as though she had stung him.

"Keep quiet," he ordered roughly.

Danielle crouched against the rock, trying to control her ragged breathing. There was a prick of tears at the back of her eyes; tears of impatience and vexation at her own weakness. She could not have gone much farther without a rest, and he must have guessed that. She knew that he thought her weak. Mentally, she might be a match for him, but physically she never would be.

"The car's coming back," he said suddenly in a low whisper.

Danielle knelt on her knees and peered over the top of the rocks. She saw the headlights. The car was crawling along now. It stopped. Danielle heard the click of the door. Then two beams of light pierced the darkness, half shrouded by the dense sheets of fat white flakes swirling around them.

It seemed like forever before those moving lights came to rest on the government car, but they reached it eventually. They reflected off the chrome on the hood and bumper first. Then they shone inside the car.

It was a nerve-wracking, eerie ordeal to crouch on the damp ground, against a cold, hard rock, watching those two lights, but unable to see the hands that were directing them. The lights flickered inside, over and around the car, but only a few paces beyond it. Evidently, the prospect of plunging about on a deserted mountain road looking for them did not appeal to the hunters.

Danielle wondered what was going through their minds. Somehow, trying to second-guess them helped to keep her own stark terror at bay. Were they thinking that perhaps they were wasting their time on such a night? Or were they thinking instead that she and Keir were already on their way back to the main road?

The snow, which had been their enemy, was now their friend. They could have been within a few yards of their pursuers and they might have failed to spot them. They must have realized that the light continued to bob up and down on the car for a minute or two longer. Then the lights moved away, back toward the road. In a moment Danielle heard the engine of the other car crank up again.

"Hot damn, we outfoxed them!" Keir said abruptly.

The gleeful satisfaction of his tone jarred Danielle's frayed nerves. It was nothing to him that she was scratched and bruised and exhausted from the mental and physical strain of the last few hours. All he cared about was outwitting those "bastards," as he called them. This was just a dangerous game to him, and he was enjoying playing it to the hilt. *Damn him!*

"You're . . . you're not the same person, just not human," she said, her voice shaking.

"I'm glad you discovered that. It will save both of us a lot of trouble," he announced calmly. "Can you make it back to the car, or do I have to carry you?"

"I can walk. You don't have to do anything where I'm concerned," she murmured bitterly. As she headed toward the car every bone in her body ached, but she'd go to hell before she asked him for help.

Shortly they reached the car, Keir before her.

He opened the door on the driver's side and peered inside. Then he motioned for Danielle to get in. Without daring to touch him, she skirted around his massive frame and scooted across the seat, far to the other side. But Keir did not follow her. Instead he slammed the door shut and began stalking around the car. In a matter of seconds, he jerked open the door and slid into the seat, bringing another rush of frigid air with him.

"Dammit, they've let the air out of one of the tires and broken out a front headlight," he said explosively. "Damnation!" he repeated as the match he was holding burned down and scorched his fingers. "What a friggin' mess. I wish to God . . ."

"That you'd never laid eyes on me again," she said, finishing the sentence for him.

"I didn't say that," he countered violently.

"You didn't have to. It's more than obvious," she said sarcastically.

"Don't push . . ."

"Well, believe me, you don't wish it any more than I do," she cried, swinging her head around, her eyes shooting darts at him through the darkness. Somehow she had managed to make it to the car on fairly steady legs, but now they were trembling convulsively and she sat wallowing in a heightened sense of frustration, doubt and fear. But one thing was certain: She almost hated Keir McBride. How could she have ever felt guilty about keeping Ann a secret from him? This cold, hard, cynical man was not father material. How could he have changed to the point that she hardly recognized him?

"Well, sitting here in the warm car won't get the job done," he said harshly.

"Can I help?" she offered begrudgingly. "Maybe hold the flashlight?"

He hesitated, then said, "Sure?"

"Yes, I'm sure," she said wearily. "It's my fault we're

in this godawful mess. The least I can do is help get us out of it."

"Then let's get to it," he clipped, opening the door and waiting for her to get out, although he was careful not to touch her.

They worked in total silence. Even if they had wanted to converse, it would not have been feasible. The cold robbed them of not only their speech, but their reflexes as well. The flashlight shook violently in spite of Danielle's efforts to hold it steady. And Keir's muffled curses sliced through the air as he strove diligently to change the tire.

Finally, the task accomplished, he dropped the jack and stood up, grabbing the light from Danielle's hand. "Hey . . . here, steady! Are you feeling faint?" He put his arm around her again roughly. "You'd better get in the car."

Too numb to fight him, Danielle leaned against him while he opened the door and then felt herself gently pushed into the warm interior. He got in after her and quickly slammed the door.

Danielle sat stiff as a rod, her teeth chattering unmercifully. It was as though every bone in her body was knocking against the other.

"Here, lean against me," Keir suggested abruptly, while unbuttoning his top coat and fitting her next to his body's warmth. He then drew her head back to rest on his shoulder. She winced.

"What's the matter? Have you hurt yourself?" he asked.

"I . . . I jammed . . . my shoulder against that rock. . . ." she said faintly.

"You didn't hit it hard enough to dislocate it, did you?" His hands trailed impersonally along the sensitive area.

Did she detect concern in his voice? In his touch? No, of course not, she told herself. She was merely hallucinating. That was all.

Suddenly she felt her coat being slipped from her shoulder as strong, lean fingers reached up and began probing gently. "Is it painful? Here?"

Even through the fabric of her blouse, Danielle could feel the callused points of his fingers. They were firm, yet gentle. It sent familiar, disturbing little tremors through her, reviving sensations she thought were long dead and buried. She should have resisted even his most impersonal of touches. To let it continue would be playing with fire. . . .

Then as suddenly as he had pulled her toward him, he pushed her away, though not roughly.

He lit a match and held it up, cupped in his hand. They stared at each other over the small, clear light. The naked hatred in those deep green eyes of his was like the thrust of a sword. She might have shrunk from it, but beneath it, submerged in those deep waters, she glimpsed other emotions . . . fear . . . and desire.

"You're lovely as ever!" he whispered in a strange, harsh tone. "And just as dangerous."

"Not dangerous to you, Keir, not anymore," she taunted.

"No. You're right. Not to *me*. I don't believe in rehashing the past."

"Do you believe in anything?"

"Oh, yes, I believe in the devil. And I believe in justice . . . in retribution," he whispered bitterly.

"Nemesis? I don't know why I find it strange that you'd serve that god. But who are you to deal out retribution?"

"What else is there?"

She grimaced painfully. "You could try having mercy. We all need that, including yourself."

"I've never asked for it and I don't believe in it. Mercy? That's another word for weakness."

"And heaven forbid if you should succumb to that like us other mortals."

"You more than anyone else should know the reason for that."

He lit another cigarette. Over the flare of the match, his eyes shone with an unnatural, gleaming brilliance. His lips curled upward into a mocking, derisive smile.

Blocking out the wrenching pain of her sudden movement, Danielle shoved herself against the door on the passenger side, his words having sent a dreadful ice-cold shock through her.

She kept her eyes averted as he began inching the car slowly forward on the snow-riddled ground. Her head throbbed, her shoulder ached and her eyes felt as though someone had thrown a handful of sand in them. Oh, God, she thought, if only she were home with Ann, soaking in a tub of gloriously hot water. . . .

"You might as well get some sleep," Keir said at length. "It'll more than likely be dawn now before we reach the cabin, provided we don't run into any more trouble, that is."

Danielle did not bother to answer him. As far as she was concerned, there was nothing left to be said. The battle lines had been drawn. Now all that was left was to choose the weapon, and no doubt that would soon follow. And he told her to sleep. Sleep. How could she even think about sleep with danger lurking around every corner and her mind a seething cauldron of emotions. But she soon found that her battered body had other ideas. Her eyelids began to droop as the warmth enveloped her like a cocoon. . . .

Keir knew when she had fallen asleep. He was glad. No point in both of them having to suffer a sleepless night. He was used to wasting as little time in sleep as possible; but this was one time when he wished he could sleep, emptying his mind of all chaotic thoughts and responsibilities. But this night he was not going to have even the few hours of rest he required. His mind raced; he couldn't slow it down.

He shifted his weight in the seat and, lifting one hand off the steering wheel, massaged the tight muscles at the base of his neck. Then he put it back quickly, since it was extremely rough going on the slick path, made even more hazardous by only one headlight. But so far so good, he thought, seeing the main road coming into view.

Removing the same hand from the wheel again, he reached for his shoulder holster and slowly drew out his revolver. He gave it its favorite place on his thigh as he nosed the car cautiously into the clearing. Closing his hand around the cold object, he looked right and then left before making the turn onto the highway. His stomach tied in knots, he eased the car slowly down the deserted stretch of concrete, his ears alert to the slightest unusual sound, his eyes searching through the inky blackness for any signs of company.

Satisfied that the "goons" had indeed abandoned their hunt, he slowly eased his foot down on the accelerator. But still he was forced to drive at a snail's pace. The road was a sloshy mess, and any sudden or wrong move could send them hurling down a ravine or into the side of a mountain.

He chanced a quick glance at Danielle. She was sleeping like a baby. Feeling the knot tighten in his stomach, he quickly forced his eyes back to the road.

But he could not lay his thoughts to rest. He began to analyze the situation, turning in his mind, looking at it from every angle. Were they truly out of danger? Was the cabin as impenetrable as he thought?

He didn't care about himself. He was not particularly impressed with danger. Other people had tried to best him in that field and had lived—briefly, in two cases— to regret it.

If he were honest with himself, he would have to admit that the single cause of his fear was Danielle— God, would he ever get used to calling her that?— worry that the Russians would get their hands on her.

Well, he would have to stick with her like a second skin. But that was going to be sheer punishment. As it was, he had to fight like hell to keep a torrent of images at bay: the haunting smell of her perfume, the feel of her naked body against his, the shape and texture of her breasts and belly and hips and buttocks. . . .

He ground his teeth together to stifle the gut-wrenching cry of agony from passing through his lips. He rubbed out his cigarette in the ashtray and adjusted his seat back. He didn't look at Danielle again; he stared straight ahead. . . .

Danielle jumped suddenly, as though an alarm had gone off in her brain. She sat up in the seat as if thrust forward by a spring, only to moan as a searing pain shot through her shoulder.

It took her a moment to realize where she was. But when she turned and saw Keir's haggard face and day's growth of beard, the horror of the past night returned to her.

"Feeling any better?" he asked, thinking she had never looked lovelier, all disheveled and sleepy-eyed.

She avoided his gaze as she licked parched lips. "A little stiff, but otherwise fine."

"And the shoulder?"

"It . . . smarts only when I move suddenly," she said, taking in the lines of strain around his eyes and mouth. *If only . . . Stop it! Don't think like that. Don't let your guard down.*

"It's probably just a deep bruise." His eyes were once more on the road.

"I . . . I take it there was no more trouble," she said hesitantly.

"So far, so good. I hope we've seen the last of our friends."

"Are we nearly to the cabin?" she asked, having drawn the conclusion they were no longer on a main road.

"Approximately two more turns and we'll be there." Danielle saw the muscle in his jaw suddenly clench before he added, "And from the way things are looking, we'll be stuck with each other a lot longer than either of us will like."

Danielle's heart sank to her toes, and what little color had returned to her face quickly vanished. Even as she told herself that he was toying with her, trying to upset her, she could not shake the sense of dread his words evoked.

Somehow she had to dredge up the strength to lay the painful memories of yesterday aside and take one day at a time.

Somehow.

Chapter 5

EVEN WITH HER EMOTIONS STRETCHED TO THEIR LIMIT, Danielle could not help but be impressed by the scene before her.

For a moment everything was forgotten: anger, frustration, fear, as her eyes surveyed her secret hideaway. It reminded her of a painting on a postcard, or better still, a magical fairyland come to life off the pages of a book. She was enchanted.

The house itself was nestled in the side of a mountain, tall pines flocked with snow surrounding it. Suddenly it dawned on her anew just how isolated they were from civilization and how totally dependent on Keir she was.

There was not a sound in the white wilderness. It belonged exclusively to them and any wild animals that were lucky enough to survive. Danielle sat transfixed and watched as the elusive dawn brightened the sky.

Would she truly be safe here, locked in this winter

wonderland? She paused in her thoughts as her eyes rose and swept across the wide expanse of mountains surrounding them like crystal clouds. Or were there more unseen dangers lurking amongst all that beauty? She shivered.

"Might as well get out and get acquainted with your home away from home," Keir said flatly. "We're here now, and there's not a damn thing either of us can do about it."

The hard, distant tone of his voice brought her sharply back to reality. The air hung heavy with the chill of the passionless tone of the few words he'd spoken. She tried to ignore the cold sweat of anxiety that caused her hands to shake, hampering her from opening the door. After several attempts, she finally managed to jerk the handle upright. But before she got out, she turned toward Keir.

"Well, at least the house is large enough so that we won't have to intrude on one another's privacy," she said tightly before planting her feet firmly in the snow and slamming the door behind her. It sounded like a bullet bouncing off its target in the early morning silence.

She waited for Keir at the door, cradling her arm against her side, easing the pressure on her throbbing shoulder. Her vulnerable mouth was twisted in pain, tears dangerously close.

Keir watched the play of emotions across her finely drawn features as he dropped the two carry-all bags at his feet and inserted the key in the lock of the heavy wooden door.

"I'll take a look at that shoulder after we've gotten cleaned up and put something to eat in our stomachs."

She refused to look at him. "Why, I wouldn't dream of putting you to all that trouble," she said, ice dripping from her voice. "Anyway, I don't need your help, thank you."

Keir's brow lowered to shadow his eyes. "I wouldn't

be too sure of that—Danielle," he said, his voice filled with contempt and a deadly sneer that caused a chill to feather up her spine. "Remember, you're at my mercy. I'd keep that in mind if I were you." Suddenly he twisted the door knob and flung the door open. Then with a mocking bow and a sweeping gesture, he indicated that she should precede him through the door.

Clutching her purse as though it were a lifeline, she took a hesitant step into the heavenly warmth, the heat lapping over her like waves. She paused inside the front entrance and gazed around, scrutinizing everything in one detailed sweep: a formal foyer leading into the spacious family room beautifully designed in cedar and aspen paneling with a loft balcony overlooking it; a great moss rock fireplace separating the family room from the dining room and adjacent to that two full-length sliding glass doors with access to an outdoor deck. The formal dining room also had a loft and moss rock fireplace. Both rooms had high, sloping cathedral ceilings.

Danielle knew immediately that this was no ordinary cabin; this was a luxurious trilevel mountain retreat aimed to please, with every conceivable comfort in mind. And it belonged to Keir's family. Was this where he had planned to spend his honeymoon? she wondered, sudden nausea sending nasty tingles through her body.

"Let me check the phone, then I'll show you to your room," he said brusquely, carelessly dumping his coat on the nearest table and lifting the receiver of the phone that occupied a portion of the table. After a moment, he slammed it down, his face dark as a thundercloud. "The damned thing's dead."

She stared at him horrified. "You . . . you mean we're completely cut off from everything?" she asked, sick with fear at not being able to check on Ann.

"That's right," he said abruptly, then added, "Your room is this way."

They moved down the foyer together and up a short flight of stairs, so close they touched as they walked.

"Who were you talking to on the phone in Cassidy's office?" he asked suddenly. They had come to a halt in front of a door which Danielle could only assume led to her bedroom. "Was it your lover?"

He said "lover" as if it were a contagious disease that she might have contacted. "That's none of your business," she snapped as she moved quickly, fearing his touch, his probing.

His breath, as he leaned his face into hers, was as cold and impersonal as his eyes. "I wouldn't be too sure of that, if I were you. Everything about you is my business. Especially if you value your beautiful skin, that is," he goaded in that same deadly tone.

Again she flinched, backing into the door.

"And damn you, stop looking at me as if you thought I was going to pounce on you. I don't like this setup any more than you do."

"I find that hard to believe," she taunted, pivoting on her heels and walking into the room. She paused in the middle, holding her breath, praying that Keir would not follow. She had decided long ago that he was enjoying this. He was being handed on a silver platter the chance to punish her and seek his revenge. And he was not about to let the opportunity pass. But she didn't know how much longer she could hold out against his jabbing barbs. As it was, her legs were barely supporting her.

He stalked into the room behind her. "What do you find hard to believe?" he asked in menacing undertones.

The blood pounded in her head. For heaven's sake why didn't he just go away and leave her alone? She kept her back turned while the silence reached a screaming pitch.

"Answer me, damn you!"

She held her silence. He was determined to pick a

fight with her, to take his frustrations out on her, but she was tired of being his whipping post. Her back conveyed exactly that as she walked farther into the room, placing considerable distance between them.

The room was lovely, decorated in several shades of green with its own bathroom. Out of the corner of her eye, she stared at the bathroom longingly, wanting nothing more than to soak her weary limbs, especially her shoulder, in the shower and try to pretend none of this was happening, that she was home cuddling Ann in her arms, reading her a book or telling her a story.

She felt his breath on her neck. A bolt of terror struck her mind, like lightning splitting the sky.

"I'm not leaving until you answer me!"

She swung around to face him, now goaded into retaliating. "Get out!" she hissed.

"No!" He grabbed her arm, stared at her, his face contorted with anger, contempt. His eyes were piercing, his mouth a harsh line, his nostrils flaring.

"You're hurting me," she cried. "Stop it." She was shivering uncontrollably.

Her cries fell on deaf ears. He neither stepped back nor relieved the pressure on her arm.

"So you're finding it hard to believe that I'm not panting to have another taste of your delectable body?" he bit out between teeth which snapped like a steel trap. The strong brown hands moved up to encircle her throat as if he would like nothing better than to throttle her. The hard masculine face grew darker by the minute. This was the second time today she had seen that look on his face.

Danielle twisted her head, jerking herself free. "That's not what I meant and you know it," she flung at him savagely, her eyes blazing with fury as her anger soared.

"Are you sure about that?" His question was an unsteady whisper as his mouth began to travel along her uplifted neck toward her chin, while a hand slid under her blouse, across the silky underwear, searching, finding a warm breast, filling his hand with its thrusting fullness. She went rigid against him, her throat flung tautly back to avoid his kiss, deeply aware that he was seeking her lips.

"No!" She groaned. "Get your hands off me."

"You're a little liar. You want it and you know it."

In a split second it happened. It was instinctive; there was no thought behind it or she would not have dared to hit him. But her hand came out and struck him hard across the face.

"How dare you talk to me like that!" she spat. And because he moved in closer: "Don't you dare touch me again. I don't want you near me. . . . Go away."

Keir might have let it end there if she had said something else. He would have endured her physical abuse, let her slap his face because she wouldn't have been the kind of woman she was if she had accepted his last insult. But it was the cry of revulsion that gnashed at his nerves and sent his temper soaring.

He had been forced into a situation that he was not at all certain he was capable of handling. He had been pulled off a much-needed vacation; he'd had to postpone his wedding. For what? To protect the woman who had told him once that his love wasn't enough.

Everything was going wrong. His carefully laid plans to remain aloof, to keep his distance, had broken down. Goddammit, she was like poison within him. She remained hostile and defiant, forbidding him to put his hands on her. Her words, *Don't you dare touch me*, continued to haunt him. All the way from Washington, throughout their long ordeal, with inhaling her scent and the feel of her body against his, he had wanted to do just that.

Suddenly he clamped his hand around her waist and drew her against the rock hardness of his chest. He bent her against his braced body and forced her head back. Her mouth fell open at the surprise and pain of his hold. She moaned in protest as his mouth came down on hers, hungrily, forcing her trembling lips apart, demanding surrender.

"Dear God," he groaned against her lips. Lust for her was like a grenade in his belly. Anything at all would cause the pin to be pulled. He was remembering how it felt to have her spread under him, to hear her moan, crazy to have him.

She refused to surrender at once; she moaned and writhed and made little sounds under his mouth, but then she suddenly went limp, her lips softening in unwilling response. It was as if she were suspended, as if time had ceased to exist. She had the feeling that she was swimming in a waterway above her head and was slowly being overcome. Nothing was real but the pressure of his body against hers; her arms were lax as they hung down, free and useless; his fingers were teasing a nipple to life while he continued the assault on her unprotected mouth.

The sensations of sight and sound escaped her. She clung to his arms, rising and falling with the rhythm of his kisses, feeling the vestige of control slipping as her arms moved upward, as if they belonged to someone else, and slid around his neck. *No!* she thought wildly. She had to stop him. Stop herself. *Think of Ann!*

But she was lost in the feeling of his warm, muscular chest under her palms. Through the thin material of his shirt the heat of his body communicated itself to her skin, and a pulsating sweetness began to throb deep inside her, a feeling that had lain dormant for three long years. Her stomach and her mouth went dry as his hands became unbreakable chains against her hips.

"Please," she whimpered before his tongue swam back into her mouth.

She was drowning. No amount of self-analysis could pry her arms from around his neck. There was never a time in the past when she had lost herself as she was lost now. She had no defense against the fire his tongue was stroking inside her mouth.

It was Keir who stopped. He pushed her away from him. Already, without conscious intent, they had both moved near the bed. Another moment and he would have pulled her down on it. He was pale, scrubbing the back of his hand across his mouth bitterly, his expression more forbidding than ever.

Danielle looked up at him, her face colorless. Tears had seeped under her lids and run down her cheeks. Recoiling in shock, she stared at him in utter disbelief.

"You're just the same!" he bit out harshly. "You haven't changed! You still don't care who you hurt. But now we know where we stand; I can take you any time I like. And I like, so be careful. Be very careful."

She shrank away, shivering convulsively, her hands held in front of her like a shield. "I didn't ask you to touch me," she countered sharply. Her emotions were churning with such a mixture of anger and pain from his unexpected verbal thrust and manhandling that she didn't pause to question why Keir's words and actions still had the power to create deep and lasting wounds within her. Suddenly the room began to spin in front of Danielle's eyes; she struggled for her next breath.

Keir stood totally still, watching her. He saw her face turn deathly white. "I didn't mean to hurt you," he said slowly. "But dammit you pushed me too far." He paused, making a helpless gesture, his jaw tightening in angry frustration before he pushed himself away from her and headed toward the door.

He stopped in the doorway and turned around. Danielle sat exactly where he had left her, trembling violently.

"I'll get you something to drink. What would you like?"

"Hot . . . tea." She did not recognize her own trembling voice. "If you have any, that is." She watched him walk out the door, heard him moving around in the kitchen, listened to the noise of glasses and cups and his heavy tread as he returned. *I should move from here,* she told herself. *I should get away from the bedroom, get off the bed. If he touches me again . . .*

"Here, drink this," Keir said. He put the half-filled cup of tea in her hand and watched while she sipped it cautiously. "I'll leave you now and let you get some sleep."

She gazed up at him, the hot liquid dulling her exhaustion. "Why . . . why did you stop? Why did you let me go?"

"You're a job I have to do, nothing more," he said grimly. "But I wanted to show you that I'm not the same gullible person I was three years ago. Now you know. You needn't be afraid. I won't touch you again."

"You made me hit you," Danielle whispered dully as though she still couldn't believe it herself. "I've . . . I've never struck anyone in anger like that, ever." After seeing him again, being thrown together in a dangerous situation from which they had narrowly escaped, she had expected to experience a painful nostalgia. But nothing she had imagined had prepared her for this instant emotional reaction whenever he simply got near her. When he had touched her, seared her lips with his, her flesh had melted beneath his fingers exactly as it had years before.

As he watched her carefully, she could feel the insistent probing of his eyes even though she averted her face. She was past caring now. All her energy was going into fighting her own rising desire. And she hated herself for this weakness of the flesh.

It was worse, she thought. His absence had managed to feed the flame of passion for him. But she knew that she could not keep on like this indefinitely. If she did, she would have to be taken out of here in a straight-jacket.

She had to get control of herself, put things in their right perspective. She had to look at Keir as her protector, nothing more, and stay out of his way, praying that he would keep his promise not to touch her. And through it all, she must cling to thoughts of her child, her home, her work. To hell with Keir McBride.

His heavy sigh brought her back to reality. She stared into his deep, brooding face. Again, she noticed how tired he looked, the grooves around his mouth and eyes taking on a bluish tint.

"I'm going to scramble eggs and fix toast," he said slowly, wondering how they were going to survive in this impossible situation, yet knowing they had no choice. Something had to give. "I'll call you when it's ready," he added, making a small effort to ease the smothering tension.

Danielle stared down at her hands. The thought of food, of sitting down at the table with him, was intolerable.

She stood up. "You go ahead. I . . . I couldn't eat a thing."

"For God's sake, Danielle, be reasonable!" Keir cupped the back of his neck with his hands as though it ached. "You need to eat. I'm not telling you, or commanding you, but *asking* you to come and eat breakfast and then let me take a look at that shoulder."

Danielle stood her ground. "No thanks, on both accounts. I'm not hungry and . . ." Her voice trailed off as she turned aside, unable to bear the penetration of those green eyes, unknowingly revealing to him the vulnerable nape of her neck.

"You have to eat," Keir pressed harshly. Then more huskily, "God, Danielle, you're nothing but skin and bones. How long has it been since you've had a decent meal?"

How could she tell him that she'd never gained her weight back after Ann was born. There had always been so much to do . . . the responsibility had been so awesome. . . .

"Please . . . will you just go away and leave me alone. I . . . I'm tired. All I want to do is go to bed. I want to be left alone."

"Goddammit, you'd try the patience of a saint!" he exploded, his conciliatory gesture forgotten as he stalked out of the room, slamming the door behind him.

The moment she was alone, she immediately began to shed her clothes, gritting her teeth against the pain in her shoulder.

Making her way into the bathroom, she opened the door and stepped inside the shower. Time was of no consequence as she let the water—as hot as she could stand it—pound her sore, aching body. But her thoughts were not so easily managed. She couldn't stop thinking. . . . *No!* she whispered silently, defiantly, as if she were pushing the horror of the last few moments back with both hands.

It did no good. The old weight of despair kept pressing down on her. The rigid anger contorting Keir's face when he had grabbed her swam before her eyes. Did he hate her that much? It was obvious that he did. And he blamed her for everything. But why? she asked herself. Wasn't it obvious that he had come through their affair and parting unscratched? He was doing what he wanted to do: roaming the globe, flirting with danger, dodging responsibilities.

She shuddered in spite of the heat penetrating her limbs. She was still finding it hard to believe that Keir had been an undercover agent for the government before surfacing and becoming a U.S. Marshal. And she hadn't known it. How could she have been so blind?

Would he be willing to change now, especially with a wife in the offing? The muscles in her stomach contracted. She would not think of things like that. But it was excruciatingly difficult not to do so with Keir being so close, touchable and yet untouchable, so distant.

What was the woman he was going to marry like? Suitable? Acceptable for him? Was she beautiful? How long had he known her? Did he touch her? . . .

Suddenly she leaned over and turned off the shower, unable to stand any more of this inner prying. It was over. What she and Keir had shared was over. She made herself say it aloud, "Over."

What she needed now was sleep. She walked out of the bathroom, nothing but a towel wrapped around her, and crossed to the bed. She pulled back the covers and very gingerly lowered her body onto the clean-smelling sheets.

Yesterday and the hellish night that followed began to recede, grew confused, grew dim, as the silence lulled her eyes closed. . . .

She slept.

When Keir stalked out of Danielle's room, he headed straight for the kitchen, determined to carry out his plan. He began opening cabinets, slinging pots and pans everywhere, searching for a skillet in which to cook the eggs. By the time he had prepared himself a full-course meal—two eggs, bacon, toast—it no longer looked the least bit appetizing to him. But he forced himself to eat, knowing he needed the strength. It tasted like sawdust in his mouth. If only Danielle were sitting with him. Danielle. *Dammit man, forget her!* Shoving the food aside, he jumped up and crossed to the window.

He was furious with himself for what he'd done to her; it was a bad sign, a sign that he was not in command of himself. The whole damn thing was crazy, he thought as he began to pace back and forth in front of the window, swearing. He would sure as hell stick to his promise not to touch her again. That was the important thing. He'd keep his distance, distance from her scent and the accidental contact in case it ignited that sexual spark again. As it was, he'd already committed the unpardonable sin, losing control. And he had a woman, a woman who loved him and was waiting to marry him. To keep his sanity, he needed to cling to that and keep clear of all involvements.

Danielle was still upset over what had happened a few days ago. So much so that she had stayed in her room as much as possible. But nothing helped. During the day she could hear Keir moving about in the adjoining bedroom or taking a shower, and then at night the creak of the mattress as he turned. Even when he slept she was aware of him.

They had tried to avoid one another when possible, give the other breathing room. During the times they had eaten together there had been a silence between them which became a strain. And he moved very carefully so as not to touch her, even by accident, when he got up to clear the table. The mounting tension between them coupled with her worry about Ann was driving her crazy.

Now, examining herself in the mirror, the luxurious bedroom reflected behind her, it was not *her* face she saw. Her armor had been penetrated. He still had the power to make her feel weak all over, to make her lose control, dangerous to the sleeping emotions which only he could arouse. That had not changed. For an insane moment an intense longing to go to him, to lean on his strength overcame her, and then she forced herself to be sensible.

"What you need is some fresh air," she said aloud, slipping into a shirt and green wool sweater with a pair of jeans, leaving her throat to rise smoothly from the open neckline. Her hair fell in silky curls to her shoulders and the only makeup she used was a faint eye-shadow and a colorless gloss for her lips. She was glad that she was able to move her shoulder now with only the slightest twinge of discomfort.

When she walked downstairs, he was sitting at the table drinking a cup of coffee.

Danielle hesitated, not expecting him still to be in the house. On previous mornings, by the time she came downstairs he had eaten his breakfast and had gone outside to do odd chores around the place. Splitting firewood took up hours of his time.

"Good morning," Keir said, standing up and reaching for an empty cup.

"Good morning." The words came in a rushed gasp as she sensed immediately that he appeared different this morning, less tense, less apprehensive, and he looked absolutely gorgeous. He was slim-hipped as ever, obvious in a pair of tight-fitting faded jeans. A rough flannel shirt clung to the muscles of his broad chest and shoulders.

"The coffee's strong enough to walk—hope you can drink it," he said, handing her a cup of the steaming liquid. She looked tired, he thought, with shadows under the eyes. But nothing could take away from the smoothness of that incredible complexion. The bright green she wore suited her exactly.

"I'm . . . I'm sure it's fine." She smiled tentatively as she took the cup from him, feeling a twinge of panic when their fingers touched. Sitting down across from him, she still did not know what to make of his sudden change in attitude. She was uneasy.

"Do you like fish?" he asked suddenly, easing back in his chair. He found himself talking quite naturally. He was determined to do away with the hostility that crackled like an electric current between them. He could afford to be generous now because she hadn't won a victory over him. The victory was his, won in that brief, explosive struggle.

Surprise robbed Danielle of her voice.

He gave her an anxious smile. "Well?"

A warm weakness invaded her body as his eyes fixed on her face for a breathless moment. Was he serious?

"Yes, I'm serious," he said, grinning, taking joy in being able to read her mind.

She flushed. "Well, in that case, the answer is yes."

"What would you say to this deal, then—if I catch them, will you cook them?"

Her eyes widened. "Of course, but where? . . ."

"In the stream at the back of the house," he said, finishing her sentence for her.

"You mean, that stream has fish big enough to eat?"

"Mmmm." He licked his lips. "You bet. Trout that will melt in your mouth."

"You're putting me on."

Keir's eyes became soft. "You really are a city girl, aren't you?"

"I won't argue that point," she murmured, giving him a tremulous smile that camouflaged her inner turmoil.

"I'll show you. How long will it take you to get ready?"

Danielle stood up. "I'm ready now except for getting my coat and hat." Through the soft fabric of her long-sleeved shirt he could see the outline of her nipples. It was like opening a brown paper bag to find that it contained something one always wanted and hadn't expected to receive, especially not in a brown paper bag.

Keir got up suddenly and walked over to the cabinet and turned his back.

"I'll find the thermos while you get your parapher-nalia." He noticed that his hand shook as he reached for the coffeepot; a smothered expletive drowned out her exit.

"I decided the weather was too perfect not to take advantage of it," Keir said. "If the fish feel the same way, everything will indeed be perfect."

They were trudging through the snow, dressed warmly—at least Danielle was. She had on her newly purchased fleece-lined coat, gloves, boots and a crocheted cap, sitting at a jaunty angle atop her head.

Keir, acting as though the twenty-degree temperature did not phase him, wore only a lined jacket over his long-sleeved shirt.

Color was in Danielle's cheeks and she smiled, though it failed to reach her eyes. "I felt the same way when I got up this morning . . . about the weather, I mean," she said breathlessly, trying to match Keir's long strides.

She could see the mountain stream that was approximately fifty feet from the back of the house. Although it looked like a stream to Danielle, the closer they got to it, the more it sounded like a river as it crashed over the rocks.

Looking around her, she was again reminded of the postcard beauty. The trees dotting the mountainside were still bowed with snow, but the sun, dancing shadows on their white covering, would make any artist eager to grab his brush. Their shimmering loveliness was unsurpassed.

"I'll build a fire so you won't freeze while I'm reeling in our dinner," Keir was saying as they reached their destination, carelessly dumping his fishing gear, a thick blanket and a bucket filled with chips of pine and wood on the white crunchy ground. For a moment he was quiet, his eyes scanning the area around them as though he were looking, watching, for an unknown presence. But when he turned toward Danielle his face was clear.

He was close to her now. She could feel his breath as it warmed her cold skin. She stepped back, ostensibly to stare at the gushing water, but determined to put distance between herself and his overwhelming male magnetism.

"You'd better quit bragging and get to work," she said saucily, feeling safe now that he was no longer within touching distance.

He chuckled. "Bragging, huh! Well, we'll see about that. You just watch an old pro."

In record time, he cleared a place in the snow, built a small but adequate fire and saw her comfortably seated on the blanket. He then grabbed his rod, already rigged, and made his way to the edge of the bank.

The pool lay in deep shadow. Water was swirling here and there on the smooth, dark surface, widening into almost perfect circles. Danielle watched in awe as he made his first cast and came up with a wiggling black speckled fish on the end of the line.

He whirled around and laughed, his eyes sparkling. "What do you think now? Still skeptical?"

For a moment, he reminded her of the Keir of long ago. The Keir she had fallen so desperately in love with. The fierce contraction in her throat made it nearly impossible to speak. "It . . . it looks easy enough."

"It is," he quipped. "Easy as falling off a log."

She took her cap off and shook her curls away from her face. "Huh, that's what I'm afraid of."

Keir stared at her for a second, thinking that her hair with the sun shining on it looked like a basket of gold filigree. "After I catch our dinner, would you like to try it?" His voice was hoarse and uneven.

Answering nervousness pressed the air from her lungs. "I . . . I might."

He couldn't draw his eyes away from her, even though he felt as if he were riding in a roller coaster in total blackness, unable to determine what lay before him, unable to prepare himself for the sharp curves, the paralyzing drops, the steep climbs. Suddenly he swung around and for the next twenty minutes concentrated on reeling in the fish.

Danielle watched and said nothing.

Finally the bucket was filled to the brim with fish. He laid down his rod and eased his gangly frame down beside her on the blanket. Neither spoke as he reached for the thermos and, using the lid, poured it full of coffee. A silence hung heavy in the air, an intimate silence that neither was prepared for, but neither could deny.

He watched her with a smoldering gaze that shattered her already-shaken composure.

"Danielle." He did not move, but she felt suddenly as if he had touched her. He seemed terribly close. The way he said her name magnified the tension between them. "I want to know, has there been anyone since. . . me?" There was an odd timbre to his voice.

Her face was a study of misery as she mulled over his question and how to answer it. *Careful, Danielle.* He was probing again—delicately, but probing nonetheless. Perhaps all he wanted was a simple answer, but things were never that easy. She was afraid of him, afraid of herself. She wanted to go—to escape the disturbing note in his voice, the handsome face so achingly close, the arm that slightly brushed hers. Buying time, she leaned away from him and made a pretense of unbuttoning her coat to expose herself to the warmth of the fire.

"Of course, there've been other men," she whispered at last. *But not the way you mean.* She felt a sudden urge to cry.

His mouth tightened. "I see."

Oh, but you don't see. You don't see that I lied to you, that I couldn't stand the thought of another man's hands on my body, nor the thought of another man being a father to your child. She stared blindly at the ground, fighting for control.

"Danielle," he repeated softly.

She felt like she was suspended in a vacuum as she stared up at him.

Red-hot desire erupted between them with a force that stunned them into complete immobility.

Then with a moan reminiscent of a wounded animal,

Keir, clenching his eyes shut, rolled over on his back, his body rigid with tension. "Oh, God, what did we do to deserve such hell?"

Silent agony.

She swallowed, trying to ease the painful constriction in her throat. "Please . . . don't. What . . . what good does it do . . . to keep rehashing old pain?" Tears flooded her eyes, and she could only gulp her words. "You're . . . you're getting married. . . ."

"God! Danielle, not now."

"It's the truth, isn't it?" Her voice was a tormented whisper.

"Yes," he clipped tersely, unable to hide the irritation in his voice. Dammit, he didn't want to talk about Natalie. He didn't want to think about Natalie. Couldn't think about her, not now, not with Danielle sitting in front of him, her warm body tantalizing his senses, her breasts showing their shape under her sweater. Not when all he wanted to do was squeeze and hug her, bite chunks out of her soft, warm, sweet-smelling flesh. . . .

An awful ache engulfed her as she sat up, searching for the words to ease the brittle tension.

"Maybe we'd better go," he said, slicing into the painful silence, and once again erecting that impregnable wall between them. She had a point; he had no right to demand anything of her, when it could only lead to a dead end road, since he had no intention of breaking it off with Natalie.

His face hardened, and he became the old dangerous Keir.

The smell of fish permeated the entire house.

"Mmmm, that smells divine," Keir said, inhaling deeply. He sauntered into the kitchen from the family room where he had been stoking the fire in the huge rock fireplace. He paused in front of the small television set sitting on the edge of the bar and flicked it on. "Thought you might like to know what's going on in the world," he added.

"Fine with me. Dinner will be ready shortly." Danielle smiled; it almost reached her eyes. "But if you want to help speed things up, you can fix the tea."

"You got it," he said and strode over to the cabinet, getting down the jar of instant tea.

Danielle watched him out of the corner of her eye, relieved that he no longer wore that terse, aloof expression. After they had come in from the stream, she was determined not to ruin the entire day by dwelling on the past and a hopeless future. So by burying her own misery, she had coaxed him back into a civil mood.

After watching him clean the fish, they had passed the remainder of the afternoon in front of the fireplace playing several games of gin rummy, careful not to touch on anything personal.

Now as she lifted the golden brown fillets out of the hot grease, ever mindful of his presence beside her, she thought how this could have been a sweet domestic scene—except for the turmoil brewing underneath the calm surface and the gun resting on the edge of the sink in front of him.

"My part's done. How about yours?" Keir asked.

"Er . . . set the french fries on the table and we'll be all set."

They had just sat down and were filling their plates when the unexpected and jarring ring of the phone split the silence. For a moment, they were both disoriented.

"Well, I'm certainly glad to have the phone working again," he said. "I'll take it in the office." He shoved his chair back and stood up, looking down into her upturned face. His breath caught sharply as their eyes met and held. She was lovely, he thought, staring at the way her caftan cupped her breasts, emphasizing their alluring fullness.

Danielle couldn't help but follow the movement of his eyes. Seconds ticked by, the phone continuing its insistent ringing. Still they stared, powerless to move. His look sent the blood pulsing through her veins like warm, heady brandy.

Finally, he jerked himself upright. "Don't let your food get cold," he said in a rough unnatural voice, before turning and walking out of the room.

Danielle let her breath out slowly. God, what was happening to her? But she knew. She had wanted to touch him so badly that it made her insides shake.

She began concentrating on her food, desperate to banish the image of his long limbs entwined with hers throughout the long nights, their heartbeats as one. . . .

She closed her eyes, fighting for her sanity. When they fluttered open again, he was standing in the doorway. Her heart jumped.

"You . . . you scared me," she stammered.

"Who is Ann?"

Chapter 6

DANIELLE KEPT THE FORK FROM CLATTERING TO HER PLATE by sheer force of will. For a moment she was a young girl again, at the orphanage, swinging high in a swing when suddenly she slipped out and watched in horror as the ground rose up to meet her, knocking the breath from her body with a savage brutality. She was experiencing the same feeling now, only much worse.

She could not say a word. Her throat and her stomach hurt as though she had tried to swallow a piece of jagged glass and succeeded.

"Who is Ann?" he repeated, his voice like a razor.

She simply gaped at him, soaking in the steely tension of his rigid jaw, the dark flush of fury staining his face. She held onto the table for dear life while she fought back the panic that threatened to suck her under. *He knows!* she told herself frantically. *He knows. He's placed a noose around your neck; now he's waiting for you to hang yourself.*

When she finally spoke, it was a poor imitation of her own voice. "It's obvious you already know," she said defiantly.

"I want to hear *you* say it." His eyes cut into hers like icepicks.

The tilt of her chin remained firmly upthrust. "She's. . . she's my daughter."

Keir's sharp intake of breath pierced the air, shattering the moment's silence. "Oh, God. No!"

He felt his heart twist and then collapse like a building in an earthquake. He held his head at an angle. "No," he repeated, not for effect, but as though, perhaps, he had been struck with an immediate and total loss of memory. It was as though he had been able to black out what he didn't want to hear. But it was true. She had a child. *His child?* God! "Danielle . . ." His hands rose and fell in a terrible gesture of despair.

Danielle opened her mouth to speak, then clamped it shut, held mute against the emotion she saw registered in Keir's green eyes. Her body was trembling unmercifully, and her heart was somewhere around her toes. She closed her eyes and breathed hard trying to relieve the pressure on her heart.

His reaction stunned her. She had expected anger, hatred, cold remoteness, but she had not been prepared for the distress, the pain. It was there, in his voice—that awful, unrelenting agony that twisted one's insides into an aching knot. She had never meant to hurt him, but she had. She had cut him to the core, and there was not one damned thing she could do about it. She could not risk telling him the truth. Ann was her life. She could face the agonies of dying a slow death easier than she could face losing her child—even to its father. Especially to its father.

She turned her back against the burning question in Keir's eyes. Her shock and anger at being caught in this situation had suddenly spent itself, and an intense feeling of guilt was rushing in to fill the vacuum. She dared not stay a moment longer, or she would come apart in front of him.

On legs that were considerably less than steady, she stood up and made a beeline for the door. She had to have time to herself. To think. No matter what the cost, Keir must never know Ann was his.

He reached the door with the agility of an animal springing to its prey. An arm shot out across the threshold. She stopped short of touching him.

"Oh, no you don't," he grated harshly, suppressed fury having taken the place of pain.

Danielle stepped back. "Please . . . let me go," she whispered.

For a few seconds, he looked away from her, his heart pumping wildly in his chest. She swayed lightly, closing her eyes.

"Who's child is it?"

Her eyes flew open. Keir was staring at her again, his face a cold mask. There was no smile, no alteration in his probing eyes. His unexpected question cut through her like a blade. But then just as quickly, she rallied, throwing her shoulders back, prepared to fight him with any and every weapon she had.

"She's mine," she answered defensively, ignoring the erratic beat of her heart. *Stay cool,* she warned herself. *Don't let him rattle you.*

"I wouldn't advise you to play games with me." His voice had a menacing edge to it.

"When it comes to my daughter, I don't play games."

"Well, we'll sure as hell see about that," he countered sarcastically.

"I don't have to take this from you, Keir McBride, not now, not ever." Although she put up a brave front, her insides were quaking.

"If she's not mine, then whose is she?" His face darkened, taking on a sinister glint.

"Mine!" Danielle repeated in a hissing tone. She turned her back on him and gazed out the window, concentrating on the huge snowflakes falling amidst the shadows of the late evening. She forced herself to gaze at the now familiar sight, the flakes adorning the weeping branches of the pines with a fresh coat of paint. Anything, she told herself, was preferable to Keir's grim countenance and merciless interrogation.

Having decided that his silence proved she had won the battle if not the war, she was totally unprepared for the next attack.

"What did you do, run straight into some other poor unsuspecting bastard's arms and have the baby?" he asked. Then before she could answer, he hammered on, "What happened, you couldn't get him to marry you?"

Every vestige of color deserted her face. "Why . . . why . . . you miserable swine!"

"Answer me, damn you!"

Hot fury loosened her tongue as nothing else could have done. She went straight for the jugular vein, just as he had gone for hers.

"But you'll never know the answer to either question, will you?" she goaded, her voice rising with every word she uttered. "Because I'll never tell you! Remember I know how you think; so no matter what I said, you'd still blame me."

His eyes narrowed and cut into her like blades. "You haven't heard the last of this, by any means. You owe me the truth and I aim to get it. One way or the other."

Suddenly the fight went out of Danielle. Seeing the fierce determination ground into the lines of his face and the icy warning in his voice, she knew she had pushed him as far as she dared. Besides, she was aware that he could easily carry out his threat once they were back to civilization. Her stomach lurched violently at the thought.

"Please . . . let me pass." Her throat was starting to close, her eyes stung with the need to cry.

He stared into her upturned face, fury lining his features. Then with a muttered oath, he turned around, swinging his tough, rangy body as if it were on ball bearings and walked stiffly into the den.

"Get out of my sight," he hissed, "before I do something that will cause us both to be sorry."

Danielle lost no time in making good her escape. But when she reached the top of the stairs, she stopped and turned around. Keir had not moved. His back was still to her, his shoulders hunched, seemingly more exhausted than she, as if his enormous strength had failed him.

Her own heart was breaking as she dragged her weary limbs to her cold, empty room and quietly closed the door behind her. She sat down on the bed, wanting to cry, to weep out all the anguish, all the hurt, all the shame. But she couldn't. The tears would not come.

Long after Danielle had gone, Keir stood leaning against the fireplace mantel, feeling sick and stricken inside.

When Cassidy had mentioned to him during the phone call about her child, assuming he already knew, he had nearly gone insane. And then to have gotten no satisfactory answers from her was driving him closer to the edge.

With an explosive curse, he crossed the room to stand by the window. Then he began to walk the length of the room. He had to believe that the child was not his or else he didn't think he could handle it. Yet, the idea that it wasn't kept him pacing the floor, sweating with jealousy. The thought of another man touching her, kissing the mouth he had kissed, loving her, then falling asleep with her in his arms, contented and warm, made him almost violent.

But no amount of pacing could calm his imagination. What the hell had become of his coldness, his indifference? Furthermore, why would anyone in his right mind want to be run over by the same train twice?

He sat down on the couch; he had to get control of himself. Because the reality was that it was over between them. After this assignment was behind him, they would go their separate ways. Somehow he had to banish the desire for her and the sickness of spirit that longed for her so desperately that he felt like a wounded animal. He had to forget what it was like to have her soft, unmarked body molded to his, the fragrance of her body, the way her nipples tasted as he tantalized them into hot points of desire, how she opened like a flower to the sun to admit his seeking, throbbing passion, how it felt to be inside her. . . .

"God!" he groaned to the silent room. *Don't think about her anymore,* he commanded himself. She was not for him. Never had been. *But what about the child?* his conscience whispered. *What if she's yours?*

Unable to sit still another second, he vaulted from the couch, crossed the room to the stairs and trudged up them to his room. He lay down on the bed and stared up at the ceiling. Think about going back to Washington, think about running for the senate, think about Natalie and your future together.

Think about anything, but the woman in the next room. . . .

Two days passed with no change. It was as if a cold war existed between them, each fighting to come to terms with misery. The strain grew more apparent every day. Danielle cooked for him, then disappeared during the day to wile away the long hours. The only bright spot of relief in the solitary hours was the phone calls home. She visited with Jusie by phone at least twice a day and never hung up until she had said a few words to Ann. Every time she heard her daughter's "Mommie, Mommie" she thought her heart would break.

She was finding the situation more intolerable by the day. No matter how hard she tried to avoid Keir, she found it impossible to do so. His hard, closed face followed her wherever she went. But what gnawed at her relentlessly was that she found herself *wanting* to know where he was, what he was doing. In spite of the tension between them she wanted to be near him.

She was just lonely, she kept telling herself. Lonely for a man. *Any man.* What she'd missed was having a man's strong arms around her. No, she argued—not any man. Just Keir. God help her, she wanted Keir. When she relived how it felt to have his talented hands caress every forbidden part of her body. . . .

No! *Don't do this to yourself!* He was getting married, for God's sake, she reminded herself brutally.

With a disgruntled shake of her head, she pulled herself out of her musings and stood up, deciding that she had time to take a shower before going downstairs to fix breakfast.

A short time later, her task complete, she was making her way back into the bedroom when the door of her room opened without warning and Keir stood on the threshold staring at her.

"I . . . er . . . knocked," he said, swallowing uncomfortably, "but there was no response, so . . ." He shrugged, his voice trailing off.

She couldn't control the tremor in her voice as his eyes seemed to burn through her robe to sear her skin. "I . . . I didn't hear you. I . . . I was in the shower."

He advanced into the room, not once taking his eyes off her, half closed the door and then opened it again as though having second thoughts.

"What did you want?" she asked huskily, uneasily, holding the sides of her robe together, aware that his painful scrutiny missed little.

Their eyes melted together. His senses stirred. She was so utterly desirable in every way.

He cleared his throat. "Cas . . . Cassidy wants to talk to you." He breathed in her perfume, staring deliberately at the open neck of her gown. It was made of some soft green stuff, with a long row of velvet buttons. He wasn't concerned about keeping his boss dangling on the phone; he wasn't concerned about anything, not with her breasts showing their shape under the row of little buttons.

He recognized the moment when she became aware of the intensity of his regard. Beneath the fine material of her robe, the hardening nipples sprang to life and were outlined in sensuous detail. His arousal was instant and painful.

Danielle tried to free her eyes from his magic spell. Her palms were damp and there was a film of sweat on her forehead as she tipped her head back and shut her eyes tightly and fought to control the desire churning inside her.

Her eyes sprang open with his next words. "I guess you'd better not keep the man dangling any longer," he said, a strained smile on his lips.

She cursed herself silently as a telltale warmth stained her cheeks. She found her voice. "He wants to talk to me?" Suddenly passion turned to fear. *Ann.* Was something wrong with Ann?

"There's nothing the matter," he said softly, reading her mind. "Cassidy just wants to talk to you."

Reassured, but not completely convinced, Danielle swept past Keir and tore off quickly down the stairs and into the den.

She found that she was shaking when she lifted the phone to her ear. "Hello, Marshal Cassidy." Her voice held a thread of uneasiness.

"How are you, Ms. Davis?" he asked politely.

"Under the circumstances, I'm fine," she lied. She was not fine. Keir was driving her crazy.

"I wish I were calling to inform you that everything had been cleared up, but unfortunately I'm not." An impatient sigh sounded over the line. "So far, the Russians have managed to elude the capable agents of the FBI. But we hope it won't be much longer until this mess is cleared up, once and for all."

Her heart sank. "Is . . . is that all you called to tell me?" she asked, trying to stifle the depression. Would she ever be able to return home to her family, her job?

"No, actually I called to tell you that we're sending another agent to your home just as a double precautionary measure." Ignoring her sharp intake of breath, he went on, "It's just that, Ms. Davis, a precaution and nothing more. But I knew if I didn't tell you first, before your housekeeper did, you would automatically think the worst."

"Are . . . you sure you're telling the truth?" There was a touch of panic in her voice. She wanted to believe him, was afraid not to believe him.

Cassidy's voice was soft, but guarded. "You can trust me, Ms. Davis. In spite of what you may think, we're not your enemy. We're trying to make this as easy for you under the circumstances as possible."

Damn him! What right did he have to make her feel guilty? And she didn't want to feel grateful to him for anything. "Thank you for telling me," she said, hanging onto her control with great difficulty.

"Bear with us, Ms. Davis," he said brusquely, before the dial tone replaced his voice.

When she hung up and turned around, Keir was watching her.

"Oh, Keir," she wailed, forgetting for a moment the animosity that simmered between them, "I . . . can't help but worry about . . . Ann."

A flicker of pain darkened his eyes for a split second, but then it quickly disappeared. He took in her white, stricken look and his eyes softened. "Don't be," he said. "Cassidy briefed me before I came for you. He's on the level. Everything is fine on the homefront."

Anxiety gripped her heart. "Are you sure?" Her voice cracked on the last word.

"I promise."

The low, husky tone of his voice left her breathless. She looked away, but not before he saw the tiny pulse pounding in her throat.

A hushed silence fell over the room.

"It's another gorgeous day. How would you like to get out of here for a while and go for a hike through the woods?" Keir asked at last, shattering the unnatural silence.

Her lashes swept up, her eyes wide with shock. "Do . . . you mean it?"

"Yes, I mean it," he said, his voice warm, a small smile tugging at his harshly etched lips.

His old heart-stopping charisma was working again. Her mind was rational, but her heart was betraying her. She was responding to his kindness like a drowning man finding a rope.

"Run upstairs and get dressed. I'll wait."

The second Danielle disappeared, the smile deserted Keir's face, leaving him looking once again grim and foreboding. Sudden irritation quickly bloomed into full anger. "Face it, McBride, you're a god-damned fool, a glutton for punishment!" he muttered aloud.

But he knew for a fact that they could not keep on going like they had been. The tension between them was like a simmering volcano—it could erupt at any given moment.

Something had to give. It was as simple as that.

"I love this weather," Danielle said. "It's certainly different from East Texas."

They were walking through the snow at a leisurely pace, following the stream at the rear of the house.

Danielle felt like she had been given a special treat by being allowed to roam around outdoors. Keir had warned her never to wander around outside alone. And since he had never offered to invite her to go along with him to cut firewood, she spent her time inside the cabin. The fishing trip was the last time she had tromped through the snow.

The sun felt wonderful shining down on her bare head.

"I agree, it's beautiful here," Keir said, his low-pitched voice echoing through the silence. She could smell the fresh, clean fragrance of his cologne as their strides matched perfectly.

Danielle glanced up at him between her lashes. "Do you come here often?" she asked rather shyly. She couldn't remember his having mentioned the cabin to her during their brief time together.

He was quiet for a moment. "No," he said. "I never have the time." He was captivated by the way her sun-kissed hair framed her face in a riot of soft curls.

"That seems such a shame." Her voice was wistful.

"Oh, it gets used quite often. My parents come here when they can get away from Washington. My mother thinks this is the greatest place in the world."

Danielle tipped her head back and looked up at the tall hardwoods. To her they seemed to have a direct communication with the heavens. "I can understand that," she said softly, wishing that she could have been here under different circumstances. But then, determined not to let anything mar this outside adventure, she shied away from any unpleasant thoughts.

Now that they had ventured about a hundred yards from the house, completely opposite from where they had gone fishing, they came upon a huge cleared area. Sitting in the middle of it was a large metal building.

Danielle halted in her tracks. "I . . . I had no idea this was here."

He peered down into her upturned face. "Does that surprise you?"

She shrugged. "Not that you have it, no. But why here?"

"It's a good thing to have around when there's an emergency, and there've been several since we've owned this place."

A frown wrinkled her forehead. "What happened?"

"My father had a heart attack a couple of years ago, and if the chopper hadn't been here or me to fly it, he wouldn't be alive today."

"Oh, how awful."

"It was at the time," he said grimly, "but he came through with very little damage to his heart." He paused and began walking. "Let's just hope we don't have to use it," he added, his eyes scanning the woods, the mountains around them.

She stopped short again and stared. "What . . . what do you mean?" she whispered. A shiver ran the length of her slender frame, a shiver that had nothing to do with the sharp, biting cold. For a moment she had forgotten the reason she was here, had forgotten because . . . oh, God . . . because of Keir and the power he held over her.

"Hey," he said gently, his gaze wandering over her face, searching eyes that grew dark with an emotion she couldn't name. "Forget what I said. Nothing's going to go wrong, you'll see." A smile deepened the dimples on either side of his cheek. "I'll let you get even by permitting you to clobber me with a snowball." He would do anything to remove that dark, frightened glaze from her eyes. Why hadn't he kept his mouth shut?

Danielle's answering smile flashed like sunlight through a passing storm. "Well, now I just don't see how I can let that opportunity pass," she said impishly.

"And I'll even supply the snowball," he said unevenly, her dazzling smile shortening his breath.

She shook her head. "Nothing doing. When the time is right, I'll make my own snowball and seek my revenge." There was a wicked gleam in her eyes. "When you're least expecting it," she added.

"Then I guess I won't be able to let you out of my sight, will I?" His voice was as seductive as a gentle caress, and a throbbing ache grew within her as their gaze continued to hold.

How long they stood wrapped in a long, sweet silence neither one knew or cared. For what seemed like eons, they were reluctant to move, to speak, to breath, for fear of breaking it.

"We'd better keep walking," Keir said moments later, his voice gravelly with suppressed emotion.

Danielle's heart was beating like a frightened deer's as she fell in step beside him, while trying to smother the empty feeling of disappointment. For a moment, she had thought he was going to kiss her.

"Are you cold?" he asked.

The silence was so long that he didn't think she would answer. They kept walking. When she spoke, her voice was just a wisp of sound. "No . . . not really . . . I . . ." Her voice faded away.

"Tell me about your work," he said suddenly, unexpectedly.

Relieved to be on safe ground, she responded quickly. "I own and manage a small bookstore."

"What kind of books do you sell?"

"All types: paperbacks, new and used, bestsellers in hardback."

"Do you like your work?"

"I love it." Her eyes sparkled like champagne. "Especially since it's in my home."

"You can't beat that for convenience."

"That's the idea."

Another silence fell between them as they climbed up a rather steep incline.

"Who . . . takes care of your daughter . . . of Ann?"

Danielle made no response.

"Does she stay with you while you work?" he pressed.

A feeling of impending disaster came to her in a sickening rush. She did not want to discuss Ann. Not with him. Oh, God, not with him. "No," she answered tightly.

"Does her hair shine like silver moonbeams, like yours?"

She caught her breath, only to find that there was no air left in her lungs. "Please . . ." she whispered desperately, "I don't want to talk about . . ."

"Why?" he demanded. "What are you afraid of?"

"Nothing," she snapped, clinging to her control with difficulty.

"For God's sake, talk to me."

She stopped and placed her gloved hands over her ears. "I don't have to talk to you. Ever."

"Danielle!"

"No!"

"Yes!"

"I don't owe you anything. You don't care about me, about Ann. How could you . . . when you're marrying someone else?" she sobbed, giving into the urge to get away from him. She whirled around, and before he could stop her, she went tearing off down the steep incline.

"Come back!" Keir yelled. "You'll hurt yourself."

Danielle paid no heed to his warning; she kept on going, tears blinding her vision.

Keir tore out after her.

She felt him gaining on her, but she could not maneuver any faster through the deep snow.

"Goddammit, will you stop!" Keir yelled harshly.

Danielle kept on going. But it was only a matter

of seconds before a hand clamped down on her shoulder.

"No!" she cried, and began twisting and turning in his grasp.

It was at that moment she lost her balance, causing her knees to buckle beneath her. She began to fall. He refused to turn her loose.

"Keir!" Her scream echoed through the silence as they both rolled and tumbled through the hard snow, down the side of the mountain.

Danielle squeezed her eyes shut and clung to Keir for dear life.

They reached the bottom, legs wrapped in a tangled heap, Keir on top.

Gasping for breath, he moved just enough to look down into her pale, stunned features. "Are you hurt?" he rasped, madly running his hands up and down the length of her body making sure that there were no broken bones.

Danielle's heart was pounding against her chest like a sledgehammer as she opened her eyes to stare into Keir's frantic eyes, so close to her own. "I . . . don't think so," she stammered, fighting for her next breath.

He groaned, his face ashen, his breathing heavy and labored. "Are you sure?"

"I'm sure."

"I'm so sorry, so sorry," he whispered, his warm breath misting her face. "If you'd been hurt, I'd never have forgiven myself."

It was a painful, aching trembling that suddenly choked her breath as their eyes locked and held.

His insides shook as his body fitted to the gentle curves of hers. God, how he wanted her. Needed her.

Lights began to pulse inside her brain. Oh, God, if he touched her now . . . *Don't let him get to you!* An anguished sob tore from her throat. "Please . . . let me up," she whimpered.

An answering sob ripped from his throat when he

saw the pleading in her eyes, begging him not to take advantage of her. He understood desire; he knew what it could do to a man's nerves. It was working on him now, wasn't it?—ripping his guts to shreds. And he knew how it could distort one's judgment. He knew it because desire was what he felt for her, but resisting the temptation to touch her now was only possible because of other feelings which he refused to give into. Love was not a word his desire would admit. At this moment, he was sure he knew exactly what a man facing a firing squad felt like.

He rolled away from her.

When the knock sounded on Luke Cassidy's door, he was brooding over the latest development in the Davis case.

"Come in," he said shortly, raising his eyes as Tony Welch came striding through the door. "Well?"

Welch came to a halt in front of his desk and eyed his boss carefully. "Couldn't reach McBride. Lines are down again."

"What the hell do you mean—the lines are down again?"

Welch stepped back. "It seems that every time there's a snowstorm in that neck of the woods, the phone lines and sometimes the power lines go down."

"Damn!"

"What . . . what do you suggest we do, sir?"

Cassidy's eyes narrowed into tiny slits. "What I suggest," he said distinctly, dangerously, "is that you get off your ass and get that message to McBride. Get the god-damned highway patrol to take it if you have to. I don't care. Just see that he gets it the quickest way possible. Understand?" Although his voice had not risen a single decibel, it sounded as though he was shouting.

Welch paled. "Yes, sir. I'll take care of it right away."

"See that you do," Cassidy said as Welch turned and walked out of the room.

The moment he was alone, Cassidy lowered his weary body back down into his chair, and cradled his head in his hands. What next? he wondered bleakly.

Danielle remained in her room the rest of the morning and most of the afternoon. She had gone there the minute they had returned to the house, her nerves and heart in a shambles. After she had stripped the clothes from her body and taken a shower, she had done nothing but sit as though in a stupor, staring into space, trying to figure out what terrible thing she had done to warrant such punishment.

It was the loud knock on the front door that finally roused her. The unexpected sound stirred her into instant action. For some unexplainable reason, she was suddenly afraid. Jumping up, she jerked open the door of her room and looked up and down the hall before making her way cautiously down the stairs into the den.

Keir was standing by the fireplace. His hand was locked around the holster lying on the mantel. He tensed when he saw her.

She felt the impending disaster as she watched him draw out the snub-nosed pistol. He raised his fingers to his lips, signaling her to keep quiet, then turned and made his way toward the door.

On legs that were not steady, she followed him, though careful to keep out of his line of vision.

He paused to the left of the door, his weapon raised. "Who's there?"

"I have a message," came the reply.

"Leave it."

"But . . . but, sir . . ."

"Leave it," Keir repeated, his tone deadly.

"Where?"

Danielle remained in the shadows, listening, uncertainty curled within her belly.

"Leave it on the doormat and then be on your way," Keir ordered crisply, refusing to take any chances.

He waited, holding his position, the silence reaching a screaming pitch. Then he moved, going to the nearest window and slipping back the curtain to stare into the evening twilight. He looked on as a tall, broad-shouldered man dressed in a Virginia State Trooper's uniform made his way down the path.

He then turned and moved quickly back to the door and cocked his pistol, opening it slowly and cautiously. Seeing and hearing nothing suspicious, he leaned down and scooped up the envelope and slammed the door.

Danielle stepped into the light, fear climbing up her spine with icy fingers. Somehow she managed to push words past her frozen lips. "Please . . . what does it say?" she whispered.

Hastily, Keir ripped it open. The contents glared at him off the page. THE HAWK IS DEAD STOP PROCEED WITH CAUTION. His oath split the silence as he crushed the paper in the palm of his hand.

Numbing terror washed through Danielle's body, threatening to stop her heartbeat. "What . . . what does it say?"

Keir looked away. "Nothing you need to be concerned with," he lied.

"Tell me, damn you!" she screeched. "Is it Ann?"

"It's John Elsworth; they found him in his cell this morning. He was murdered."

Chapter 7

DANIELLE INSTANTLY WENT WEAK WITH RELIEF THAT nothing had happened to Ann. Then suddenly she turned cold. The implications of what it could mean to her and to Ann hit her like a vicious blow. If they had gotten to Elsworth in prison, they could surely get to her . . . or to her child.

"Oh, no," she whimpered, putting her balled fist up to her mouth. Her insides began to shake as the futility of the situation overwhelmed her. Then she breathed deeply, struggling for composure. Now was not the time to fall apart, she scolded herself brutally. Ann would be fine. Cassidy would not let her down. He had promised, hadn't he? Besides, it was her they wanted. She was the only one who could identify Letsukov. Now, however, it was of paramount importance that she keep a cool head.

"It's not as bad as it sounds," Keir said softly, seeing fear pinch her features. He heaved his huge frame to an upright stance. "First thing, they don't know where we are, and the second thing, they have to go through me to get to you." His voice and eyes reminded her of cold steel.

She swallowed against the lump in her throat and nodded weakly.

A chill shook his body as he saw the worry and fear remain in her face. "Why don't you go sit down in the den, and I'll get you a shot of brandy," he said with gentle insistence.

"Thank . . . you," she muttered inanely, though she continued to stand still, her face a waxen mask, her body unnaturally stiff. The concern in his voice nearly triggered her tears. Would this nightmare ever end?

Keir stared at her, taking in her pale solemn face. It was all he could do not to pull her into his arms and reassure her again that nothing or no one was going to harm a hair on her head.

She looked so vulnerable, so uncertain, so haunted, yet there was a strength about her that surprised him. He had never felt protective of a woman before, not even Danielle when he'd first met her. And certainly not Natalie; his attitude toward her was like that of an older brother. But there was nothing of that in his feeling for Danielle; there never had been. She was a mixture that had always confused him, constantly arousing new impulses which he had never experienced before. And with each passing moment he was with her, the situation became more explosive, more unbearable . . . and more dangerous.

Her movement shattered his thoughts. Danielle crossed to a chair in front of the fireplace and sat down, lowering her head in her hands.

He stood a moment longer, watching the firelight play over her. Suddenly every nerve in his body began to twitch. He wanted her; he wanted her in bed. He wanted her so badly it was ripping his insides to shreds. *But you're not going to touch her, goddamn you! Get a hold of yourself. Do your job. Forget everything else.*

He moved in a jerking motion, striding toward the bar, angry at himself.

Shortly he returned to the den with glasses in hand.

"Thanks," she murmured, raising the glass to her lips and downing a small portion of the amber liquid. Although it seemed to explode, creating a burning sensation in the bottom of her stomach, it did nothing to ease the dull ache inside her heart.

Keir sat down heavily opposite her, like an old man whose body had seen the end of the road. He placed the tumbler, unsampled, on the arm of the chair.

Danielle watched him carefully, her expression grave, but questioning.

"Why . . . why do you think Cassidy sent a message instead of calling?" she asked nervously.

Suddenly Keir jumped up as though he'd been shot and in two agile strides covered the distance to the phone and snatched up the receiver and placed it against his ear.

"Damnation," he snapped, "just as I thought. The lines are dead again."

"Oh, no, not again," Danielle cried in disgust, hating the fact that she was again cut off from communicating with her home.

"I can't say I'm surprised," Keir said soberly while chewing on his bottom lip. "We lose power here several times during the winter months." He sighed. "I only hope they're working around the clock to get it repaired by morning."

"Do you think you should've talked to the messenger, tried to find out a little more?"

"No," Keir answered. "Because I know that he was a go between and nothing more. Knowing how Luke's mind works, he got me the message the fastest way possible. Don't worry, he'll be in touch again soon, you can count on that, especially if there's to be a change in plans."

"You seem to have a lot of confidence in him."

Keir's lips twisted. "He can be a bit trying at times, but he knows what he's doing and I can only respect that in a man."

"It's obvious he feels the same way about you."

"Let's just put it this way. He more or less pulled me up by the bootstraps and took me under his wing at a time when I didn't really care if I lived or died."

The bitterness in his voice stung Danielle's ears. She looked away. *Oh, Keir,* she cried silently. *Why do we keep hurting one another?*

She was aware of him with every fiber of her being, even though she kept her face averted. He was wearing jeans and a tan crew-neck knit shirt, a tan down-filled vest being his only concession to the biting cold. The silver threads running through his dark hair were highlighted slightly by the flickering light.

Out of the corner of her eye, Danielle saw him reach for his glass, gripping it tightly. His long legs, stretched forward in an apparently relaxed attitude, seemed tense too. He was gazing broodingly into the crackling fire. Was he as aware of her as she was him?

Danielle turned her head and stared into his face, and immediately wished she hadn't. He was looking at her speculatingly, not at her face but at her lips.

She felt her cheeks burn as the silence lingered.

"Who . . . who do you think was responsible for Elsworth's death?" she asked suddenly, desperately.

Keir gave her a guarded look. "Letsukov must have a contact on the inside who was willing to pull this nasty job for him."

Danielle shuddered. "But why would they want to kill him now? The damage has already been done. He's already testified."

"That's the point," he said, a sardonic brow slanting upward. "They were determined to get even, and they apparently succeeded."

She sank her teeth into her lower lip to keep it from trembling. "If . . . if they were determined to get to

John . . . then it means they'll be that much more determined to get to . . . to me. . . ."

Her words hung heavy in the air, followed by a frightening silence. Keir finally shattered it, his voice like ice. "If they do, they're as good as dead."

"Oh, God, Keir, how . . . how did all this get out of hand so quickly?" she asked, the hardening twist of his forbidding jawline and his menacing words frightening her almost as much as the bizarre murder of Elsworth. The thought of Keir actually taking another person's life—well, that didn't bear thinking about. Tears of hopelessness were gathering on her eyelashes.

Upon seeing those tears, something snapped inside Keir, an explosive fury at everyone involved in this escapade, including himself. In spite of the brave front she was putting on, she was terrified, and it shook him to the core. He inwardly railed at Cassidy for having gotten him into this fiasco, himself for having broken the first rule and becoming personally involved. Again. For whether he wanted to admit it or not, he *was* involved—had been since the moment he walked into Cassidy's office and saw her standing there.

And his hands were tied. The frustration of not being able to do anything but wait, possibly becoming sitting ducks while they did so, was placing a heavy strain on his patience. If Letsukov had been able, through connections, to get someone on the inside to murder Elsworth, then Letsukov was capable of getting to Danielle.

But for now all he could do was sit tight and wait to hear from Cassidy. If his superior thought that they were in any immediate danger here, he would have signaled a move. Why then did he continue to feel an uneasiness crawl up and down his spine?

"Are you going to be all right?" Keir asked, thick, sweeping eyelashes partially shielding his expression.

"I'm . . . I'm fine."

A deep frown etched across his brow. "Are you sure?"

"No, but I'm working on it," she replied faintly.

"Dwelling on it won't do any good, you know."

"I know, but I keep thinking about John. . . ."

"Don't," he demanded in a soft whisper, "don't say it. Don't even think it. In order to get to . . . Ann . . . uh—they would have to go through two professionally trained U.S. Marshals. And nothing is going to happen to you." His voice trembled, as a barrage of emotions ricocheted through him. He didn't dare define what he was feeling, but it was there.

"I . . . I hope you're right," she murmured, her eyes glued to the fire.

"In spite of what you may think, you can trust me, you know," he said softly.

His words, like an arrow, pierced her soul. A ragged breath tore through her as the tension crackled in the air between them. Their eyes, through the shimmering firelight, met and held.

"I think I'll go outside and take a look around." He had to get away from her.

Danielle experienced another twitch of panic at the thought of him going outside alone. "Is . . . that necessary?" She couldn't seem to stifle her feeling of paranoia.

His eyes were hooded as he stood up and looked down at her, the firelight emphasizing her drawn, tense features.

Again, he had to fight the urge to haul her into his arms, while damning himself and his weakness.

"Nothing's wrong," he replied, more briskly than he intended. "I just want to take a look around."

"You'll . . . be careful, won't you?"

Keir's breath caught in his throat. "I . . . will," he said thickly, unable to pull his eyes away from hers. "I'll be back shortly."

The remainder of her strength suddenly drained from her and a warm, heady longing stirred within her. "I . . . I think I'll rustle us up a bite to eat while you're gone." The thought of going back upstairs to her empty room upset her worse than sharing an intimate dinner with Keir. Or did it?

"That's not necessary," he said. "You just stay put, and I'll take care of that chore when I get back," he added lightly, then stared at her a moment longer before pivoting on his heels.

His footsteps appeared as heavy as her heart as she rested her head back against the cushion and listened to him walk to the door.

Why had fate suddenly decided to pit her against such overwhelming odds? she wondered despairingly. All she had wanted since losing Keir was to live her life in peace, create a loving home for her daughter and do the work she loved best. Nothing was working out as she had planned. She was holed up in a cabin, hiding from a maniac, only to run headlong into another problem, equally as dangerous—Keir and the rebirth of her love for him.

She saw her neat, tidy world being ripped apart at the seams, and there wasn't one thing she could do about it. She was beginning to depend on, to need, him again. And that was something she had promised herself would never happen. Where would it all end?

"You've barely touched your food," Keir said, eyeing her plate filled with a steak, baked potato and a fresh salad.

After having taken a quick look around the place, his flashlight and his Smith and Wesson as companions, Keir had come back inside to the cozy warmth, finding that Danielle had taken him at his word and remained where she was. He had noticed the empty glass of brandy on the table beside her before discarding his coat and making his way into the kitchen to begin preparing dinner.

Now as he watched her, taking in the dark shadows under her eyes and the weary slant to her mouth, he longed to make her pain disappear. *Sadist!*

"It's delicious, really it is, and I'm grateful to you for fixing such an elaborate meal."

Nervously, she took a tiny bite of the steak, licking her lips with the tip of her tongue as she grew more and more aware of his gaze.

"I'm glad you approve. It's not often I take the time to put together a decent meal." He was becoming mesmerized by the tiny flick of her tongue.

"I'm sorry," she apologized suddenly, pushing her plate away, shattering the tension. "I thought I could eat, honest I did. But . . . but I feel my stomach beginning to rebel. When I think of John . . ."

"Hey, take it easy," he pleaded earnestly. "You're only making matters worse. How about another glass of brandy or wine?" A gentle smile touched his lips, driving another kind of pain straight to her soul, a pain filled with an aching, driving need. "It's guaranteed to calm even the worst case of frayed nerves," he added.

"Promise?"

"Scout's honor."

"Go ahead, fill my glass."

"Full?"

"To the brim."

"You'll get drunk."

"I hope so."

"Why?"

"Then maybe I'll forget."

"If it works, will you let me know?"

They were no longer referring to the murder and they both knew it.

Danielle felt herself flush betrayingly. "Yes," she whispered, then looked away to cover herself. Her heart was racing as though she'd just run a mile.

Keir got up suddenly and went to get the bottle of wine out of the bucket that he had left chilling on the bar. Careful not to touch her as she lifted her glass up to him, he poured it full. Then he filled his own and sat down.

A long silence fell between them.

Danielle suddenly turned her head away to hide the tears stinging her eyes. She must stop this now. She had to get a tighter reign on her emotions. Keir was getting married, and besides, hadn't he made it eminently clear how he felt about her? There was no future for them.

"Danielle . . ."

Her name was whispered in a kind of incredulous despair. But she had to resist. If she gave into the feelings churning inside her, she would be lost.

Keir watched her, could feel her pull back. God! Was he ever going to get over wanting her? Hadn't this living hell gone on long enough?

He searched for words, but found none. Once again he remembered how they used to be—he saw her naked again, all the angles and curves of her body; he felt her mouth, the surrender in it.

Why her? Why didn't he feel the same burning passion when he looked at Natalie? Why was this woman so special? Had he forgotten all the pain, the disillusionment he had suffered at her hands? Why in heaven's name couldn't he hate her? Yet, he did not. He still wanted her. But how could he justify this feeling to himself, to Natalie? It was wrong for him to betray Natalie, even though she knew he did not love her the way she loved him. He and Danielle still wanted different things out of life. But neither could deny the thread of passion that bound them together, yet kept them apart.

She deserved to be loved carefully. And often. And he still wanted her as much now as he ever had. He would never forget the swell of her breasts, her rib cage, her belly and long thighs as she fitted to him like the missing pieces of an ancient puzzle.

She belonged to him. He would die if he never saw her again.

"Keir?"

He realized then that his thoughts were plainly written across his face for the whole world to see. He quickly turned away. He could not afford to make public his innermost thoughts. He wasn't going to let her make a fool of him again.

"I think I'll go up to my room now, if you don't mind," she said uneasily. "It's been a rather long day."

Keir stood up immediately. "I think that's a good idea." He avoided her eyes. "Good night."

"Good night," she replied. "And thanks for everything," she added softly.

Danielle sat straight up in the bed. Her heart was pounding wildly, and her mouth was so dry that it hurt to swallow. Was it her own cry that had awakened her? Her body began to shake; her teeth began to chatter. Then she remembered; she was dreaming, dreaming about John Elsworth. She had imagined his white, terrified face as she had begged and pleaded with his assailant not to hurt him, only to then have the life strangled from his body.

"Oh, no, please," she cried, burying her face in her hands. Her shoulders shook violently as uncontrollable sobs pounded her body.

She did not hear the bedroom door when it opened. She wasn't even aware that she was no longer alone until she felt the mattress sag beside her. She jerked her head back and stared into Keir's deeply troubled eyes.

"Are you all right?" he whispered, a jagged note to his voice. "God, when I heard you cry out, I didn't know what to think." On the sly, he leaned over and eased his gun down on the carpet.

When he straightened up, he noticed how the moonlight bathed the room in a delicate glow. He could see the warm tears overflowing the shuttered rims of her eyes.

Danielle shivered. "I . . . was dreaming . . . a nightmare." She gulped. "It was awful. I . . . dreamed about John. . . ." She couldn't go on.

"Shhh, don't cry," he soothed, her tears cutting him to pieces. "It was just a dream, nothing more." He couldn't stop himself from touching her. For a moment, his hands closed over her bare shoulders. It was a mistake to touch her, a dangerous indulgence he had promised both of them would never recur. He felt her stiffen and immediately withdrew.

"You don't have to be afraid of me," he said. "I told you that."

"I . . . I'm not afraid of you," Danielle whispered, the tortured words barely audible. "Only myself."

His groan penetrated the silence. "Oh, God, Danielle, don't say that. As it is, I can't answer for myself much longer." He dug his fingers into the palm of his hands to keep from pulling her into his arms. "I'd better go now. It would be better. Better for you."

Still he did not move as the moonbeams illuminated the entire premises, dancing across the strained, tormented expressions on both their faces.

"Please . . . don't go." She swayed toward him; he looked down into her eyes. "Don't go away. I don't want you to leave me. I . . . know what it'll mean if you stay, but I don't care. Do you understand? I don't care." She loved him, had never stopped loving him. It was as simple as one, two, three. And right now she needed him as never before. She thought that she'd surely die if he didn't hold her.

"Are you sure?" he asked. "Once I touch you . . . it'll be too late."

She put out her hand, and he caught it, turning her palm against his lips. The moist softness of his mouth against her skin set her insides on fire. It had been so long . . .

"Please," she whispered.

They moved toward one another, and he closed both arms around her. He simply held her for the longest time, the pagan beat of their hearts throbbing in unison as a cloud blocked out the moon, plunging the room into total darkness.

After a while, he pulled back, his hands coming up the sides of her face.

"Can you see me?" she asked.

"I don't have to see you; I can feel you."

"I'm glad."

He leaned down and placed his mouth against her lips, softly, tenderly. She tasted of tears, and her face was cold as he continued to hold it between his hands, stroking the smooth skin. It was a kiss that unlocked her fears.

Her chest ached beneath this gentle assault, matching the ache in his own chest as his hands wondered across her breasts, seeking hungrily.

"Oh, God, how have I stood not touching you?" he asked. The pain of wanting and owning and possessing was no less now than it was that first time he held her. If anything, it was worse, heightened by his having made love to her, having known her passion and tenderness.

The alcohol she had consumed had turned to honey on her breath. "You taste so good, smell so good," he whispered into her mouth. He stifled a moan. He thought that his body would explode for want of her as he felt her softness against him, the softness he had dreamed about for three long years. "Please, I'm not sure I can wait. I'm so hot . . . it's been so long . . . I'll try to be gentle . . ."

"Oh, please love me," she pleaded. "Now."

"Yes, oh, yes."

With quick adept fingers, he removed her gown, feeling her fingers pressing hard into his flesh, her mouth a moist flower opening and closing over his. He wanted to prolong the kiss, to explore her mouth and savor the intimacy, but he could not wait, nor could she.

He pulled away to discard the pair of jeans he had slipped into when he heard her cry. Kicking them aside, he lay down beside her, his body pressing warmly against her.

Suddenly their behavior turned savage. His mouth touched her everywhere. His hands caressed her sweetly, familiarly, following the hungry quest of his lips.

"Sweet, oh, so sweet," he murmured as he grasped her and pulled her on top of him. She melted like hot wax against his aroused body, kissing him deeply, exploring his mouth, building a tremulous stirring heat while she curled her fingers in his hair, over his shoulders, feeling his muscles bunch beneath her hands.

He moaned, shifting to capture a nipple between his hot, moist lips. A slow ache grew deep within her as his tongue began licking wildly. When he entered her it was swift and frantic. She arched her back and began to move slowly, sensuously.

Keir felt the top of his head nearly come off. He could only pray that this would not be the end—surely only the beginning. Yet, she was like a rainbow; at any time, he could open his eyes and find that she had faded to a sweet memory. But what she was doing to him was no memory; it was excruciatingly real.

Quickly he clung to her hips, joining her in her movement, lifting her, kneading her flesh as he accelerated to meet her in this extraordinary incidence of simultaneous timing. He knew in that moment that he had never stopped loving her.

They fell sideways, still joined and lay panting, breathing in the air from each other's lungs.

"Oh, Danielle," he whispered.

She held onto him, unable to speak. He was her

fortress where she could hide. His shoulders, chest and arms formed a shelter in which she could rest safe from her fears. She did not want it to end. Ever.

He held her tighter, spreading himself about her like a protective shell.

They slept.

Waking at dawn, Danielle passed her hand over his face to make sure that he was real, not just a figment of her imagination. She did not feel the least bit guilty. Just content, satisfied, replete. And in love. She could no longer deny it. She loved him. She wouldn't think about tomorrow and its painful responsibilities. It would come soon enough. Surely she deserved this tiny sojourn in paradise.

She lay still, eyes closed, stroking the bristly hair at the back of his neck, enjoying the rough tickling sensations on her hands.

His eyes opened in time to catch her smile. He smiled too. She put her arm around his chest and hugged him, mutely and reverently.

"Good morning." His heart swelled with the pressure of ecstasy that was almost like a terrible grief.

He leaned an arm over the side of the bed and fumbled through his jean pocket for a cigarette. After lighting it he fell back on his pillow and looked at her under half-closed lids.

"What are you thinking about when you look at me like that?" he asked huskily, then drew smoke deep into his lungs.

She seemed to give herself a mental shake. She touched his chest. "I'd forgotten how beautiful your body is." And it was. Broad and muscular at the shoulders, narrow at the waist and hips with long, strong legs. "Except for this scar, I might add." She traced her fingers the length of the puffy gash while he ground out his cigarette in the ashtray on the bedside table. "How did you get it?"

Keir trapped her hand against his chest and lifted himself on one elbow and looked down at her body, his hand straying to a breast, cupping its warmth in his hand, thinking how firm and perfectly shaped it was.

He smiled, feeling for her nipple. "Let's not ruin this beautiful moment," he said hoarsely, "by talking about my beat-up body."

"But I like talking about your body." Still, her resolve was weakening.

He fell to the pillow, carrying her with him, bringing her lips down to his. She had a soft mouth, and he loved running his hands through her curls. It was always the same—like fine silk. *You're a fool.* He had said this to himself a dozen times. A damn fool for living in a fantasy, and what he was doing was insane, for both of them. But he couldn't stop what was happening. It had gone too far. He couldn't stop making love to her, and now he couldn't stop the deadly, insidious joy of loving her.

He smiled at her and she smiled back.

Suddenly she moved.

"What are . . ." He broke off in midsentence, about to ask her where she was going. But she was sinking beneath the covers. She kissed his flat stomach, licked at his navel.

"Danielle," he muttered thickly.

"I want to please you." Her hands clasped him around his lean, strong thighs and her hair fell forward to dance on his flesh.

"You do please me, baby. You do."

His moans of pleasure exalted her and embraced her.

When it was time, he flowed inside her. It was slow, and relaxed, like the rhythm of the sea on the beach. It was beautiful.

They were quiet for a long time.

That explosive night of love set the pattern for the next few days. On the surface they were contented and happy, basking in their rediscovery of one another, making love incessantly.

And if underneath that thin layer of contentment, uncertainty and worry simmered, playing havoc with their souls, they ignored it. And if they were both aware that they were escaping from reality, that nothing had changed between them, that they were both still harboring resentments and bearing scars, they ignored that too. They pushed aside the danger that surrounded them, forgot that time was their number one enemy. In essence they were living for the moment.

For Danielle, those were days filled with magic. She was where she longed to be, and that was locked tightly in Keir's arms, letting him absorb her fears and her anxieties. She knew that she was playing a dangerous game, that she was existing on borrowed time, and it made her much more determined to cram the memories of a lifetime into those days.

She refused to speculate on tomorrow and the pain and heartache it was certain to bring. Instead she seized the moment.

And that was exactly what she was doing when she came downstairs early one morning to a quiet house. Where was Keir? she wondered as she breezed into the kitchen. Then she saw a note in the middle of the breakfast room table. EGGS AND BACON IN THE OVEN. K.

Danielle's heart leapt at his unexpected thoughtfulness. Dropping the note, she quickly rushed to the window and looked out. Just as she thought; Keir was hard at work swinging the axe. Boldly perusing his every movement, Danielle's eyes devoured him hungrily. Absently it struck her that he needed a haircut. Longer, looser now, the frosted curls bounced on top of his head, clinging wetly to his face and neck.

For a moment, she enjoyed the free perusal, taking untold pleasure in watching the hard-toned strength of his muscles as they rippled under his shirt. Her skin tingled at the memory of caressing the taut skin that covered those rippling muscles.

Suddenly an idea formed at the back of her mind. She stood still, nervously twisting her fingers together. Now would be the perfect time, she thought. A grin lit her face. Dare she follow through with her plan? After all, he had promised. Hadn't he?

Chapter 8

With an impish grin warming her face, Danielle dashed back upstairs, struggled into her boots, stuffed her curls into a knit cap, slipped into her coat, grabbed her gloves and bounded back downstairs.

Pausing at the window again, she noticed that Keir was still swinging the axe, his back to her. Cautiously she opened the door and tiptoed across the deck, down the stairs and stepped into the snow. With a grin still plastered across her face, she reached down and scooped up a handful of snow, and began squeezing it tightly in the palm of her hand, forming a ball. From time to time she added to it until she had it molded into a nice-sized ball.

Then she began to sneak closer, stopping ten feet away from him. Was her nerve going to fail her after all?

"Keir," she called sweetly.

Just as he raised up with his arms full of wood, the

snowball flew from her hand, landing with a thud square on the side of his temple.

A silence followed as Keir shook his head several times, trying to fling the cold liquid out of his eyes.

Danielle stifled a giggle. Then turned and ran like a frightened deer. From where she deemed a safe distance, she paused and swung around.

A leering grin replaced the shock on Keir's face and without taking his eyes off Danielle, he slowly let the heavy wood dribble piece by piece out of his arms to land with a thud in the snow.

"I hope you're prepared to pay for that," he yelled, taking a step toward her.

Danielle backed up. "No . . . please . . . Keir!" she pleaded before twirling and running through the snow as fast as she could go, lengthening the distance between them.

Keir followed.

Her laughter sang out in the silence. It was music to his ears as he gained on her.

"You told me I could do it!" she squealed over her shoulder.

He should have heard the sound, recognized it for what it was. But he did not. Not until it was too late.

"Danielle!" he screamed.

At his terrified warning, Danielle froze. Suddenly hearing the loud noise, her eyes followed the sound. She looked up to the top of the mountain peak. She saw it then, a slew of rocks mixed with snow lumbering down the mountainside toward her. She stood stricken, her stomach twisting violently as she saw the dangerous debris sweep and grind everything in its path.

"Move, Danielle!" Keir shouted above the devastating roar, breaking free of the self-paralysis that gripped him, rendering him powerless to move.

She began to run, forcing her feet to break through

the snow, only to realize that she was heading in the wrong direction. She heard Keir's frantic voice calling her back.

Fear gripped her as the adrenaline flowed through her body and her heart pumped viciously against her rib cage. Rooted to the spot, she stared at the terrifying spectacle. There was no dramatic roar, no rushing momentum, only the steady slide of the whole mountain on the move toward her. It was like a wave coming at her in slow motion, a wave of tumbling rock. Her legs buckled beneath her, and before she could stop herself, she plummeted into the wet, white snow. Then desperately she pushed herself up, again trying to make her way to Keir.

She stumbled again, this time sobbing as she tried to stand up. But she could not move. Sharp needles of pain shooting through her ankle and down into her foot rooted her feet to the ground.

His whole body trembled with fear. Suddenly he knew he would not reach her in time and even if he did, the powerful blow of the rocks would hammer them both into the wet earth. Nevertheless, his feet never faltered as he raced desperately against time to get to her, though the ground was shaking so violently at times that he had trouble maintaining his own balance.

Then he saw her fall again. Absolute fright gave him superhuman strength to try to reach her before it was too late. He was panting heavily, realizing that she could not get up. Nothing could protect her from the violent onslaught. The rocks were crushing to pulp everything in their way like matchsticks.

Oh, God. Sweat oozed out of every pore on his body. He had to get to her. He just had to.

Danielle began to crawl through the snow, away from the thunderous roar. She looked over her shoulder and saw the rolling devastation only a few yards away.

"Get up and run!" Keir yelled, closing the gap between them. "Run to me!"

"I can't!" Danielle cried. "My ankle!"

Looking behind her she saw something that made her freeze again. It was too late. The huge rocks bounding down amidst the white dust were almost upon her. A scream froze in her throat, and she knew that she could do nothing to ward off the cascading death.

She crumpled to the ground in a heap, covering her head with her hands, her only way of protecting herself. Then suddenly she felt a blunt numbing sensation on the side of her head, heard Keir's bone chilling cry as he lunged across her, felt the cold snow on her face and then there was nothing. . . .

Hidden from view by a row of trees and several large rocks, a man stood up, instantly bringing relief to his stiff legs. He moved around for a moment, giving a vigorous shake to one leg and then the other. Slowly but surely he felt the blood begin to move through his numb limbs.

A heady sense of excitement built steadily inside him as he watched the scene unfold below him. It seemed as though the two figures in the distance were actors and he was the director, carefully, artistically plotting the heartbreaking demise of the leading lady. A cruel smile thinned his lips as he removed his glasses from the bridge of his large uneven nose. He looked on with suppressed glee as the rocks crashed to the ground, burying their target beneath the rubble.

With anticipation, his grin widened in his sallow face. His superior would be proud of him. He was to be commended; it was a job well done. He couldn't wait to deliver the good news. Yet, something held him back. Caution maybe? Years of disciplined training? It did not matter. His entire political future, his entire life was riding on this assignment. It must be perfect down to the last detail.

But he had to be sure. Nothing must go wrong. He waited and watched. . . .

Danielle awoke to a muted glow hovering around her. Slowly, painfully she opened her eyes, feeling every bone and muscle in her body rebel against even that simple action. Where was she? What happened? Then out of the corner of her eye, she saw movement. She saw Keir. Instantly her confusion receded. Tears of panic shadowed her eyes.

Keir watched silently as she opened her eyes. He moved closer to the bed and peered into her colorless face, blinking back his own tears.

"Hi," he said, bending low and placing his mouth next to her ear, concern and worry contorting his features.

Danielle moistened her dry, cracked lips with the tip of her tongue. "Hi, yourself," she whispered, her eyes fluttering shut for a moment, but when she opened them again, he was still there.

"How do you feel?" Keir asked, his voice a raspy whisper.

"I'm . . . I'm not sure." Again she tried to lick her parched lips.

"Don't try to talk," he said, reaching for her hand and bringing it up to rest against his bristly cheek.

Danielle squinted her eyes in the subdued light, longing to bring his features clearly into focus. Deep lines creased the corners of his eyes and pulled down the edges of his lips. He looked completely bedraggled, worn out. Even in her fuzzy state of mind, she could see the red streaks in his eyes; they reminded her of a road map.

"How . . . how long have I been . . . unconscious?"

He flinched visibly. "Long enough," he whispered, laying her hand down beside her, but not turning it loose.

"What time is it now?"

Keir turned and glanced at the clock on the bedside table. "It's six o'clock," he said wearily.

"What . . . caused those rocks . . . ?" She couldn't go on, the horror of it all robbing her of speech.

He forced his voice to remain calm, unruffled. "I'm sure it was just an act of nature. Anytime you have snow, ice and rock, it can happen." His eyes softened. "But you don't need to worry about that or anything else right now. All you need to do is concentrate on getting your strength back."

Suddenly he averted his gaze, unable to keep his feelings from showing. His eyes narrowed to tiny slits. Gut instinct told him that the rock slide had been no accident. It smelled like a professional job. But unless he could garner tangible proof, what he thought wasn't worth a damn. As yet, he had not been able to scout the area. He had not left Danielle's side since he had bathed her wounds and put her to bed.

"Oh, Keir," she whispered, "I'm so sore. I feel like every bone in my body is broken." A sob rattled in her throat.

"I know," he said in a torture-ridden voice. "But thank God there are no broken bones. You're suffering from multiple bruises and a mild concussion where a rock struck you on the back of the neck."

"When . . . is all this going to end?" She lifted round, helpless eyes to his face.

He sighed heavily. "I wish I knew. Oh, God, how I wish I knew."

A painful silence fell between them.

Finally Danielle whispered, "I . . . remember you threw your body over mine just as the rocks . . . reached me." She paused. "Were you hurt?"

"Just a few bruises, that's all." His voice was gentle. "But I'm tough; it's nothing this old body can't handle."

"Are you sure?" she asked, concern for him beginning to weigh heavily upon her.

"I'm sure."

A deep relieved sigh escaped through her lips before her eyes fluttered shut. She was so tired. . . .

Thinking that she was falling asleep again, he leaned back in the chair and reached in his pocket for a cigarette.

Suddenly her eyes popped open, wide with fear. "You're . . . not going to leave me, are you?" She reached for his hand.

Keir felt his heart turn over as their fingers entwined. He leaned toward her. "Not unless you'll let me warm you some soup; it'll make you feel better to put something in your stomach."

She smiled faintly. "Thanks, but not right now. I think I'll sleep a while longer."

"I'll be here when you wake up," he said softly.

"Keir."

"Yes."

"Thank you."

"Shhh. Go to sleep."

He watched her until she was breathing evenly and then very gingerly he got out of his chair and strode to the window to stare outside, his jaw clenched so hard the bones hurt. What now? Pain and frustration gnawed at his insides until they were raw. Pain for Danielle. And frustration because he was unable to do anything about it.

Still he blamed himself. If indeed the rockslide had been started deliberately, which he was still convinced that it was, then he should have been aware of it. But no, he was too busy letting his heart overrule his head. As a result, Danielle's life was in grave danger. Unless, of course, Letsukov thought she was dead.

But he could not go on that assumption. Those Russian agents were professionals. They would be sure the job was finished before they backed off. Yes, he was certain there would be another attempt on her life. The only thing that had been in his favor was that the phone lines had been repaired, enabling him to talk to Cassidy. Together they had discussed the best course of action to take. He pushed his hands through his hair and then rubbed the back of his sore neck. He just hoped they were right in planning their next move. He knew Danielle would not be able to handle much more.

Oh, God, just thinking about those rocks sliding down the mountain, determined to crush the life from her, made him crazy. If he had been a mere second later . . .

Reaching up, he wiped the perspiration off his brow with a trembling hand and rested his head against the cool windowpane. Why did this have to happen now? When things were going so well between them? For days there had been no bitterness, no harsh words, as their bodies had become one, night after night. But now it must end.

No! his mind rebelled. He did not want it to end. But he knew that he could not go on like this. Dammit, he'd been trained to think like a professional. Where was his self-discipline and training when he needed it? Why was it failing him now? If he had been doing his job, Danielle would not be lying in that bed, having barely escaped death itself.

But how could he give her up a second time? His fingers curled into a tight ball as his mind replayed the pleasures they had shared: her whimpering moans as her tight warmth surrounded him like a velvet sheath, the way her nipples felt like rough silk against his tongue, the way . . .

No more! Don't do this. Don't do this to yourself!

Why couldn't he remember that nothing had changed? he asked himself brutally. *Because you love her, that's why,* he cried silently. He loved her! And he couldn't have her.

Suddenly a feeling of such intense desolation overcame him that he wasn't sure he could stand up under the weight of it.

Danielle was scared. "What do you mean, we may be leaving?" she asked, with difficulty keeping her voice from rising. She didn't want to take one step out of this lodge unless it was to go home. And she could tell by the tone of his voice that she wasn't going home.

"Cassidy and I talked, and we think it may be time to move you to another location."

Her eyes narrowed furiously. "Just like that, without any explanation?"

"Just like that without any explanation," he echoed tersely. Then he cursed himself for his rude tone when he saw her wince. But dammit, how could he tell her the truth, that if he'd kept his mind on his business, she would not look like she had just fought the battle of Armageddon and lost. And how could he tell her that the accident was *no* accident, that it had been purposefully planned and meticulously carried out. And that he feared for her life.

Danielle glared at him a moment longer before turning her back and walking with heavy steps to stand in front of the fireplace with the pretense of warming her hands. They had been battling back and forth all morning and still she hadn't gotten a satisfactory explanation as to why they were suddenly going to pack up and leave. In fact she hadn't been able to get a satisfactory explanation about anything from him since the day after the accident.

When she had awakened the following morning, still sore, yet feeling fine otherwise, it was to encounter a distant, cold Keir. Oh, he had been attentive to her every need as far as her physical well-being was concerned, but that was as far as it went. No more of the intimate looks or touches and no more sharing the same bed.

At first she had been hurt, then furious, then bitter, only to come full circle to hate herself for having sacrificed her values, her self-respect for stolen moments in his arms. But even at that, she had swallowed her pride and had tried to reason with him. Had it been only two days ago they had exchanged those bitter words?

She had been sitting outside on the deck, brooding, wallowing in her own misery when she looked up and watched as Keir stalked through the door. He sat down across from her with a frown on his face, a frown that had been there constantly since the accident. She knew that part of his problem was that he blamed himself for what had happened, but she could not understand why. . . .

"Keir," she had said tentatively. "I know you blame yourself for my injury, but . . ."

A harsh expletive had aborted her sentence. "But what?"

"Why are you being so hard on yourself?"

"Because it was my fault, that's why," he bit out savagely.

She spread her hands. "But you . . . you said that . . . any time you have the combination of ice, snow and rock . . ." Her voice trailed off.

Keir stood up and in a jerking motion walked to the railing bordering the deck and propped his foot on the top plank. "Spare me. I know what I said."

"We're not talking just about the accident, are we?" she asked, taking great pains to keep her voice from trembling.

He swung around to face her, his expression suddenly guarded. "Danielle . . ." he began, only to stop and jam his hands into his jeans in total frustration.

Danielle immediately dismissed the notion that she heard panic in his tone. Anger? Very likely. Panic? Forget it! More like disgust. Guilt.

"Why don't you go ahead and admit the truth?" she retorted.

"And what is the truth?" His voice was ragged with an emotion she couldn't identify.

"That . . . you're sorry . . . you got involved with me. . . ." Oh, God, she felt sick.

"I just wish it were that simple," he replied harshly, lifting his hand to his forehead in a weary gesture.

"Oh, it's simple to me. Simple that you're having second thoughts." She scrambled to her feet and glared at him. "Well, don't worry, from now on you won't have to worry about me. I know when I've been had." She tilted her chin as though to keep it above water. "Was this your way of getting revenge?"

Before he could answer her question, she turned and fled with his words, "Dammit, Danielle, come back here," ringing in her ears.

She did not go back, and from that moment on, they had existed with a polite wall of silence between them. Now they were involved in another verbal slinging match from which no doubt he would come out the victor.

Danielle strove hard to hang onto her patience and tried to figure out a way to get across to Keir that she was not leaving here today, tomorrow, or any other day for that matter unless he told her why. She could be just as stubborn as he.

"Would you like to talk to Cassidy?" Keir offered soberly, breaking into the frigid silence.

"Not unless he'll tell me what's going on."

"Well, I can't guarantee what he'll say, but maybe he'll make you feel better, anyway."

Danielle's mind was in turmoil. There was something that he wasn't telling her. She felt it. And because of this feeling, she was becoming more paranoid by the minute. She was conjuring up all sorts of terrible events in her mind. Maybe she was indeed going crazy. If she didn't soon get back home to Ann . . .

Her shoulders slumped in defeat; she turned away from him. Why did he have to choose now to turn on her? She loved and needed him now more than ever. But pride mingled with fear and anger kept her silent. She would just have to endure on her own. She had made it without him for all those years; she could do it now. Couldn't she? Suddenly a numbness settled over her, and she felt like her soul was withering and dying within her. Damn him!

There was an answering grim set to Keir's jaw as he studied her in the lingering silence. In spite of his resolution not to weaken, he longed to beg her to forgive him, to tell her he was sorry that he had hurt her. But how could he when he was hurting as deeply as she? Dammit, he had to protect her, didn't he? Keep her safe? Of course he did. In order to do that, he had to keep his mind and heart clear, clear of her sweet smell, the feel of her smooth, gentle curves. And though he knew that he could never have her, it didn't stop him from loving her.

"Danielle," he said softly.

She faced him, her face devoid of expression, her eyes dull with that haunted look he knew so well.

He cursed himself silently. "The move isn't set in concrete, you know." His voice had changed, the pitch was deeper. "But remember, if we do have to go, it will be for your own good."

Danielle's conscience pricked her sharply, making her feel guilty for her behavior. She swallowed hard. "I . . . know," she said, pushing back a wisp of hair that was tickling her cheek. "It's just that . . ."

"I understand," he cut in.

Their eyes met and held while once again that heady, explosive, magic crackled between them.

Then a sudden boyish grin captured Keir's mouth, easing the sophistication, the cynicism, the hardness. "Would you like to sit with me and soak up some sunshine while I finish cutting and stacking the last of the firewood?" He waited in breathless anticipation for her answer.

Relief flowed in her veins. Would she ever understand the complexities of this man?

Danielle's eyes raked the sky, looking for a cloud, but there were none to be found. It was another of those truly incredible days. The heavens were an incredible blue making it appear solid, the snow-covered mountaintops so sharp and vivid, the craggy outline of each rock and tree so distant. No city haze or fog existed to deaden the color or blur the lines. It reminded her of the fairy tales of her childhood, the enchanted dangerous places and forests. Places she used to dream of escaping to, always yearning for something more than the confining loneliness of the orphanage. The landscape too was enchanted, almost haunted, as though something frightening and hostile lurked in all that beauty.

She shivered suddenly, then scolded herself for letting her imagination run wild. But then, ever since the rockslide and Keir's abrupt change of attitude, she had been on edge, felt a renewed sense of unease. And now that a move was in the offing, it was worse.

"How does it feel to be a lady of leisure?" Keir asked, swinging the axe as though it were made of air instead of steel.

Keir's deep voice jerked her out of her unsettling thoughts. She squinted against the glaring sunlight bouncing off the snow and smiled at him after seeing the teasing glint in his eyes.

"I'd love to help, only I didn't think you'd let me."

"Huh! You think you'd like to help, but once you began working those sore muscles, you'd lose interest in a hurry, believe me."

She frowned and flexed her arms outward and then

upward and then around. "Oh, I don't know so much about that," she said. "I only feel a slight twitch when I move."

Keir's eyes were unexpectedly tender. "Well, you don't worry about doing a thing. I just want you to sit right there where I can keep an eye on you, and rest." His voice had grown serious, with an undercurrent of possessiveness that left her weak.

She took a faltering breath, then rushed on to cover her confusion. "If . . . if you insist. . . . But how am I ever going to get the soreness out of my muscles if I don't get some exercise? You haven't let me lift so much as a dish towel since . . . since the accident."

"That's right." He paused, supporting himself on the handle of his axe and looking at her carefully. "And I don't see any reason to change it now."

She was quiet for a moment as she studied his features: the dark skin leathery, the dark tangled hair that fell across his wide square forehead. With the sun lighting his upturned, relaxed face, his features lost their shadowed, hard look.

"All right, you win," she said at last, making a face. "I won't argue. I'll just sit here, soaking up this wonderful clean air and sunshine and watch while you slave away." A smile teased her lips.

How long she sat there, she didn't know. She lost all track of time. But it must have been hours, she thought. Yet, Keir showed no signs of tiring, nor did she tire of watching him. It was as though his big, brawny body were made of iron, the way he split one log after the other, stopping only long enough to stack them. She was mesmerized by his display of untiring strength. And he was so good to look at.

She never knew, could not remember later what made her suddenly turn and stare off into the distance. But it was that small unconscious action that saved her life.

Stark terror dug at her chest, cutting off her breath. *No!* she screamed silently. Lurking on the mountainside adjacent to them, a man was scurrying around as though looking for a place to hide. Heart thudding, her throat parched, her mouth dry, she watched. The fact that he was there was horrifying in itself, but the rifle he was wagging in his hand made the nightmare shockingly real.

For a moment—stunned—she couldn't react. Then she raised wild, rounded eyes to Keir, stretched her arm toward him in a silent plea.

As if aware of her panic, Keir whirled around. It was then that he caught his first glimpse of the metal flashing in the bright sunlight.

Then he saw the man crouched down in the snow.

Then he heard the brittle, echoing crack of a shot, heard wood splinter behind him on the tree opposite Danielle.

"Danielle! Get down!" he screamed, slinging the axe aside before ducking and crawling on his hands and knees, dragging his rifle with him, to where she was sitting in a frozen stupor.

"Danielle!"

This time his cry freed her frozen limbs, and she dove head first in the snow, behind the wood, landing on top of Keir just as another bullet passed by their heads.

Out of breath from her fall and shaking as though her bones were coming apart, Danielle clung to Keir, still unable to utter a word.

Above her, Keir's mouth was set in a straight grim line, lips tightly compressed. His face was pale. Fury wound him up as if he were a watch spring; under the strain, the muscles in his neck popped up, taut, impressive, ready to strike.

"Are you all right?" he asked, speaking against her mouth, his body remaining a shield over hers.

"I . . . think so," she whispered.

Satisfied with her answer, Keir reached for his rifle and cocked it, looking at his target, an evil glint in his eye.

Danielle's heart was pumping crazily, and she felt curiously lightheaded, as though she were a character in one of those old horror movies. But reality returned with a vengeance when she heard a bullet bounce off the front of the wood pile, cracking like a bullwhip.

"Listen to me," Keir demanded savagely. "And do exactly as I tell you. Understand?"

She nodded, biting down on her lower lip, drawing blood.

"When I tell you, I want you to get up and run to the side door of the cabin."

She began twisting and turning beneath him. "No! Not without you!"

"Dammit, you'll do as I say. It's our only chance. I'll cover you by firing in succession. He'll be so busy covering his own hide, he won't be able to get a clear shot at you."

"Oh, God, Keir," she cried as he helped her to her knees.

She clung to his hand, tears streaming down her face.

He looked at her for a brief second, his heart in his eyes. "When I give you the signal, you crouch down and run like hell." He then rolled over on his stomach and began firing. "Now! Run!"

She ran.

Keir did not let up until he saw Danielle reach the side door of the lodge, frantically yank open the door and dart through it.

From the warm interior, Danielle stared panic-stricken as the play of gunfire continued. She was sobbing openly now, beside herself with fright for Keir. *Oh, God, please, don't let anything happen to him. Please not because of me.*

From where she was standing she could see Keir stop to reload and then suddenly try to get up, only to stumble forward while forcing bullets from his own rifle as a cover. He labored toward her, firing the heavy gun.

It seemed to happen in slow motion, yet everything happened in a split second. Was he hallucinating or did he see the assailant fall just as he felt his own head explode with a force that seemed to lift his feet from the earth? He felt his body being hurled and suddenly he was flat on the ground. He was looking up at the sky and trying desperately to breath. He groaned as the world started spinning. Everything dissolved into blackness. . . .

"No!" Danielle screamed.

Chapter 9

DANIELLE COULD NOT STOP SCREAMING. NOT UNTIL SHE saw Keir move, that is. He was alive! Thank God, he was alive. But her jubilation was short-lived. She had to get to him. Now. Before it was too late. Suddenly without conscious thought of her own safety, she crashed through the door, hit the ground and began frantically crawling toward Keir, tears of relief and terror streaming down her face.

But there were no sounds of gunfire to disturb the uneasy, eerie silence that now filled the air as she thrashed her way through the snow on bowed hands and knees.

"Keir, oh, God, Keir," she cried, reaching out to him. Her fear trembled on the edge of panic as she took in his face, white and stark.

He lunged toward her; she caught him in her arms and bore the brunt of his crushing weight, grinding their bodies deep into the snow.

"Danielle," he rasped. "Go . . . may . . . try

. . . again." His words were pushed past his lips, an awesome effort.

She was sobbing. "Don't, don't try to talk. Let me help you."

The afternoon remained silent.

"Can you move enough to get to the house?" A quiver of icy dread tore through Danielle. Keir was right; they were nothing but sitting ducks in these wide open spaces. If the sniper should return again . . . Or was he dead? Or had Keir only wounded him? If the latter, was he just lying low, waiting for his chance to cut them both down?

Like a demon possessed, Danielle began tugging and pulling on Keir's massive frame. "Please," she pleaded, "you've got to help me."

He tried to get up.

She tugged again, making little headway. She couldn't do it. *Yes, you can! You have no choice.* But he was just too big, too cumbersome, too hard for her to handle.

He groaned.

Cradling his head against her chest, she placed her ear close to his lips. "Are . . . you trying to tell me something?" she asked desperately.

He nodded, then groaned again, as a piercing pain shot through his head.

Danielle panicked, thinking he'd passed out again. She touched his cheek with her gloved hand.

"Keir . . ." Her spine prickled.

"Just . . . a scalp wound . . . nothing . . . worry . . . about."

She went weak with relief that he was somewhat rational, coherent.

"If I stand up, can you get to your feet with my help and lean against me?"

He shook his head in the affirmative, struggling to stand, using her as his crutch. She gained her footing, Keir's body resting heavily against her.

Danielle felt as though her bones would crumble under his staggering weight, but taking slow laborious steps, they inched forward, terror giving her muscles the lift they needed.

Finally they made it to the door of the lodge.

Managing somehow to wedge her body between the door and Keir, she was able to get him across the threshold.

"Just a little farther," she encouraged, panting, her breath coming in short, uneven spurts, her chest feeling as though it would burst at any moment.

The couch. She had to make it to the couch. One more step, she kept telling herself. If she lost her burden in the middle of the floor, she would never be able to get him up again.

Again he sagged heavily against her. Her heart skipped a beat as she whipped her head around to look at him. Blood was trickling down his face, down onto the collar of his shirt, staining the fabric a dark crimson.

Pushing back her hysteria, she gritted her teeth and took that final step. Sick, weak-kneed, exhausted, she felt at last her leg clunk against the wooden trim on the couch. Sobbing openly now, she held herself at an angle and lowered Keir's body down onto the soft cushions.

She then collapsed against him like a tattered rag doll, sobbing her heart out.

Thank God, Keir was alive. And thank God they were safe. . . .

"How's your head?"

Keir almost smiled. "Other than feeling like I've been beat with a baseball bat, I'm fine." But his face belied this; his skin was deathly pale against the dark beard stubble.

They were huddled in front of the simmering fireplace, the afternoon sunlight only moments before having succumbed to the full moon and twinkling stars. It would soon be time to make their move.

Danielle drew a shallow breath. "Please . . . don't joke about it. I . . ."

"I'm sorry," he interrupted, looking contrite, "but I had to try to do something to ease that tense, frightened look pinching your features." He paused, leaning over and laying his hand on hers, giving it a gentle squeeze before withdrawing it. "I'm all right, truthfully. You know how profusely head wounds bleed. They always seem much worse than they really are. After my head quits hammering, I'll be as good as new."

"I . . . I still can't believe the sniper's bullet only grazed your temple." Her chin wobbled. "When I . . . I saw you fall . . ."

Even now, hours later, she still could not wipe the scene from her mind. Had it been only a few hours ago that she had bathed his face to find that he was right, that the bullet had grazed his temple, giving him nothing more than a dizzy, pounding headache at the base of his skull?

A tremor shot through her, and she began rubbing her hands briskly up and down her arms, trying to generate some heat to her limbs, which were cold in spite of the red-hot fire.

"Hey," he pleaded gently, leaning toward her once again, "don't fall apart on me now. You've come through like a champ so far; don't ruin your record. What do you say?"

"I'll try," she whispered, her eyes fluttering shut for a brief moment as her head fell against the back of the chair. Her face was waxen in the yellowish glow of the lamplight. Fear had left its mark.

Keir felt his chest tighten with longing to hold her. But if he touched her now, it would be fatal to them both. The fight had just begun. They still had the dangerous task of getting to the helicopter undetected and getting away before their tormentor or tormentors returned, whichever the case might be, and tried again. Danielle might not be so lucky next time. He had no way of knowing yet if he had fatally wounded the sniper. More than likely he had not. The only thing he could remember before he blacked out was seeing him fall. How the hell had they tracked them down?

But there was no doubt in his mind that they were no longer safe in the lodge. After Danielle had cleansed his face and doctored his flesh wound, he had gone immediately to the phone to get an emergency coded message to Cassidy. But lifting it off the hook, he hadn't been surprised at what he'd heard: nothing. This time he was certain the lines had been cut. They were on their own.

He felt her eyes on him. He turned and faced her.

"We're not out of danger yet, are we?" she asked.

"No, we're not," he answered bluntly, then expelled his breath heavily, lean features suddenly grimly etched in the subtle lighting of the room. "If we do make it to the chopper, then we have to assume they might have tampered with it, although when I checked it a while ago and untied the back and front blades, things appeared normal. If anyone had fooled around, I couldn't tell."

She tugged her fingers through her hair. "You took an awfully big chance scouting around in the dark by yourself."

Keir's eyes glinted dangerously. "Not as long as I'm packing my hardware. If anything had moved other than the trees, I would've blown a hole through it."

Danielle's eyes dipped to the revolver lying on the hearth only a hair's breadth away from his right hand. Close to his heavy booted foot and resting on his thigh, was a long-barreled rifle. Looking at those menacing objects, she was again reminded of the dangerous game they were playing. A game of cat and mouse with high stakes—their lives.

She recoiled, whipping her eyes away from the guns,

feeling her insides curl with yet another kind of terror. Death. Oh, God, she wasn't ready to die. But for the first time since the nightmare began, she realized that she might not come out of this alive. And because of her, Keir could lose his life as well.

Hadn't he already taken a bullet that was meant for her? She was finding it all extremely hard to cope with. And the fact that it was his job, what he was trained to do, made not a whit of difference. After all, he *was* the father of her child, the man she loved. Didn't that count for something in this insane world? And now, even though she knew that he did not love her and was planning to marry another, she did not care. All she wanted to do was curl up next to his strong, warm body and beg him to love her. She needed him, his warmth, his strength. Just this one last time. Her vow to rely on no one but herself evaporated in the mist like a phantom horse and rider.

Yet she knew that her deepest yearning was impossible. As she peered at him now, he was again wrapped in a cloak of hostility. As he'd so brutally reminded her before, she was a job, an assignment, nothing more.

She felt the pain within her abate to the dull ache that had become her silent shadow. If only she could stop loving him. . . .

"It's time to go," he said, bringing her sharply back to reality. There was a brittle, controlled edge to his voice.

Getting up, Danielle marshaled every bit of self-discipline she possessed to keep her mind clear. She would not be a burden to him. But the thought of slipping through the inky blackness trying to get to the helicopter made her limbs knock with sheer terror. However, she let none of this show as she faced him.

"I guess I'm as ready as I'll ever be," she answered, somehow managing to keep her voice even.

But Keir was aware of her fear. It was so strong that it was almost tangible. He glanced at her one more

time, taking in the lovely picture she made standing
straight as an arrow, her shoulders squared stubbornly,
her eyes wide and trusting, yet glossed with a touch of
uncertainty. She reminded him of a tiny soldier ready
to do battle without even the slightest idea of how to go
about it. The soldier's only arms, guts and determination. But hadn't some of the mightiest wars of all been
won with soldiers such as this? In that moment, he had
never loved her more.

"Keir . . ." She searched his darkening eyes.

He took a deep breath and let it out slowly, wondering what sort of madness held him in its grip.

"Let's go," he muttered brusquely, reaching down
and effortlessly lifting the pistol and ramming it down
into his shoulder holster. Then he slipped into his
jacket and picked up the rifle.

Danielle, already having donned her coat, reached
for her cap, gloves and purse.

They were ready.

"I want to go over the plan one last time," Keir said
as he switched off the lamp, plunging the room into a
muted darkness. They began to make their way slowly,
cautiously across the floor to the side door.

"Remember," he went on, "you're to hug my back-
side like a leech. But if you hear anything that sounds
like gunfire or anything out of the ordinary, run for the
nearest cover and hit the ground immediately." He
paused. "Now you tell me what you're supposed to do
if something happens to me."

"If . . . if I can, I'm to get the rifle and run to the
chopper, barricade myself in and . . ."

"And shoot to kill."

"Oh, Keir," she whispered, moving her head helplessly from side to side, "please, don't . . ." She broke
off as her body jerked violently. "I . . . don't want to
even think about anything happening to you."

"Dammit, Danielle, you have to think about that,"

he countered tersely. "It's a reality—a god-damned reality. I thought you understood that." He heard her whimper and hated himself for having to use such harsh language and tactics to clear her mind and sharpen her nerves. It was an old intelligence ploy, but it worked. He had to keep her together until they reached the chopper and were airborne.

At present, she was too weary, too heartsick, too scared to argue. She would follow Keir wherever he led. And remembering too her promise not to be an albatross, Danielle said steadily, "You can count on me."

"Atta girl," he said, his voice having suddenly gone hoarse. Then he touched her hand and she responded by gripping his briefly. His hand was warm as love. Her throat tightly constricted, she followed him wordlessly out the door.

Danielle was positive that she did not breathe the entire time they stole through the dark, cloudy night. She smelled snow in the air. That's all they needed was another storm, she thought. Crouched down, they darted in silence from one massive clump of trees to the other.

Keir dragged her relentlessly, his grip on her arm like a steel trap, never faltering in his determination to outwit his unknown assailant and get her to safety. But with every step they took, she could feel Keir's frustration, hear his muffled curses as the deep snow made their progress slow and difficult. The only thing in their favor was the low, swirling cloud cover.

Yet Keir's sensitive ears were attuned to every sound no matter how slight or insignificant. When he deemed it safe, they pressed on. The moaning wind whipping through the bare treetops was the only sound between them.

When at last the helicopter came into view, she went

weak with relief. She knew then the gods were smiling on them. They were going to make it.

She could feel the steel in Keir's body as she leaned heavily against him while stopping one more time before springing to the chopper.

Keir waited, his eyes searching, his rifle raised and ready. Fear and tension spread between them like a cancer.

Danielle stood in paralyzed silence, still not breathing. Had Keir seen, heard, something she hadn't? Had they come this far only to be fair game now as they made their last bid for freedom? Suddenly their destination seemed a lifetime away.

Then Keir yanked on her hand, giving her the signal to move. Bending low, they began to run.

Sucking in the cold air, Danielle felt her lungs laboring as she lifted her legs high in the deep snow, matching Keir's brutalizing gait step by step.

It wasn't until Danielle slammed the door of the helicopter shut that she breathed.

Wasting no time, Keir began flipping toggle switches on and off, checking needles and dials.

Then he glanced at Danielle, sitting reed straight in her seat, her teeth chattering. Delayed reaction, he thought.

Reaching over behind him, he came up with a blanket and laid it in her lap. "After you put on your headset, bundle up in this," he said. "And stop worrying. Since they haven't made their move by now, they're not going to." He gave her a reassuring smile.

Danielle stopped her teeth from banging together long enough to give him a weak smile before putting on the cumbersome headset and untangling the thick blanket and wrapping herself in it. She felt somewhat better now, content to leave everything in his capable hands.

Keir flipped more toggle switches and the cockpit lit up. A few seconds later the blades overhead began making a whop, whop, whop noise. After that Keir pulled back the stick, and the helicopter rose swiftly in the cold Virginia night.

"Are you going to try and contact Cassidy?" Danielle asked, her heart no longer palpitating.

Keir raked a hand over his hair. "I'm tempted, but I'm afraid to break radio silence. Once they realize we're airborne they'll tune into our radio frequency."

"Is there any chance at all that they won't?"

He hesitated. "A slim to none."

"Do you think we should risk it?"

"Do you?"

"No."

His jaw tensed. "I agree. I don't want to give those bastards another chance to get at us. I'm going to fly us to our training camp where I know you'll be safe."

She tried to ignore the tiny throb behind her temple, but after a while it was hard to do so. It just would not go away no matter how much she kept telling herself that she was no longer afraid.

"Are you warm enough now?" Keir asked.

"Yes . . . I'm fine, except for my pounding head," she answered honestly.

His eyebrows furrowed as he fumbled in his pocket for a cigarette. "You can relax, you know. The worst is over." *At least for the time being,* he added silently.

"You're sure?"

"I'm sure."

"Why do you think they weren't waiting for us?"

Keir looked grim. "It's my guess they're operating one man short now and have probably gone back to regroup."

"You . . . you mean you think you actually . . . killed . . . ?" She broke off, shivering.

"It was either him or us." There was no emotion in

his doubled-edged voice. Just a deadly calm statement of fact.

Danielle shivered again and fell silent.

"Why don't you try and get some sleep," Keir said at length. "Maybe by the time we meet Cassidy, everything will be over. When he gets my message, the FBI will be swarming around the lodge in addition to combing the mountains around it and setting up roadblocks. If they are still in this area, they're good as caught." Was it his imagination or were the controls getting stiff?

"Do you think that it was Letsukov and his partner, Zoya, who shot at us?"

"More than likely. But there's still an outside chance that Letsukov's hired someone to do the dirty work for him. It's awfully risky for Letsukov to get personally involved, but now Zoya, that's a different matter altogether. Again, it's all conjecture on my part."

He paused and drew on his cigarette, watching her tense, pale features reflected in the moonlight. Again he felt that tight squeeze on his heart while suppressed fury gnawed at his belly. How much more could she take? Dammit, it wouldn't do for him to get his hands on those sons of bitches. . . . It was fast becoming an obsession with him. He tightened his knuckles around the wheel, feeling them almost snap in two under the pressure.

Then forcing a calm to his voice that he was far from feeling, he continued soberly, "Rest now. I'll wake you when we get ready to land." Sweet Jesus! It wasn't his imagination; the controls were jamming.

Reassured by his smooth, confident tone, Danielle threw him a faint smile and eased her head back. For now, they were safe. She refused to think beyond the moment. But she had no more than closed her eyes when Keir's loudly vented curses jerked her upright.

She swung terrified eyes to stare at Keir's rigid profile. "What's . . . what's wrong?" she asked over her hammering heart, watching him struggle with the controls.

"We're losing god-damned pressure, that's what!"

"What does that mean?" There was a waver in her voice.

"From the way the chopper's behaving, the hydraulic line's sprung a leak," he said roughly.

Danielle's features mirrored her disbelief. "Does . . . does that mean we're going to crash?"

"No, but it does mean I'm going to have to set her down. Now!"

"But . . . but how? It's dark . . . the mountains . . ."

They didn't want to believe it, but they *knew*.

The terror had begun again.

"Don't panic," Keir pleaded urgently. "Just tighten your seatbelt and hold on."

Feeling as though her insides had been kicked out, Danielle stiffened and tried not to think, tried to blank out what was happening. But she couldn't; it was too horrifyingly real. Oh, God, had they come this far only to end up crashing in the mountains, their bodies mangled and burned beyond recognition? She stared down at her hands, which were clenched, thinking: *This is it. I'll never see my child again. I'm going to die!*

Keir knew that he was gambling, but he had no alternative. It was either land her now in the mountains or die.

It was a curious sensation of helplessness, with not even a button to press, as his only link with reality seemed to be four closing points of orange lights. He could feel the sweat beneath his arms, running down his sides. He knew that under the weight of the grip he was exerting on the lever, his hand was shaking fiercely, his head was pounding, causing his stomach to heave. He prayed . . .

He threw the lever forward, hoping against hope that

he was wrong. No such luck. The gears were jammed. Quickly he adjusted his airspeed, at the same time checking the hydraulic circuit breaker. He was right. The sign flashed: OUT—hydraulic failure confirmed.

Losing no time, he switched to manual override, allowing him to steer the chopper manually. Next he reached over and flipped on the bottom landing lights, searching desperately for a place big enough to land.

He dared not look at Danielle, but he didn't have to. He knew that she was going through hell, and there was nothing at this point he could do to relieve the fear. Dammit to hell, he cursed silently. No wonder those Russian bastards weren't waiting for them. Just as he'd feared, they had indeed tampered with the chopper.

"Keir, are we going to make it?" Her voice shook.

His face grew black with determination. "You're damned right," he hissed, though it took all the strength he could muster to manipulate the lever.

Danielle's eyes were glued straight ahead, her hands digging into the seat as Keir continued to fight the lever. It seemed like forever, but in actuality it was only minutes before he guided it onto a flat strip sandwiched between two mountains.

Her heart was in her throat as she felt the helicopter make contact with the hard ground.

Keir sat for a moment, rigid and immobile. Then he wiped the sweat from his brow and faced Danielle.

"Are you all right?"

"I . . . I think so," she whispered, her eyes slowly filling with tears. "What . . . what about you?"

"I'm fine," he said, his eyes holding hers.

"Do . . . do you think they'll be waiting for us?"

He hesitated, his heart still knocking. "Probably," he answered honestly.

She turned away, not wanting him to see her fears, her weakness, and peered out into the grim, silent night. What now? They were stranded in the mountains, cut off from the world, no food, no shelter except the plane, and more than likely still being pursued. She wanted to scream. But she did not; it would be fatal to allow herself that luxury.

Keir saw the tears pooling in her eyes, sensing that she was close to the breaking point. But he couldn't have her falling apart now, any easier than he could have earlier, even though he was worried about that possibility. She had been through hell and not once had she complained or cried. But he did not know how much more she could take.

No doubt, it would be morning before they were rescued, if then. It was definitely going to storm. That meant they were looking at spending the night in the chopper and then tomorrow—well, he wouldn't think about tomorrow. They still had to get through this long, cold night. He glanced through the windshield. Despair hardened his features as he heard the snow mixed with sleet hit the glass.

He sat still for a moment and then reached for Danielle.

Luke Cassidy was worried.

"Amy," he bellowed into the intercom, "get me Tony Welch in here on the double."

"Sir, are we going to make our move now? Join the FBI?"

Cassidy swung around to face the other occupant of the room. His name was Ray Tanner, a tall, slender man with red hair and freckles who could pass for fourteen instead of forty. But that was as close to a boy as he came. Next to Keir McBride, he was the agency's top man. He was a crackerjack shot and also like McBride had nerves of steel. But he was missing that certain instinct that set McBride apart from other men. However, for this job, he was exactly what Cassidy needed. "We don't have any choice, especially after

what we've just learned." Cassidy's features were
bleak.

"Do you think they're still alive?"

"If Letsukov and his god-damned muscle men
haven't gotten to them first." He pounded his hand on
the desk in frustration. "Dammit, how in the hell did
they find them?"

"Forgive me if I sound hardhearted, sir, but McBride
can take care of himself. He's a mean son of a
bitch."

"By himself yes, but not with a woman along."

"Do you think—"

A sharp rap on the door interrupted Tanner's sentence.

"Come in, Welch," Cassidy said sharply.

Tony Welch strode into the room, his forehead
creased in a perplexed frown. When his superior sent
for him on a moment's notice, he knew something big
was going down.

"Sir," Welch said respectively. "Tanner."

"Sit down, Welch," Cassidy said, "and let's cut the
polite crap. We've got trouble, big trouble."

Tony Welch flushed and sat down.

"A forest ranger sighted a chopper in the mountains
not far from McBride's lodge. We wouldn't have
thought much about it except on their radio frequency
they picked up a scrambled message from what
sounded like two Russians. One was demanding help
while referring to their target being in range."

He paused, holding their gaze. "It's just been confirmed that McBride's chopper is definitely gone from
the lodge. But due to the snowstorm, the FBI is afraid
to risk sending any choppers in there."

"Where do we come in, sir?" Tony asked, finally
getting a word in edgewise.

"Storm or no storm, we're leaving at first light of
dawn."

Both men stood up and nodded their assent.

Cassidy walked to the door, yanked it open and turned around. "Meeting adjourned, gentlemen."

The shack was securely padlocked. That was obvious from his position on top of the slope that angled down through the pine trees toward the front door. The window next to it was boarded up, as he assumed the others would be. The place looked like no one had been around for a while, but he couldn't be sure. He was taking no chances.

He crawled down from the top of the slope, not standing until he was sure that he could not be seen by anyone from below, and began winding through the trees, stopping from time to time to study the shack from a different direction. It still appeared deserted. His eyes kept dipping to the ground checking ahead of him for any tracks where someone might have gone down to the shack, but there weren't any, although that didn't particularly ease his mind. Anyone after them would know enough to hide their tracks. All the same he couldn't be too cautious.

Keir tromped carefully through the trees, tapering off to one side as he descended. The snow whipped around him. He glanced at the dilapidated structure, glancing around him, continuing to circle. Since he had found the shack, they could have too, and since this was the only one nearby, they could have easily guessed that this was where they might come for food and shelter.

Shelter. Up above where he had first been studying the shack, Danielle was waiting, and if he had to take his time and check out the shack thoroughly, he also had to hurry. Danielle couldn't make it much farther. She was utterly exhausted. From the moment they had awakened in the chopper at dawn, stiff, freezing cold and hungry, they had been on the move. They'd had to take a chance on finding some type of roof over their heads or risk freezing to death. He'd been afraid that any type of rescue was impossible in light of the storm.

Now, all he was concerned about was getting Danielle out of the elements and safe from their pursuers. His gut instinct warned him that the worst was yet to come. Danger stalked them like a tangible evil.

He bolted over to the side of the shack, stopped, pressed himself flush with the building, peered around the corner, gun raised.

No one.

Then he placed his ears next to the shuttered window for any sound from there. Hearing nothing, he made his choice. He spotted and picked up a broken piece of metal, ducked around to the front door of the cabin and worked the metal between the lock and the door. One quick yank and the lock cracked away, wood splintering. Dropping the rusty tool, he angled in through the door, gun ready.

Deserted.

Once his eyes adjusted to the dark, they darted around the room, taking in the old rickety wooden bed frame leaning against the left wall, mattress gone, no springs, just wooden slats, a black potbelly stove to the right with metal ducts going up through the ceiling, a few cans of food stacked on a propped-up shelf. The place smelled clean but damp.

It was a moment before he relaxed enough to move, breathing slowly. Then going to the door, he waved for Danielle to come down.

He met her halfway.

While Keir reached for a weak and trembling Danielle, three men with binoculars watched them from the top of the opposite mountain peak. And when the two weary figures turned and made their way back toward the shack, one man let the glasses fall to his chest and took a sip of cold coffee from a cardboard container while watching the door of the shack close.

He smiled at his companion, oblivious to the pain this brought to his large nose, his thick frozen lips. "We've got them right where we want them now, Comrade Letsukov," he said speaking in Russian. "We won't fail this time."

The second man was as pale as a pallbearer, but nothing could mask the cruel twist of his thin lips. "You had better not, comrade, you had better not." With an evil smile, he took a sip of cold coffee. The third, beefy-looking man kept his silence.

Once the door creaked shut behind them, Danielle slumped down onto the hard, cold floor, chills wracking her body.

Concern hurried Keir's actions. Although he knew that it would be suicidal to build a fire, he was going to chance it anyway. He had to bring some warmth to Danielle. She had endured a perilously long and hard day. And it wasn't over yet, he thought with a harsh sigh.

"Hang on," he said. "As soon as I bolt the door and put that old bench in front of it, I'll build a fire." He wasn't about to take any chances on being slipped upon unawares.

She nodded weakly.

His eyes searching the room, he saw an old tattered sleeping bag wrapped in plastic on a corner shelf. Quickly, he crossed the room, pulled it down, gave it a hard shake and then threw it on the floor.

"Here, slip into this. It'll help until I get the fire going."

Refusing to think about how filthy it was or who might have used it, Danielle scooted over onto it and numbly let Keir zip it up to her chin, her wide, frightened eyes watching his every move.

"You're doing great," he whispered gruffly, before transferring his concentration to the stove.

"Is there anything I can do to help?" she asked after a moment, struggling to sit up in the sleeping bag.

He was hunkered down, breaking the dry splintered wood into small pieces, making a pile of them on the inside of the stove.

Swinging around to face her, he was struck anew at how fragile she looked. He felt his heart turn over. The creamy skin under her eyes was stained a bluish color, enhancing the vulnerable twist of her mouth. Her features wore a white, stricken look. But again she wasn't complaining. If Natalie had been in similar circumstances . . . *Damn you, McBride! Stop it.*

"No," he muttered at last, his nostrils tightening, furious with himself for the turn his thoughts had taken. His hands were unsteady as he dug his lighter out of his pocket and lit the kindling.

Misinterpreting his sudden grimace, Danielle caught her lower lip between her teeth and turned away, fighting back the tears. A knife turned in her stomach, knowing that he was wishing he had never laid eyes on her again. She had brought him nothing but pain.

A silence followed as Keir continued to fiddle with the fire. He looked terrible, she thought. His eyes were sunk deep into their sockets, the bandage had come off his head, exposing the angry scalp wound, lines were deep around his mouth. Her heart ached for him. He was just as cold and weary as she was, but he was putting her needs first. Because of that, and because she loved him, she wanted him to hold her. She wouldn't think beyond that.

"Keir."

"Yes."

"I'm . . . sorry."

"For what?" he asked tautly.

He was looking at her now, the fire making spitting noises behind him.

"For . . . getting you in this mess."

"Don't be. I'm not."

He watched her with hungry eyes. He knew that he ought to turn away. But he was aware that she did not want him to and that he did not want to, that now more than ever their desire remained unspoken. It hung in the air, in her half-hidden figure against the weakening light.

And with the closeness of tomorrow, the end of this stolen moment was intolerable. . . .

She too ignored the danger surrounding them, the hunger gnawing at her stomach, the aches in her body, the approaching darkness, the sleet hammering against the crude shed, and lost herself in those eyes. They were gentle, almost tender, and seemed to draw her very soul from her.

His sharp intake of breath shattered the silence.

She held out her arms.

"Are you sure?" His voice was a hoarse whisper.

Watching him in the firelight, she saw the vein in his neck rise, beating, then fall back.

She breathed achingly. "Yes, I'm sure."

Chapter 10

WORDLESSLY AND WITHOUT TAKING HIS EYES OFF HER, Keir removed his boots and then stood up and discarded his jacket.

Still not saying anything he crawled in beside her and folded her into his arms. With a sigh, Danielle melted against him, feeling him absorb her pain and misery.

"Danielle," he whispered, "I . . ."

She reached up and placed a finger across his lips, silencing him. "Please. I don't want to talk. Not now. I . . . I just want you to hold me."

With a groan he tightened his hold, and buried his face into her soft, damp curls.

At this moment, the only thing that was real to her was being in his arms, close to his heart. She had been through so much that nothing else seemed to matter. She could no longer separate the bizarre from reality, except when his arms were around her. And he had never held her this way before. Never. Tender and careful and strong. As if his arms under the flesh were made of steel with all the power in the world to crush her or protect her. And that was the way it felt. Safe. *It's the way I hold Ann,* she realized, her heartbeat suddenly staccato.

That was the way it was with Keir. She had come full circle; she had come home.

Time passed and still they clung. They were both aware of the quiet darkness and of the sleet as it continued to fall on the tin roof. But they were reluctant to break the spell that so tenaciously bound them together. After all, she wasn't asking for a lifetime with this man; she knew that was impossible. She just yearned for the moment. Was that asking too much?

Keir was the first to stir, to speak. Easing her back against the tattered fabric, he propped his head on his elbow and peered down at her. "Are you warm now?" he asked huskily.

"Definitely," she whispered, shifting her gaze beyond him to the smoldering embers of the fire. She smiled. "You did good."

"How's that?" he asked, the grooves around his mouth deepening to suggest a smile. Unconsciously he began stroking the side of her face with a finger. Her skin was smooth and soft beneath his touch.

She was finding it difficult to breath, once again blocking out everything except the pressure of his big, warm body against hers.

"You . . . you built a cozy fire out of nothing," she murmured rather incoherently, his touch doing crazy things to her insides.

"I'm glad you like it," he drawled, giving her a teasing grin, letting her know what he thought of their inane conversation.

There was another disturbing silence as she tried to subdue the butterflies in her stomach.

He smiled at her and she smiled back.

Then suddenly as though their smiles had lighted a

torch, the smiles disappeared. A hint of something hung in the air between them, a sense of waiting, a kind of awareness.

She reached up and traced the outline of his lips with her finger, watching his eyes, seeing a deep dark glow that shook her to the very core. She wished he'd kiss her—not just wished—she *ached* for his kiss.

As though reading her mind, he lowered his head and laid his lips against hers without speaking, and her hands touched where his day's growth of beard grew coarse under his chin. She rubbed her fingers into the dark growth, then she traced the formidable structure of his nose.

He kissed her again, hard and fierce, and something inside of him was angry and frustrated at not being able to graft her slender body to his. God, how he wanted her. Here. This minute. In this crude mountain cabin. He wanted her so badly he hurt. Because he knew being inside her was like that, like grafting her body to his, and each time with more and more permanency until they were truly and entirely inseparable.

"Oh, God, Danielle," he muttered, "I want you so much." He moved his lips against her temple, her forehead, caressed her face, causing her eyelids to droop heavily. His touch was tender, too soothing; she couldn't resist it. Her mouth parted. He kissed her eyelids, then paused to stroke her face again before kissing her ears, the sides of her throat, her chin. Her mouth quivered. She began to moan, unable to withhold her response to the gentleness of his touch.

She put her arms around his neck. "Oh, please . . . yes," she whispered, kissing him softly on the mouth, moving her hands around to bracket the sides of his face.

Unlocking his hands, he turned her toward him, sliding them around under her sweater and up over the wings of her shoulder blades, feeling the tension like flat stones lying beneath her skin.

"Are you sure?" he rasped, kissing the base of her throat.

"Yes." She would treasure these few hours. She would spend each moment like a miser, as if it would be her last.

He had to bend his head to her lips to hear the simple three letter word. Sighing, he pressed her close, breathing in the smell of her hair, aware of the sudden heat rising from her body.

"Oh, God, I care . . . so much," he whispered thickly, his hands unbuttoning her clothing; unzipping, unsnapping, unfastening. She kept moaning, feeling his lips and fingertips making their way over her face and neck.

She lay naked in the ghostly glow of the firelight, too beautiful to be real.

He stripped off his own clothing, laid down next to her and once again took her in his arms, placing his hands on her hips bringing his body into perfect alignment with hers. She felt him become hard with the eagerness to place himself inside her.

After a while, she could hear his heart pounding—or perhaps it was her own. She sighed deeply and held him.

He explored and worshiped her with kisses. Keeping hold of her, their mouths avidly joined, he turned with her, his thighs closing around her, so that he was holding her completely.

Yes, yes, she thought. *Hold me, love me!*

His hands stroked her shoulders and down the middle of her back, curving over her buttocks as he rocked gently beneath her, creating a pressure at the apex of her thighs, causing her to moan, to rock with him, heightening the sensations. His tongue in her mouth made her dizzy with desire.

"So lovely," he murmured. "All softness."

He shifted, turning once more, making her gasp as he teased her nipples, luring her just a little closer to the edge. His touch seared her sensitive skin as he moved her down beneath him, his mouth replacing his fingers on her nipples, turning them hard.

Keir ached for her. She was so warm. So fresh. So vibrant. So real. Her flesh trembled as his touch spoke the language of her body, his thumbs gently tracing an invisible circle around the bumpy, dark halo.

She began to groan softly, excitedly. Her breathing grew ragged and fast as he moved to squeeze her breasts in the large gentle cups of his hands as though they were holy and fragile objects. No longer could she think, only feel.

His head moved down. He kissed her taut, concave belly, pressing his face into her, both his hands relishing the smooth, hard curve of her hips. He moved. Lower.

"Oh, Keir!"

His head dipped knowingly. His mouth, his tongue, his fingers all caressing her, so that she groaned, laboring, opening still more, her face, breasts flushed, burning.

She thrashed about. His caress seemed different, new. Yet deliriously familiar. Unlike anything she'd known. Yet so right, so perfectly right.

Soon he came up and covered her body with his once more, and she took him between her hands, reaching; taking him in, holding her breath.

He looked down into her face, into her eyes, his own glazed.

"Now," she pleaded. "Sweet man. Now . . ."

He filled her completely. Binding him to her with her arms, she met his mouth greedily like a starving child.

He stirred inside her, then moved back, exciting a response, then forward, her hips lifting to meet him, her thighs parting still more. He drove into her with both power and gentleness, and she felt herself dissolving beneath him.

Magic. Pure magic. Slowly climbing higher, increasing the pace; she was feeling nothing but pleasure;

exquisite pleasure, revived in every pore, magnified, all-consuming.

She whimpered and called his name under the onslaught of the engulfing, painful pleasure.

He wanted to hold back, to make this moment last forever, a lifetime, but for once he found it almost impossible to restrain himself. For him, this was more than an act of sex; it was a rejuvenation, a reawakening, a kind of reincarnation.

Danielle cried out, tearing her mouth away from his, withering against him. He moved more quickly. "I love you," he whispered. Knowing she did not hear, he returned his mouth to hers hungrily, wildly, as she arched against him and was hopelessly locked there, trembling as he kept on and on, until she cried out again, sobbing.

He had to stay inside her, feel the fullness of her response. Feeling it, made humble by what they had together achieved, he collapsed gently upon her breast.

She felt his sudden stillness, then the ecstatic flow as he moved again, again . . .

It was then that she knew. She could never willingly give him up. . . .

That was only the beginning of a night with no end. . . .

Three o'clock in the morning found them hovered around the fire, feasting on the contents of tin cans of food like they were delicious delicacies from a fine restaurant.

"I never knew food straight out of a can could taste so good," Danielle said as she munched on the last of her beef and beans.

Keir smiled, watching her, having already downed his portion in two bites. Although there was not much to eat, only five cans, it was enough to last several more days if they had to remain there, he thought grimly. He shook himself. He wouldn't think about that now. Not with the firelight playing across Danielle's flawless skin, highlighting its silken sheen, shadowing the hidden places he had sought and found with his lips and hands. And the thought of embracing her again made him tremble.

"I . . . agree," he said, his voice uncontrollably husky.

Still, after hours of lovemaking, he wanted her again and again and again. How was he ever going to give her up?

He smiled at her, his eyes narrowed into a lazy measuring look.

The tip of her tiny tongue suddenly darted between her lips and circled after swallowing the remainder of her food. The center of him swelled and grew hard.

Danielle was not without her own discomforts. Her senses were drugged with the look, the touch and the feel of him. Madness. Sheer madness, that's what it was. But a madness that neither was prepared to ignore or control. They were running for their lives, hiding out in a log cabin in the mountains, with a snowstorm reeking vengeance on the outside. Yet none of this seemed to matter. Nothing mattered except Keir. She would savor these moments in his arms like a rich, heady wine. And because it was forbidden, it was that much more exciting.

Her head was spinning and her mouth was dry as she silently raised a finger to his lips and began to rub across the inside of his plump lower lip. She felt the moistness seep into her fingertips as she continued her gentle assault.

"Yes," he managed to whisper, before he trapped her finger between his teeth and began sucking on it.

A moan escaped from deep within her as he finally let go of her finger and reached for her. "Come here," he whispered again.

As their bodies gracefully eased back onto the bed

roll, their lips met in another of those soft, closed-mouth kisses, followed by a hug. He held her, making her eyes close and her skin ripple with excitement as his hand moved up and down over her hair and back.

Then he released her, studying her quietly for a moment, trying to understand what it was about this particular woman that aroused him so fiercely and made him want her so desperately.

Danielle's eyes were closed now, her head resting contentedly in the curve of his arm, the burgeoning fullness of her breasts grazing his chest. He stared into her face, an ache around his heart, seized by love for her.

Her face. He could spend the rest of his life sitting here looking at her face. Lovely woman with her delicate features, fragile eyelids lined with the finest threads of violet, the curve of her cheek, her jaw, her throat. . . .

"Hey," he said suddenly, snapping his mind back to the moment at hand. "Hey, don't go to sleep on me now."

Her eyes opened slowly and she gave him a sleepy smile, pulling his hand up to her breast and holding it there.

Yawning, she whispered, "Why can't I sleep?"

Her breast felt warm against his palm; he cupped it tenderly.

"I want to talk." His voice was deep and raspy.

"What time is it?"

"Does it matter?"

"No."

"Good girl."

"What do you want to talk about?" she asked, disinterested, breathing in the tangy smell of his flesh.

"You."

Her eyes widened. "Me."

He gave her an indulgent smile, then leaned down

and kissed her unhurriedly. When their mouths parted, she looked up into his eyes, basking in the pleasure of simply holding him.

"Yes, you," he murmured.

"What could you possibly want to know about me that you don't already know?" *Please don't let him ask me about Ann.*

"Everything." He smiled. "But mostly what it was like being in an orphanage. You never told me."

Relief made her weak. But yet she hesitated, perplexed that he would ask something like that now. He never failed to amaze her. But he didn't seem to think his question strange at all. He was perfectly serious and he expected an answer.

"I . . . I don't know," she stammered, trying to remember. How could she describe the long years of an existence so uniform that time itself had no meaning. The routine, the antiseptic smell, the discipline, the crushing lack of privacy. There was only one word to explain it.

"It was lonely," she said at length. "Lonely because you knew you were cut from a different mold, no matter how hard you tried to tell yourself that you weren't. I remember when I finally convinced myself that my mother didn't want me." She grimaced and was quiet for a moment. "Believe me, it was a bitter pill to swallow."

"How could she have done that?" Keir demanded angrily. "How could she have just abandoned you?"

"I used to think that," Danielle said. "I used to sulk about it and call her terrible names—whoever she was. But as I said, I finally understood a little. She must have been poor, frightened. And somehow I got the feeling she was on drugs, and had been seduced and left with no one to turn to. I'm . . . I'm sure it wasn't easy for her."

"It wasn't easy for you either," he said sadly. "Were you treated well?"

"Oh, yes. But there were so many of us that it was difficult for the sisters to give us special attention. One sister singled me out and gave me extra attention. She asked me to keep in touch after I left and though I call her often, I have not once returned to the orphanage." She paused, as if uncertain how to continue, and then with a deep sigh, went on, "Now you know . . ."

There was such a bleakness embedded in her voice that he was beginning to regret having asked her. Yet he felt that he had to know.

"Thanks," he said gently. "I appreciate your telling me."

She turned and buried her face into his chest, remembering the things she wouldn't tell him. The countless foster homes she'd been forced to endure, where more times than not, she had been mistreated. Agony. She was remembering the agony of knowing she would never be adopted, never have a real home, having learned at an early age that couples were afraid to take a chance on adopting a child with no past, especially one whose mother had been on drugs. It had seemed as though she was tainted.

The day she walked out of the orphanage, she had promised herself that she would never look back. And she hadn't. Until now. But somehow, she didn't feel resentment against Keir for making her talk about the past. In a way, it was a link with the danger surrounding them, and it even had a cleansing, healing effect on her heart, knowing that this sometimes dangerous, sometimes gentle, giant of a man had cared enough to ask. . . .

Keir lit a cigarette and smoked it silently, holding her next to his heart, absorbing her pain, making it his own.

Again she ignored the little warning bell in her mind as she raised up and kissed him with renewed passion. Their time together was only fleeting, she knew. But for her it would have to last a lifetime.

"Make love to me again," she whispered.

With a smile they loved through the night, lost in the magic of their own making.

With the dawn came the knowledge they were no longer alone. They were both up and dressed and Keir was preparing to take a look around outside when he heard the noise. He froze.

Keir was never quite sure what followed—Danielle's scream or the small explosion that blew apart the left front window. It could have been Danielle's scream first. Or she could have been screaming from the explosion. He never knew.

His first thought was that someone had thrown something through the window or that the wind had ripped it apart, but then it registered on him that two bullets had whacked close together into the wall beside him, and he dove toward Danielle and the floor.

"Dammit, they're out there. Get down," he hissed before crashing to the floor. As he landed, he covered his face and neck and waited for the debris to settle. When he looked up, his eyes searched the room for Danielle, his breath coming in gasps and his heart pounding a hole in his chest.

After the first stunned moment and hearing Keir's hissing command, Danielle had likewise hit the floor, rolling across to the dark corner of the room, burying her head in her hands, too terrified even to whimper. Then peeping through her fingers, she watched with her heart in her mouth as Keir tried to make his way toward her.

The wind was shrieking outside; snow gusting in through the shattered window, bullets splitting the air.

Keir raised and pointed, he inched his way on his belly toward Danielle.

Although paralyzed with terror, she managed to reach out and latch onto the front of his shirt, drawing him toward her. He made a terrible sound, one that cut through her as he flung his arms around her, seizing her with all his might, holding her crushed against his chest.

Her lips shook violently as she tried to speak. "What . . . God . . . what are we going to do?" she whispered, clinging to him, shaking as another round of bullets riddled the cabin.

Keir reached for his rifle behind Danielle, while slamming the pistol in Danielle's hand. Then he aimed the rifle toward the window and the door.

"It's just a matter of seconds before they'll be on us like a swarm of bees, making sure we're dead." He paused, searching for breath and feeling Danielle's bones as they seemed to rattle in her slender frame. His eyes found and locked on the back door that was in reaching distance of his foot. Deliverance. Maybe. Better than nothing.

Cupping her cold face between his hands, he forced her shocked eyes to meet his. "When I shove open the door, I want you to start firing and take off running. I'll be covering you from both the back and the front. Whatever you do, don't stop shooting as you run toward the woods."

She clung to his hand, her eyes wild. "But . . . they'll kill . . . you," she cried, thinking that this was a replay of the day before.

He shook his head roughly. "No, they won't. Don't argue. Remember I won't be far behind you." Dammit to hell, where was Cassidy and the FBI when he needed them?

Positioning her hands on the trigger, still crouched, he slammed his boot against the door, shoving it open. "Go!"

With her mind completely divorced from her body, Danielle darted through the door, struggling to fire the pistol, both hands gripping it tightly. She battled the snow, spotting a clump of trees to her right. Sobbing, her chest heaving, bullets dancing through the air, she pushed on, sometimes stumbling, sometimes not. How long she ran, she didn't know.

She was freezing. Her heartbeat exploded and her breathing grew rapid. She felt as though every muscle in her body had been pummeled with a club.

Reflexes took over. One more step and she would have it made.

Then suddenly she stopped dead in her tracks.

Her heart slammed into her throat.

A man's booted feet blocked her path.

Fear rendered her motionless. *Oh, God, I'm going to die after all.*

She forced down the scream and slowly, defeated, she raised her eyes.

"Thank God, you're alive."

She fell in a dead faint into Luke Cassidy's arms.

Keir saw the man follow Danielle, cutting across the snow. Keir halted, spun around, dropped to the ground, rifle aimed and shouted, "Zoya, take another step and you're dead!"

There was not a flicker of emotion in Keir's eyes as he kept them pinned on the Russian.

Then suddenly from another angle, a bullet whizzed by his head. Lunging to the side, Keir leveled his rifle and fired. Zoya dodged. His bullet only grazed him. Stumbling, Zoya continued to follow Danielle's path.

An expletive flew from Keir's lips simultaneously with another bullet whining past his ear, driving him to seek cover. Dammit, he cursed again silently. If only he could see where the shots were coming from or how many there were to contend with.

He brushed the snow out of his eyes and licked it off his lips as he tried in vain to find his culprit. If it was only Letsukov, then he was in good shape, he thought.

He could outlast him or waste him. One on one. But it wasn't himself he was worried about. It was Danielle. His only hope was that the bullet he had put in Zoya had slowed him down, keeping him from getting to her. Danielle. He had to have all his wits about him to get out of this and help her. With him dead, she did not have a chance.

"Come out, McBride. You're covered," a heavily accented voice shouted. He saw him then. It was Letsukov all right. He, too, looked exactly like his picture. Good. It was between the two of them. He liked it that way.

"I'm going to get you!" Letsukov shouted again in broken English.

Keir didn't bother answering. He edged sideways, through the thick falling snow, the scattering clumps of tree and rocks providing him with cover. He slipped, slid and scrambled in the snow, hoping to circle to the rear and come up behind Letsukov. He thought of Danielle in Zoya's clutches and did not pause to catch his breath. With luck, he'd get one clean shot.

As soon as Keir spotted Letsukov, his luck ran out. There wasn't one man to face, there were two.

Suddenly a beefy arm circled Keir's throat and lifted him high off the ground. He felt the tightening of that forearm on his windpipe. He was losing consciousness. Fast. He had to escape. Kicking back, Keir smashed his heel hard into a kneecap.

"Damn!" the man grunted in pain, but the hold didn't slacken. Desperate now, Keir raised his leg, sending his heel into his groin.

The goon fell with a thud as he released Keir. It took both of them the same length of time to recover, the man from the intense pain Keir had dealt him and for Keir to get precious air back into his straining lungs.

Both of them rose to hands and knees, then dropped

to a crouch. Like wary animals, they circled. He was big and strong, a head taller than Keir, with the physique of a wrestler, a street brawler. But he didn't have an edge on Keir in that department. Keir was like a bull moose. And he knew every alley-fighting technique in the book.

Suddenly Keir feinted. When the goon straightened slightly to catch his blow, Keir again went for his kneecap. Keir felt the kneecap yield.

"Ahhh!" the man howled in pain, bending over to clutch his injury.

Taking advantage, Keir spun and aimed his foot for the point of jaw.

Crunch!

That one blow was all it took. The man lay sprawled face down in the snow, out cold.

Letsukov. The only one now between him and Danielle. Just as Keir hurled his body toward the Russian agent, a sharp sting in his side doubled him over.

The Russian's laugh filled the air. Using the beefy man's inert body as a shield, Keir rolled over behind him, clutching his side.

Keir peered over the man, but Letsukov wasn't anywhere to be seen. Keir, oblivious to the pain, scrambled for his gun. Reaching it, he slipped it between his stomach and the snow laden ground.

He waited, gritting his teeth, growing weaker by the moment.

He saw the feet, before he saw the face.

"Surely you didn't think you could outsmart us, McBride." Letsukov's voice held an icy sneer. Raising his gun, he pointed it at Keir's head and laughed. "Too bad you won't be around to watch Ms. Davis suffer the same fate."

Reacting instinctively, a strangled cry erupting from his lips, pain blinding him, Keir came up and rammed against the man.

He heard it then. The sharp crack of a rifle. *Oh, God, please, not Danielle!*

Letsukov slouched on top of him just as he seemed to hear a voice, distant and high, and feel a hand on his shoulder, pulling at him. . . .

He knew no more as a sweet darkness sucked him under.

Chapter 11

IT WAS ONE OF THOSE RARE WINTER MORNINGS IN EAST Texas when both the sun and the temperature are in complete accord. By mid-afternoon, the weather forecasters were promising the temperature gauge would rise to the upper fifties. If the weather did indeed hold, maybe she would leave the store in the hands of her assistant and take Ann to the zoo, Danielle told herself. Maybe an outing would help.

The last month's weather had been horrendous. The constant dampness, combined with the low mercury readings, had taken their toll on everyone's temperament.

Dangling her feet off the edge of the bed, shaking in spite of the blaring central heat, Danielle stared at the cream-paneled walls just as she had the day before and the day before that. An unbearable loneliness consumed her as she rose and tightened the quilted robe around her waist and walked into the bathroom.

She tried to ignore the weariness dragging at her

spirit as she stepped into the shower, letting the water cascade down her skin. Why couldn't she get a hold of herself? Why couldn't she be thankful that she was back home with Ann and Jusie? Why couldn't she be thankful that her life had been spared? Why couldn't she be thankful that the nightmare was over, that she was out of danger?

But she *was* thankful, she argued. Thankful for everything, but— It was the "but" that was her problem, that was filling her days and nights with mental anguish and despair. She had not heard from Keir.

Since she had boarded the plane for home in the company of Tony Welch, she had lived in silent agony. Thoughts of Keir filled her heart and mind every single moment of every single day. Oh, she knew that physically he was going to be all right. He was recovering from his wound satisfactorily. Cassidy had assured her of that each time she had spoken with him by phone. And he had also assured her that both Letsukov and Zoya would never bother her again, nor would their sidekick. And that once she came to Washington and gave her deposition, she would never hear from the U.S. Marshal's office again.

Yet his confident words did nothing to stifle her concern or her fear. Keir had nearly lost his life twice because of her. That was a burden she was finding hard to bear. The nights were horrible. She would wake up sobbing, her gown drenched with perspiration.

Each time this happened, she would get up and stumble into Ann's room and sit by her bed and stare at her. Other times she would just sit and hold Ann and cuddle her. She was her lifeline.

Still nothing relieved the pain of not hearing from Keir. Was she wrong? Had she just imagined that he still loved her? Had he gone home, married his fiancée? No. She would not, could not, believe that. She had seen the look in his eyes; she had seen love.

And when she did hear from him, what then? Would

he forgive her when he learned about Ann? And if so, would they be able to overcome their other differences? Would he be willing to change? To give up his dangerous job?

With tears gathering in her eyes, she slipped back into her robe after completing her shower and walked with purpose out of her room and into the kitchen. It was early yet, not even seven o'clock, she noticed, her eyes glancing at the wall clock, her hands busy with the routine of putting the coffee on to brew. Once that chore was done, she opened the refrigerator and poured herself a glass of fresh orange juice.

With a deep sigh, she sat down at the table and sipped on her glass of juice, disinterestedly watching the coffee as it dripped into the glass pot. When the wall phone jangled, she jumped; then her heart began racing. She stared at it a moment longer before gathering the courage to answer it. She had been disappointed so often. . . .

"Hello," she said tentatively, lifting the ivory receiver.

"Good morning," a chirpy voice countered on the other end of the line.

Her caller was Marge Beckman, a close neighbor and bookstore customer.

"Hello, Marge," Danielle said, trying to keep the disappointment out of her voice. *You're a glutton for punishment, Danielle Davis!*

"Did you hear what I was saying to you?" Marge was asking in her hyper little voice.

Danielle shook herself, feeling all chewed up on the inside. "Sorry. Would you mind repeating it."

Marge hesitated, before rushing on, "Oh, it was nothing really. I was just apologizing for calling you so early. But I saw the light on in your bedroom. . . ." Her voice faded out.

"That's all right. I was up," Danielle said, rolling her

eyes upward, preparing herself for another of Marge's long-winded conversations.

She could picture her friend, sitting in her den, her feet propped up on a footstool, smoking incessantly, her bright brown eyes a perfect combination for her red hair and freckled face.

"How's Ann?"

This brought a smile to Danielle's lips, as did any mention of her daughter. "Oh, she's fine. Her usual contented self."

"Huh," Marge said, "you should've seen her while you were gone. She wouldn't stop crying. Jusie had her hands full, but she managed just beautifully, as she usually does. Have I ever told you how much I envy you Jusie?"

"Many times," Danielle answered wearily.

For a brief moment, a short silence fell between them. Danielle feared what was coming next, and she was prepared for it.

"When are you going to tell me where you were those days you so mysteriously disappeared?"

Danielle prayed for patience while calming her racing heart. "I'm not," she said bluntly. And rudely. But she had no intention of going through a replay of a conversation of two days ago. Ever since she had returned from her ordeal, Marge had tried every way she could, using every ploy she could think of, as had several of her other friends, to find out where she'd been only to return looking as though she had been to hell and back.

Well, she hadn't explained then, and she had no intention of doing so now. She hadn't even told Jusie the whole bizarre story, only the parts she deemed necessary. And even that had been somewhat of a trauma. But she'd had no choice; she'd owed it to Jusie. She owed Marge Beckman nothing.

"Well . . . er, what I really called for was to invite

you to a party," she said hurriedly, rebounding from Danielle's bluntness. "At my house. Friday night."

"I don't . . ."

"Please, don't say no, Danielle," Marge cut in before she had a chance to do exactly that. "It'll do you good to get out."

"Marge, you know . . ."

"Promise me you'll at least think about it," Marge interrupted again before she could answer. "Relax and enjoy yourself for a change. I know the pace you've been keeping at work since you've been back home. When I left the store the other day, you looked like you'd had it."

Perhaps being around people bent on having a good time would do her good, she told herself.

"All right, all right. I'll think about it."

"Good. Now for the best part," Marge said. "Hal has a new assistant. Mmmm, he's a hunk: tall, six feet plus, unattached, and he invited him to the party . . ."

Danielle's skin went cold. "No. Absolutely not."

"But Danielle . . ." The frustration was plain in her voice.

"No, Marge," she stressed again, panic-stricken. "You . . . know how I feel about that."

"Oh, Danielle, your attitude just proves you're in some kind of trouble," Marge whined. "Why won't you tell me, let me help you?"

"Good-bye, Marge," Danielle said without emotion and dropped the receiver on its cradle, oblivious to Marge's continued frantic prattle.

Trouble. Is that what one called it when a person's heart ached and her soul was plunged into the very depths of despair? When one kept hearing the bullets, seeing the blood, Keir's blood. Trouble. Such a small word to hold so much devastation.

Getting up, she strode jerkily to the cabinet and poured herself a cup of coffee only to have it slosh all over the counter top. "Damn," she muttered, mopping up the spill. Forcing her hands to stop their trembling, she poured herself another cup of the hot liquid. Then holding the cup carefully, she walked to the table and sank into a chair.

A shudder shook the entire length of her body.

For the first time she allowed herself to remember the last time she had seen him, every detail as vivid as if it had happened yesterday. Closing her eyes, Danielle could hear Cassidy's voice. . . .

"Thank God, you're alive," he'd said.

But when she had come around a short time later, a stranger was hovering over her, anxious to make sure she was all right.

Blinking several times, she'd tried to sit up. Gentle hands were holding her down, a blanket thrown haphazardly over her shoulders.

She looked around wildly. "Keir!" she cried, struggling to stand.

"Shhh, calm down," the strange voice ordered. "You're not to worry about him; he's being taken care of."

Danielle struggled that much harder against his restraining hand. "No . . . no . . . needs help . . . must get to him!" Her heart was in her mouth and her lips were dry as she remembered the harsh sounds of bullets, Keir bounding out of the cabin, covering for her as she ran for safety. "Must go to him," she said again, frantically scrambling to her feet, pushing the stranger's hands aside with determination.

"Please, Ms. Davis," he begged, "my orders are to get you to the helicopter, keep you out of danger."

Danielle began to back away from his pleading eyes, shaking her head. "No. Not . . . not until I see Keir!" Turning suddenly, she began to stumble in the direction of the sounds. The sounds of gunfire. Oh, no, Keir! Was she too late? No!

Hurry! Hurry! Hurry! A voice taunted her as she plowed through the snow, praying.

"Ms. Davis, come back," her protector yelled, though following close behind.

Another voice came out of nowhere. "Dammit, Mason, you were supposed to get her to the chopper. Cassidy'll have your ass for this!"

Danielle never paused. She kept on running.

She saw Luke Cassidy the same time he saw her. He was bent over, staring at a body. Keir's body! She gasped in horror, slamming her hand to her mouth to keep from screaming. Cassidy's eyes were on her as he rose. God, no, please. She couldn't stand it.

Cassidy reached for her as a team of men carrying a stretcher hovered over Keir, lifting him gently. But Danielle couldn't move, couldn't speak, couldn't cry. She was locked in a web of pain so intense, so powerful that it was crushing the very life from her.

"What the hell are you doing here?" Cassidy demanded. "They were told to keep you . . ." Then he broke off, seeing the look of dazed shock on Danielle's face.

For a moment he just stared at her tragic, lonely figure standing as straight as a reed, the snow curling about her face.

She looked up at him.

Cassidy swallowed against the lump in his throat. "He's not dead," he said softly, "seriously wounded, but not dead."

Her chin trembled. "I . . . want to go with him," she whispered, her eyes glazed with pain.

Although Cassidy's eyes held sympathy, he spoke with soft authority. "I'm afraid that's impossible. He's on his way to the hospital. But don't worry, McBride's a tough old dog." He cleared his throat. "But then, you ought to know that. He saved your life." He paused again, a bright light flickering in his eyes. "He'll survive. He doesn't have much choice. He's got a wedding date to keep. Remember?"

She reeled as though he had physically struck her. *No, No!* she screamed silently. *You're wrong. He loves me!*

He was staring at her strangely, though his voice was gentle. "How would you like to go home, Ms. Davis, home to your child? At last, you're a free woman."

Free? Oh, God, if he only knew. . . .

"Mommie, Mommie!"

A shudder raked Danielle's slender frame. How long had she been sitting there tormenting herself? She couldn't seem to stop. But when those men had lifted Keir's still body onto the stretcher and had taken him away, she had wanted to die.

"Mommie!" Ann called again.

Brushing the tears from her cheeks and breathing deeply, she stood up, calling softly, "I'm coming darling. Mommie's coming."

Something disturbed him. A noise? What was going on? He couldn't seem to focus his eyes. He felt a heaviness in his left arm.

"Mr. McBride?" He heard a strange feminine voice. "I think he's finally coming around, doctor. His eyelids were flickering a minute ago, and I just saw him move his arm."

Keir felt fingers probing around his side. He gasped painfully as they touched the area around his chest.

"Mr. McBride!" came a firm voice. "Mr. McBride, can you hear me?"

Keir tried to force his eyes open. Yet it was proving impossible. He wanted to tell them that, but all he could manage were inarticulate grunts.

"Just relax, Mr. McBride. Relax your body and try to open your eyes," he heard the man say.

He breathed deeply and let his body go limp as he exhaled. Now with practically no trouble at all, he opened his eyes. Two faces were peering down at him. They broke into smiles.

"What's happened?" Keir whispered as best he could. He felt the heaviness in his arm again. It felt like a red hot poker was pressed to it. He turned his head and tried to focus his eyes to see what it was.

"No, please, take it easy," clucked the nurse. "You've got a hole in your side and you're bandaged tighter than Dick's hatband. You've been drifting in and out since surgery three days ago now. You're at Walter Reed Hospital."

Surgery? What was she talking about? What hole in his side? "What happened?" he moaned weakly. His speech was clearer now. The doctor began examining him. He heard the door open and recognized Dr. Samuel Calcutt, the organization's physician, as he breezed into the room.

"Well, Keir, you're back with us," he said, crossing to the foot of the bed. "You had a close call. How are you feeling?"

"Head hurts, side bloody aches," Keir mumbled.

Dr. Calcutt smiled. He stepped to the side and pulled back the sheet. "In addition to the hole in your side, you have a few fractured ribs. Do you remember anything of what happened?"

Keir wrinkled his forehead, trying to think back. He let out a groan as the pieces began coming back to him. He looked back at Calcutt wildly, frantically. *"Danielle!"*

"Calm down, Keir." He patted his arm. "She's all right. She's at home. You're at Walter Reed."

Keir's head was raging, his tongue dry, heavy.

"We had to perform surgery. You'll be out of commission for quite a while."

Keir tried to look down at his side, but quickly turned his head back as the pounding worsened.

"It's going to be all right, Keir." Calcutt smiled.

"It hurts," Keir breathed, closing his eyes. "I hurt all over."

"You're going to do that for several more days. But you're out of danger now."

Keir was still somewhat confused. "My head is pounding."

"You need more rest," Calcutt said.

Keir stared as the nurse stuck a needle in the IV tube. The room began swimming. Keir didn't like the feeling. Suddenly he was back in the cabin in Virginia . . . with Danielle. . . .

"Keir, Keir, my boy," he heard from a distance. He opened his eyes. As the blur sharpened in focus, he recognized Cassidy. His head wasn't pounding as badly as before, but his side was throbbing. He saw Sam Calcutt beside Cassidy.

"Is he going to be all right now?" he heard Cassidy ask the doctor.

"Let's give him time to wake up. He's doing well. Vital signs are good. I would say he'll be able to talk, yes. He's out of danger now and he remembers pretty well."

"Cassidy," Keir whispered.

"Oh, good, you know me," Cassidy said.

"What . . . what happened?" Keir asked, still groggy.

"I was hoping you could tell me." Cassidy laughed.

Keir moved. He felt awfully uncomfortable. He looked over and saw the tube, then the needle in his right arm. "Who put that crap in my arm?" he moaned.

"Ha!" Calcutt laughed again. "Anytime he's conscious enough to remember his dread of needles, then he's going to be just fine." Still smiling, he turned and left the room.

Cassidy watched the doctor leave and turned back to Keir.

"Well, my boy, you've done it again." He smiled, shaking his head. "An excellent job." He bent over the bed. "We've finally got those two Russians where we want them, flat on their back in the hospital and then off to the clinker."

Keir looked at Cassidy. "You mean neither are in the morgue?"

Cassidy laughed outright. "Not yet, but close. Zoya's in critical condition from the wound you gave him. And the same goes for the beefy goon they hired. You did a number on him. He was on the operating table for several hours."

"What . . . what about Letsukov?"

"He's in intensive care."

"Why the hell didn't you let me do the honors?"

"I can certainly understand why you feel cheated, but when we arrived on the scene, it looked to be fairly even. Then just as I pulled the clip and aimed, deciding to shoot, you got the drop on him, had him right where you wanted him. But then again I was afraid to gamble even for a second with your life. I knew you were badly hurt, so I pulled the trigger. End of story."

Keir shook his head as he thought back to the incident. He had never been so scared in his life, scared for Danielle, himself. "I didn't . . . even know you were there. All I could think of was killing that bastard and the pain in my side."

"No wonder, your side had a hole in it as big as the Grand Canyon."

"Calcutt told me . . ." Keir groaned.

"But you're going to be fine—just fine."

"Sounds like it," Keir said sarcastically.

"Now, calm down, don't get excited. I know you hate being flat on your back, but we'll compensate you handsomely, you know that. Anyway, you're in no condition to argue with the doctor. And Calcutt is insisting on a rest period."

"How long?"

"Oh, I'd say a month, maybe six weeks at the most."

"Dammit, Cassidy," Keir said, struggling to sit up. "I can't stay here for that long. Sweet Jesus, I'll go out of my friggin' mind."

"Hey. Take it easy." Cassidy patted his arm, gently pushing him back down in the bed. "Don't you know it won't do you any good to argue with Calcutt? Anyway, you don't have to stay in the hospital all the time."

Keir felt relieved, though his head was banging again. He grimaced and closed his eyes.

Cassidy looked down at Keir, a worried frown on his face. "Don't worry, we'll have you back on your feet and one hundred percent fit in no time. After all, we can't keep the bride waiting forever, now can we?"

Keir's eyes flew open as his heart skipped a beat. Natalie! Oh, God, he hadn't even thought about Natalie. *Only Danielle.* "No, I guess I can't," he said quietly, knowing, though, that he could never marry Natalie. He turned his head to the side.

Following a long moment of silence, Cassidy asked, "Are you up to talking?"

Keir twisted his head around and grimaced, the sudden action sending a sharp pain through him.

Before he had a chance to speak, Cassidy went on, "It's not over yet, Keir."

Keir's facial expression didn't change. Cassidy might as well have said it was raining outside.

"Although we did put Letsukov and Zoya out of business, they're just the tip of the iceberg. There are others just like them here in Washington, operating right under our nose. Only these are much bigger fish. Computer high technology."

"What the hell does that have to do with us, with me? That's the FBI's problem. Not ours."

Cassidy fingered the railings on the bed. "They want to make it our problem, your problem."

Keir eyed him carefully. "Luke, what do you say you quit beating around the god-damned bush and tell what's going on?"

Cassidy prowled around the room, stopped, looked at Keir. "What I'm trying to tell you is that Lofton, assistant bureau chief, has been hounding me day and night to let him talk to you."

"So."

Cassidy sighed heavily. "So, they want to use you on a special assignment."

Keir suddenly felt the weight of the world on his shoulders. "Dammit, Luke, why me? They've got more competent men now than they can say grace over. Why the hell do they want an aging beat-up body like mine?"

"Huh!" Cassidy snorted. "Who are you trying to kid, McBride? You know why they want you. You're the best and they damn well know it."

Keir remained silent. The last thing he wanted to think about now was another assignment. God forbid, he had barely survived this last time with his life. Since regaining consciousness, all he wanted to do, ached to do, was see Danielle, hold her, touch her. . . .

"Well?"

Keir closed his eyes wearily. "Maybe later, Luke, I'll consider it. But not right now. I don't want to even think about it now." His voice was bleak.

"Well, you have an advantage in your favor, if you can call it that. You have to recuperate for a while yet. Then we'll take it from there. But for now all you have to worry about is getting well and keeping Natalie happy." His sober eyes now held a twinkle.

Keir was quiet.

"What's the matter?" Cassidy smiled. "You getting cold feet now about tying the knot?"

Keir sighed. "If . . . if you don't mind, I'd rather not discuss it."

"That's your choice, my boy. Didn't mean to pry." Cassidy began buttoning his coat. "All you've got to do is lie here and get well; then go home and think about the big fat check you'll be getting every week for lying on your ass."

"The money's not important and you know it," Keir said tersely.

"Sorry, I forget you're not one of us struggling American citizens." He shrugged. "Somehow, you don't look like a millionaire."

"Luke!" Then he saw the impish grin that spread across his face. The man had the weirdest sense of humor.

Cassidy held up his hand. "I'm going. You get some rest and I'll see you tomorrow."

Keir nodded and watched as Cassidy made his way to the door.

Placing his hand on the doorknob, Cassidy swung around. "One more thing before I go. What's Danielle Davis to you?"

The surge that went through Keir made the hair on his neck stand on end.

"Why do you ask that?" he snapped, suddenly on the defensive. His head was beginning to throb again.

"Cool down, Keir, my boy, your bandages are beginning to smoke."

"Dammit, Luke!" he said, his eyes flashing with rage.

Cassidy laughed. "See you later, Keir." He shut the door softly behind him.

For a while Keir lay with his eyes closed, feeling exhausted. And thinking of Danielle. Suddenly he felt an ache for her so intense that it almost overwhelmed him. But he was helpless with nothing left of her but memories, memories that were slowly ripping him to pieces.

He couldn't stop his mind from churning, thinking . . . the way she looked as she lay naked on the tattered bedroll in the firelight, her hair shining, gracing her shoulders the way he liked it . . . the way he kissed her sweet mouth, her fresh-smelling skin . . . the way her eyes had changed as she awakened him with a half-strangled cry and lowered her face, opening her mouth over him. Oh, God, the pain of remembering . . .

He groaned and turned, careful not to disturb the needle in his arm. But still he couldn't halt the flow of restless thoughts. She hadn't even called to check on him. Gut instinct told him that. But why should she? he chided himself unmercifully. She was out of danger now, back in her nice, secure little world. Fear had caused her to turn to him, nothing more.

Whatever was happening to her now, whatever she was doing, he knew that he was the last person she wanted to see.

Keir walked slowly across the grounds. He'd been at his parents' estate outside of D.C. for a few days now. His stay in the hospital had turned into almost a month due to an unexpected bout with pneumonia. But he was stronger now, much stronger.

Cassidy was still clucking over him like a mother hen, as were his parents and . . . Natalie, until yesterday, that is. Had it been just yesterday that he had told her he couldn't marry her? He winced against the pain. He had been walking as he was now when he heard someone calling his name. . . .

He had looked back and saw Natalie running toward him. Why couldn't he love her? She was pretty. She had a thick crop of neatly kept dark brown hair, nice full breasts and long shapely legs that accentuated her tiny waistline.

She swung her arms around his neck and kissed him warmly.

"Aren't you going to eat dinner with us?" she asked.

"I'm not very hungry right now, Natalie," he declined wearily.

Natalie looked away.

She didn't understand, he knew. And he despised himself for what he was doing to her. To himself.

Natalie fell in step beside him, her eyes shadowed. "What's the matter, Keir? You're different." She lifted her shoulders. "I know you've been seriously ill, but . . ." She paused, as though groping for the right words. "It's all right if you want out," she said softly.

He told her then. Told her that he couldn't marry her now. Not ever. The words simply spilled from his lips, and with them a heavy burden fell from his heart. Oddly enough they had parted friends.

Yet his misery was immense. Even now, his aimless wanderings did nothing to help him. He thought distance would help. Distance, he expected, would make him free. But it hadn't. The merest thought of Danielle made his pulse race. She was inside him, in his head and in his heart. Finally, he gave up and let the pain, the loneliness and fatigue drive him back to the house.

Raymond McBride saw the change in his son. Breaking his engagement to Natalie was the first indication that something was wrong. What had this last assignment done to Keir, made him a blasted eunuch? He noticed his son's tenseness increase as each day passed. Something was definitely on Keir's mind, and Raymond McBride was going to get to the bottom of it.

He looked up as Keir came into the house.

"Come here, son," he said.

Keir looked surprised at the tone of his father's voice. He entered the den.

"Please, sit down." Raymond indicated one of the plush velvet seats.

Keir sat down with a sigh, wondering what this was all about. Although he and his father weren't close, he admired him greatly. And he had seen the anxiety on Raymond's face and knew he was concerned, as was his mother. He was sorry to have put this strain on their lives.

"What's wrong, son?" Raymond asked. "What's gotten you down like this? Your work? What?"

Keir smiled, thinking that his father had lost none of his sharpness. When it came to sniffing out a problem, he had the instincts of a bloodhound. That was why he was a born politician.

"It's a combination of things—nothing special," he lied.

"Who is she?"

Keir leapt to his feet, stunned. "How . . . how did you know?"

"I may be old, son, but I'm not senile."

Keir laughed outright for the first time in a month. "I agree. You're not senile." Then he suddenly became serious again. "It's someone very special. But . . . oh, what the hell, there's no point in discussing it. It's hopeless."

"Do you love her?" Raymond frowned.

"Yes."

"Have you told her?"

Once a long time ago. "No," he said.

"Then how do you know it's hopeless?"

Keir stared at his father as though he was seeing him for the first time, and remained silent.

"I know you don't believe this, but all your mother and I want is your happiness. I . . . you're all we have." He paused. "Oh, I'll admit we're disappointed about you and Natalie. But if it takes another woman to put the life back into you, then I'm all for it."

"Oh, Dad, there's so much you don't know. . . ." Dare he hope? Take a chance? Once in the cabin she had looked at him with love. And there was still the unsettled question of Ann.

"I've never known you to give up so easily," Raymond said.

"I haven't ever before."

Suddenly Raymond picked up the newspaper and

headed for the door. Before walking out, he turned around.

"What are you waiting for, son? Go to her." With a determined step and the slam of the door he was gone.

A smile softened his lips. The old man had a point. What *was* he waiting for?

As it turned out, Danielle did not go to the party. Ann was sick. Thursday morning she began running a temperature. She lost her breakfast, conked out immediately after that, then got sick when she woke up. Danielle called the doctor for an afternoon appointment and spent the rest of the day imagining that Ann had all kinds of rare, terrible diseases and telling herself she was being ridiculous, overimaginative.

Ann behaved well through the examination, but Danielle couldn't stop herself from fearing the worst.

"It's just a virus," the doctor said. "I'll give you a couple of prescriptions. If she isn't better by Friday, call Lucy and make another appointment."

Friday dawned clear and crisp, finding Ann much better.

"Are you going to Marge's party?" Jusie asked over coffee that morning. It was early and Ann was still asleep.

Danielle shook her head, noticing how her shoulders ached. From too much bending and stooping in the store, she thought fleetingly. "I don't think it would be a good idea, do you?"

Jusie pursed her lips. "Sure do."

"Well, I don't," Danielle said stubbornly.

Jusie's brown eyes wandered over Danielle's wan, pale features. "You can't keep this pace up much longer. You're working too hard, not eating—why you're practically a skeleton. The only time you relax is when you're with Ann. And even that doesn't seem to help much."

"Oh, Jusie," Danielle wailed, fighting back the tears, "don't you start too."

"What do you mean, too?"

Danielle curled her fingers tightly around the coffee mug. "Marge. She raked me over the coals the other day, asking questions, telling me how awful I look."

Jusie snorted unbecomingly. "She's nothing but a nosy busy body. But at that, she has enough sense to know you're flirting with a nervous breakdown. Even Ann senses it."

That was the crowning blow. Danielle withered like a flower on a broken stem. Tears began trickling down her face. Dear Lord, Jusie was right. She was grieving. Grieving for Keir and for what might have been. How much longer could she endure being torn between love and fear?

"Oh, honey," Jusie said softly, seeing the spasms of agony cross Danielle's face. She got up and put her arms around Danielle's heaving shoulders, pulling her against her bosom, rocking her like she did Ann. "Don't cry. Maybe if you talk about it, it'll help."

"I'm . . . I'm so mixed up, Jusie, so unhappy," she sobbed. "I . . . I love him, yet . . ."

"Shhh, don't cry," cajoled Jusie. "You'll make yourself sick." She smoothed Danielle's curls away from her face. "I think the time has come for you to get it all out of your system."

Danielle pulled away, struggling to get a hold of herself. But she couldn't stop trembling. "I . . . I don't know if I can."

"Of course you can," Jusie encouraged softly.

Danielle forced the words through stiff, dry lips. "You remember . . . I told you about the marshal that was with me in Virginia." She paused. "Well, I . . . uh . . . had known him before . . . a long time ago. I . . . I didn't think I'd ever see him again."

"You loved him." It was more of a statement than a question.

"Yes," Danielle whispered.

"What's so terrible about that?"

Danielle swiped at the tears drenching her face. "It's . . . you don't understand. . . ."

"Go on."

She fought for her next breath. "Ann is his daughter," she said dully, "and he doesn't even know it."

For a moment there was nothing but a profound silence in the room. Then Jusie stood up, her expression never changing. "I'd better make more coffee. I feel like we're going to be here a spell."

Danielle was late opening the bookstore. But it didn't matter. She felt much better, her heart lighter, having unburdened it to Jusie. She had told her everything, except of course, those intimate moments she had shared with Keir. They were too private, to sacred to share, even with her beloved friend. Some things were better left unsaid.

After that, she had dragged her weary body to her room and gotten dressed and then checked on Ann to make sure there was no recurring fever. Ann had been cool as a cucumber. Still Danielle wasn't about to leave her and go to Marge's party.

Now as she turned the sign around, indicating that she was open, she felt hope for the first time in weeks. Maybe it wasn't hopeless after all, she thought. Maybe when he came, they could work things out. But why hadn't she heard from him? It had been over a month. Could she have been wrong in thinking he still cared? No! She would not think about that. Not now.

Hazel Standley rescued her. "Good morning, Danielle," she said, breezing through the door, leaving the chimes tinkling behind her.

Danielle could have hugged her. "Good morning. How are you?"

Hazel smiled. "Just fine, that is if you have something new to read."

Danielle's eyes brightened. "You're in luck. Your favorite romances came in yesterday."

"Great," Hazel chirped. "Those *are* my favorites. Now how about novels?"

"Mmmm, let's see," Danielle said, weaving between the racks to stand in front of the displays filled with historical romances. "How about this one?" She reached out and plucked it off the shelf. "It's wonderful."

And so it went. Although the day was long and tiring, it was fulfilling. With the fireplace blazing she visited with customers, worked up orders, crawled around on her hands and knees unboxing books and straightened the romantic fiction section.

By the time she turned the sign around to read "Closed" at six o'clock, she was bone weary. It was all she could do to make it up the stairs. Uppermost on her mind was a hot bath and crawling into bed.

It was a while however before she got her wish. Ann wanted to play. After thirty minutes in the water, she laughingly told her daughter, "Darling, if we don't hurry and get out, we're going to look like prunes."

Ann giggled as she splashed water. "What's punes, Mommie?" Mixing tears with water, Danielle grabbed her daughter and hugged her fiercely, thinking she had never seen her look more like her father.

"How did you sleep?" Jusie asked, watching Danielle like a hawk as she walked into the room, dressed in a plum-colored suede jumpsuit. She was stunning, except for her eyes, Jusie thought.

"Fine," Danielle lied, smiling her thanks as Jusie handed her a cup of coffee. She hadn't slept at all. Restless dreams of Keir had kept her awake.

"Well, you sure don't look like it to me," Jusie quipped. "If your eyes sink much further in your head, you'll lose them."

Danielle laughed, although it never reached her eyes. "Hope not. Couldn't read then."

But she hadn't fooled Jusie, not for a minute. "Why don't you let Judy mind the store today. It's Saturday; you won't be very busy. Go shopping, eat out. It'll do you good."

Danielle chewed on her lower lip. "Oh, Jusie, I don't know." But she was tempted. It was a beautiful day and she did need a break.

Jusie saw her weakening. "If the weather holds, I'll take Ann to the zoo. She had such a good time with you the other day, I thought I'd take her back."

Danielle smiled, this time transforming her face. "Oh, Jusie, I love you," she whispered.

Determined not to brood, Danielle made a day of it.

Finally, too weary to take another step, she piled her packages into her car and headed for home. North Street was practically deserted as she drove down it, the majority of the college students having gone home for the weekend.

Feeling better than she'd felt in a long time, she parked the car in the driveway and scooped up her packages in her arms. Then carefully she made her way to the door, opened it and began climbing the stairs. "Jusie, Annie, I'm home," she called.

Silence.

Frowning, she crossed the threshold into the family room, only to freeze suddenly in her tracks.

"Oh, God!" she mouthed as the packages fell from her arms and scattered across the floor.

"Why didn't you tell me?"

Chapter 12

IF DANIELLE LIVED TO BE A HUNDRED, SHE WOULD NEVER forget the scene that greeted her eyes. She blinked several times. Nothing changed.

Keir, his massive body filling the rocking chair to capacity, was sitting by the fireplace rocking a sleeping Ann. The child's dark curls were tumbling across his muscled arm, and one rosy cheek was nestled against his chest. A tiny hand was wrapped possessively around his thumb.

Keir looked up at her, tears clinging to his thick lashes. "Why didn't you tell me?" he repeated brokenly.

Danielle felt the bottom drop out of her stomach as she stood motionless. Was he furious with her? Would he follow through with his threat to take Ann away from her? No! She would find some way to stop him. Even if she had to change her identity again, flee the country. She couldn't bear being separated from her child.

Fear held her mute as she tasted the bile that rose in the back of her throat, threatening to strangle her.

Their eyes locked and time stood still.

Dread filled Danielle's heart as the standoff continued. She felt panic seep into every part of her body. *Oh, Keir, is that hate I see in your eyes? Please don't hate me. At the time, I had no choice. Please understand . . . I love you. But I can't give up my child, not even for you.*

The atmosphere sizzled with suppressed emotion and expectation.

She wet her lips and tried to speak, to plead with him, to grovel if necessary, if he would just understand how very sorry she was. It was obvious that he was hurting—this big, proud man, who faced danger every day of his life without flinching, was torn apart by the sight of his daughter. And seeing father and daughter together for the first time, the likeness uncanny, it hit her squarely between the eyes what he must be feeling at this moment, knowing that he had been deprived of the first years of their child's life. But again, she cried inwardly, what choice had she had?

Neither spoke.

Suddenly, a whimper escaped from Danielle's lips, and she jerked her head around and the room began swaying. She struggled for breath, fighting off the waves of nausea that were washing over her like a tide.

"It's going to be all right, you know," he whispered, smiling through his tears, though his heart was breaking.

Stunned, positive that her ears were playing tricks on her, she swung her head back around, tears glistening in her eyes, streaming down her cheeks. He was still smiling.

"Oh, Keir," she groaned, feeling herself yield to the pressure on her heart. Broken sobs began pelting her body, robbing her of speech.

His own eyes still filled with tears, Keir rose slowly, and clutched his precious burden against him. "Please don't . . . I can't stand to see you cry."

Danielle fought to get ahold of herself, knowing that if she did not, she would never be able to stop crying. Seeing Keir like this after a month of uncertainty was almost more than she could handle.

"Show me her room, and I'll put her down," he said. His voice trembled fiercely.

Wordlessly, Danielle glided on legs that were made of air instead of bones and preceded Keir out of the family room, down the hall to Ann's room. *Everything is going to be all right. I just know it is.* She crossed the threshold and then paused just inside the door, switching on the Alice-in-Wonderland lamp. Suddenly the room was bathed in a warm, cozy glow.

She stood by helplessly as Keir strode across the room to stand in front of both a baby bed and a twin-sized bed. He turned toward her and raised his eyes in question.

"Please," Danielle whispered, "put her in the baby bed. She's been sick and . . . and restless. I don't want to take a chance on her falling out of the bed," she finished lamely.

"Aren't you going to undress her?" he asked.

"Later." Danielle moved to stand beside him as he gently laid Ann's relaxed body on the bed. "She'll probably wake up and howl, then I'll give her a bath and put her back down for the night."

"Why wait? Let's make her comfortable at once." He laid the child down and with gentle, awkward fingers began to unlace her shoes.

"Please, Keir, I'll do it," Danielle said with a somewhat strained smile. What if she was wrong about his motives? What if . . .

"You're afraid to let me touch her, aren't you?" His mortified tone, his hurt eyes, sent a stab of pain through Danielle's heart.

"I only mean—well, if you want to, then do stay and help me," she finished in a warm, sweet, rushing fashion. "Can you slide her sock off? That's right." She watched as he managed to draw off the socks without disturbing the child. "Now for the clothes." But Ann awakened as her mother attempted to unbutton her top. She did not cry, however; she gazed at them both drowsily and said, "Keir," in a satisfied voice.

Danielle shouldn't have been surprised that Keir had managed to worm his way into her daughter's heart and charm her, she thought as she crossed to a chest of drawers and drew out a tiny fresh nightgown. Ann lay holding tight to Keir's thumb as he leaned over the rails for her greater convenience.

"She's perfect," he murmured.

"Yes." Danielle's voice held an odd, hurried note. "At . . . least I think she is." To busy her hands, she latched onto Ann's teddy bear at the foot of the bed and placed it against her stomach.

"She reminds me," he went on, "so much of myself."

One of Danielle's hands went to her breast. *Oh, please just let him be proud and not greedy. Don't let him want more than I'm prepared to give.*

"Let me put the nightie on, Keir."

"Oh, of course." But he did not move, still studying the exquisite little figure, the flushed baby face and tumbled black curls. "I have it! That painting of me when I was about three. I had forgotten it, except for her eyes. The shape of her face, her mouth—even her hands. Look at that." He measured a long, sensitive hand against the baby one, which was a miniature of his own.

Danielle uttered a faint, choked sound as if she had attempted to speak and found her voice gone.

Keir swung around abruptly and saw her standing there, white as paper, clutching her breast.

His face was filled with awe. "My God," he breathed, "she's really and truly mine." It was as though he still did not, could not, believe it.

Ann, neglected, gave a protesting whimper. As if released from bondage, Danielle bent over her, put on the nightgown, covered the child and kissed her.

For a brief second, green eyes fluttered open again. "Mommie," Ann murmured softly.

"It's all right, love, Mommie's here. Go to sleep," Danielle cooed. Then she turned to Keir. "If you'll go on," she added in a whisper, "I'll turn off the light."

He left the room and she followed him.

In the den he stopped and faced her. "What possessed you not to tell me?" He struggled to keep his tone even.

Her stomach revolted. She wasn't out of danger yet. "Tell you? How could I? And even if it had been possible, I'd rather have gone to the stake," Danielle cried passionately, "than have told you in that way. Remember you weren't ready for a home with a white picket fence around it and a family."

"Oh, God, Danielle, we could have worked something out."

She remained silent.

"Was this your revenge?"

"There . . . there was no revenge about it. It was over between us. You weren't interested in . . . in settling down."

"But I didn't know. I never dreamed—do you suppose, for one instant, that if I'd known, I wouldn't have turned over heaven and hell to have found you."

"I tell you, Keir," Danielle's eyes were lit with anger, "nothing would have induced me to make such a plea."

"Don't be a fool," he cried roughly. "You had no right to conceal this. The child was mine as much as yours."

Her shoulders slumped in defeat. "How . . . how was I to know you'd still want me? Anyway, it was too late. After I became involved with the government . . . nothing was the same." She spread her hands.

"Oh, God," he groaned, "if only I'd known. The

agony of all those years without you, without seeing my child is almost more than I can stand."

Danielle's face changed, her mouth trembled and her eyes, a moment before brilliant with rage, darkened pitifully.

A muttered curse split Keir's lips, followed by a harsh sigh. "God, I'm sorry. I've no right to turn on you now, reproach you—I'm making a blasted idiot of myself. I was just as pigheaded and stubborn as you were, and I got exactly what I deserved and ought to be kicked for raking you over the coals."

"I didn't do this to hurt you. I just . . ."

"God in heaven, if only one could turn back the pages," he whispered, his voice raspy, broken.

"It's too late; one can never do that," she said gently, keeping her own tears at bay by the greatest of effort.

They looked at each other; Danielle's heart began to throb, Keir's hands closed until the knuckles were white and the fingernails bit into his palms.

He smiled through his tears. "No, my darling, it's not too late. Not for us."

"Keir. I . . ." Her voice failed as she watched him brush a tear off his cheek with a clumsy finger and felt the renewed sting of tears behind her eyes as the lump in her throat grew too big to swallow. She could stand most anything, except his tears.

Unconsciously her head began to weave from side to side. "I'm sorry, so sorry," she whispered.

He turned toward her then and folded her within his arms.

She nestled into his warmth, letting it surround her like a soft veil.

He held her as though he'd never let her go, but still he did not say what she so desperately craved to hear, that he loved her and wanted to marry her, that he wanted to make a home for her and Ann.

After a moment, she lifted her eyes, searching for his, unable to hold any longer what was in her heart, her soul. "I . . . I love you," she said sweetly, then was as startled by her own boldness as Keir appeared to be, but she couldn't stop herself. She could only plunge ahead recklessly, speaking too fast, in too much of a rush to express what could no longer be left unsaid. "I love you, Keir McBride. And if you want me to, I'll stand here the rest of the evening and night saying it over and over until my voice wears out."

He stared down at her, his beautiful green eyes a darker and more intense green than she had ever seen them before. Yet he remained silent and just looked at her.

She tried to read those eyes, but she couldn't tell a thing about the thoughts behind them.

As she waited for him to respond to her declaration, Danielle wondered with a sinking heart if she had misunderstood his words of a while ago, misinterpreted the message in his eyes. Yet how could she be mistaken about the way his arms were folded around her now and the hammering of his heart as it answered the hammering of her own?

When his silence reached a screaming pitch, she almost wished that she could call back the words she had spoken, roll back the clock just one minute. But no, she could not take back a word of it. She loved him, had always loved him, and after what he'd done for her she owed him that and much, much more.

Then he kissed her.

His lips pressed against hers, tenderly, yet forcefully, both giving and taking, seeking and demanding. She responded to him instantly, with a heat that made her dizzy, made her lose touch with reality.

The kiss involved not only lips, teeth and tongues, but passion, hunger and need. He cupped her face, holding her gently but firmly, as if he were afraid that she would reconsider her commitment and would pull away from him.

"Oh, Danielle, Danielle," he whispered against her lips, "there are thousands of things I want to hear, to ask, about Ann—us, but right now all I want to do is to hold you and never let you out of my sight again. But even more than that, I want to make love to you, to show you how much I love you, how much I've missed you, how my life these past weeks has been hell without you."

"Me too," she echoed softly.

It was a healing, cleansing time for both as they remained locked steadfastly in one another's arms, oblivious to the sounds around them, aware of nothing but their own happiness.

The revelation concerning Ann had shaken him to the core; still, he could not resolve his emotions, could not get his swirling brain into any sort of order. *Ann.* That precious baby, that exquisite little figure with her silky black mop and dark-lashed green eyes and rose-colored face. Ann was his—his own child, his and Danielle's. Oh, God! he groaned silently. Fool that he had been, mad, blind fool to have given up so easily, to have thrown away the gift God had given him.

But now, miraculously, he was being given another chance. And this time he would not blow it. He would love her and Ann, take care of them, cherish them for the rest of his life.

His arms around her were like bands of steel as he tightened them around her slender frame. "Where's your bedroom?" he asked, his warm breath bathing the inside of her ear.

She shivered. "Mmmm, down the hall."

"What are we waiting for?"

"I haven't the foggiest."

He laughed and gave her another of those breathtaking hugs.

When he let her go, she looked up, then frowned. "Jusie! Where is Jusie? We . . . can't . . . I mean . . ."

He leaned over and kissed the tip of her pert nose, drinking in the fresh fragrance of her skin, her hair. "Don't worry about Jusie. She's gone to visit friends. For the night, I might add."

Danielle's eyes widened in surprise, and her mouth fell open.

"Shut your mouth," Keir ordered, grinning. "She wanted to make sure we had plenty of time alone to do our thing. At first she was reluctant to let me in, but when I told her who I was, a complete change came over her." He grinned. "We had quite a conversation."

"You're crazy, you know," she said breathlessly.

"Crazy about you." He couldn't get enough of her. His need was raging. He craved the taste of her lips, was starved for the feel of her skin and the soft tension of her flesh. He wanted to undress her slowly and kiss her breasts and slip deep inside her.

Her lips touched his throat. She did not kiss him. Not exactly. She prolonged the feeling of passion in the artery that stood up and thumped in his neck.

He turned to her, moved into her, and they pressed harder together, belly to belly. Her breasts were squashed pleasantly against his chest. He kissed her forehead, her eyes.

She felt slightly intoxicated as she slipped her fingers into his hair, feeling, touching, loving. . . . For this moment was the culmination of all her hopes, her dreams for the future. The sins of the past were forgiven, the hope for tomorrow was bright and shining as a beacon. Perfect. Everything was perfect. He would ask her to marry him; they would settle down, no more running, no more hiding, no more danger, and no more being parted. What more could she ask for?

"Ah, my darling, you cause such a storm in me," he whispered as he bent down and scooped her up in his arms. She seemed weightless, and he felt as if he could lift the earth.

She clung to him. In her clear eyes there was a vulnerability that touched his heart.

"I want you," she whispered.

They went into her bedroom. "I love you," he said. "I nearly went crazy without you," he added before kissing her deeply, sweetly, reaching for her soul. When he drew away, she brought him back. His kisses sent darting spasms of response through her. He was so strong, so solid and positive and whole. And he was hers.

When they separated, she found herself taking in air in small gasping gulps, taut with expectation as his hands unzipped her jumpsuit and the cool air touched her skin.

Her hands sweetly touched him before moving down to unfasten the snap at his waist and sliding the zipper down. Then she put her mouth on his collarbone, the side of his neck, the base of his throat. His skin was smooth and warm and fresh. It felt good against her lips, even the scar where the bullet had pierced his side had healed nicely.

They took their time undressing one another, stopping to kiss and touch, finally lying down on the bed together.

He circled her nipples with his tongue, bathing them in the dew of his mouth, causing her to suck in her breath with exquisite pain. Her hand fell lightly on the back of his head to keep him there.

"Oh, Keir, I can't believe you're here, touching me like this," she whispered, opening under him, drawing him down to her.

"I love you so much." He traced a finger down her thigh.

"And I love you. Oh!" She quivered as his fingers dipped into her. "Keir!"

She placed her hands between them, guiding him forward. But she no longer needed to direct him. He was there, parting her, entering, his hands caressing her breasts as he knelt between her thighs and immersed himself fully into her, then stopped, resting there. She raised her arms and brought him up to her breasts, anxious to please, to love him.

His hips shifted, beginning a counterpoint, playing a melody that was perfectly timed to his slow-thrusting theme. He held her, filled her more completely, more perfectly than ever before.

"God, you're perfect," he whispered.

She closed her eyes as he moved inside of her, stirring something deep, something profound, something so wonderful that a soft dying cry came from his mouth. She shuddered and clung to him moaning softly, her eyes still tightly shut as she rose, then fell, gasping. A minute later, as the last of the spasms were passing, she felt him come inside her.

He was aware of her rising even closer to him in great love and gladness, his own hopes and love reaffirmed.

Her thoughts and fears suddenly seemed unimportant because whatever happened, he really was going to be there. She simply knew it all at once, believed it absolutely; he was going to be there always.

"I'm so happy," she said, a long time later.

"All I want," he said as he caressed her arm, "is for you to be happy."

"And that makes you happy?"

"Need you ask?" He pulled her on top of him. "For the first time in years—well, since you all but threw me out—I feel alive."

"It's just that all this seems like a dream come true."

He smiled. "Well, if it's a dream, I never want to wake up."

Snuggling close to his warm body, she said, "Me neither."

"Speaking of waking up, hadn't we better go check on our daughter?"

She smiled up at him thinking the word "our" was suddenly the most beautiful word in the English language. "Oh, you don't know Ann," she said. "The minute she wakes up, she starts calling, and if I'm not around, she calls for her Jusie."

"Then you think we're safe?"

"Trust me, we're safe. In fact, she may not, probably won't, wake up until the morning. I'm sure Jusie fed her before she left, so she won't be hungry."

"She did," he said and grinned. "Jusie was just beginning to feed Ann dinner when I got here, and by the time Jusie was finished, we were fast friends."

Danielle felt a glow around her heart. "You had both Ann and Jusie eating out of your hand, is that what you're saying?"

He chuckled. "That's right."

"Did Jusie feed you too?"

"No."

"Are you hungry?"

"Terribly."

"Want to sneak in the kitchen for a midnight snack?"

"Thought you'd never ask."

Keir got up and slipped into his pants as she scooped up his shirt and put it on, holding her arm up to her nose, sniffing at his sleeve.

He laughed. "What are you doing?"

"Inhaling you. It's like putting a part of you on, wearing you around."

"Crazy!" He took her arm and steered her toward the kitchen.

Together they prepared an omelette, bacon and toast, and by the time they consumed the food, checked on a peacefully sleeping Ann, Danielle's eyes had begun to droop.

"It's back to bed with you, my sweet."

"But I'm not sleepy." She smiled. "Really, I'm not, just relaxed, satisfied."

He gave her a leering grin. "Let's go back to bed anyway."

She laughed and grabbed his hand and led him toward the bedroom. Immediately they rid themselves of their scanty clothing and, straightening the covers, crawled back into the bed.

He put his arm around her and held her warmly in the crook of his arm. After a moment of contented silence, he confessed softly, "You know, you've never been off my mind. I kept finding you in every revolving door."

"I've never been without you," she answered, turning toward him with her heart in her eyes.

Thus began a play in separate acts with intermissions of kissing, talking and touching.

He told her about Natalie, how she was a substitute for her, that she was a wonderful person but he had never loved her. He also told her about taking dangerous assignments, one after the other, in order to keep his mind and body active so he would not think about her. The more dangerous the job, he said, the better he liked it.

His hands were warm against her flesh by the time she spoke of the loneliness she had endured after they parted. He wanted to know the details of Ann's birth, and she told him. She told him how in the hospital she had longed for him to share in that miracle but had known that no matter how much she ached for it, it was impossible.

After they had emptied their souls to one another, they lay quietly on their backs, close together, her head on his arm, exhaustion apparent in the drooping flutter of her eyelids and tired slant of her mouth.

"I love you," she whispered, burrowing closer.

"Go to sleep, my love." He brushed his lips across her forehead.

"You too?"

"Me too. We'll talk in the morning."

Long hours into the new day, arms wrapped tightly around one another, they fell into a deep sleep.

Sensing that she was alone, Danielle awakened in a blissful state of happiness. Keir. Their coming together had all been everything she had hoped for and more. At last they were to be a real family, she thought. Stretching contentedly, her eyes strayed to the numbers on the clock. Suddenly she jerked upright. Good Lord, it was nine o'clock. Ann. Surely she wasn't still asleep? And Jusie. Where was Jusie? She didn't hear her banging around in the kitchen.

After bounding out of bed and making a quick detour by the bathroom, Danielle paraded into the kitchen, tightening the sash on her robe as she went.

"Mommie, me full," her daughter greeted her the minute she crossed the threshold.

Danielle lovingly glanced at a happy Ann, who straddled Keir's knee, egg mixed with grape jelly staining her cherub face. Then she raised her eyes and collided with Keir's brilliant green ones.

For a heady moment, they were alone in the room.

"Good morning." Keir spoke softly, but his eyes spoke another message. *You're wonderful,* they said.

"Good morning." Could that weak, wispy voice be hers? Clearing her throat, she moved closer to Ann and leaned down and kissed her on the cheek. And for the first time, her daughter didn't hold out her chubby arms to her. It was apparent that Keir was still an unqualified hit.

"Your daughter's a little pig, no doubt about it," Keir said, running his big hand through Ann's curls affectionately.

Danielle merely stood there, her heart swelled with love and pride at the picture father and daughter created together. With Jusie nowhere in sight, it was obvious that Keir had opted to feed and bathe Ann while she slept. Then a sudden sting fanned her cheeks as she remembered how little sleep they had actually gotten.

As though reading her mind, Keir grinned, darkening her blush even more. "Hungry?" he drawled, helping a squirming Ann down from his lap.

"A little."

"Good. Sit down, and I'll prepare you a McBride special."

Danielle laughed, scooping her daughter up in her lap and giving her a squeeze. Then, unconsciously, she reached for a napkin and began wiping the goop from her daughter's face. "Hold still, little wiggle worm," she demanded when Ann began turning her face from side to side. "All right, get down, but first give Mommie a kiss, then go get your coloring book and colors and show Dad . . . Keir . . . how well you can color."

"When are we going to tell her?" Keir asked a moment later as they watched their happily occupied daughter in the corner of the den.

"I'm . . . ready when you are."

Suddenly his eyes narrowed as he leaned toward her. "Aren't you forgetting something?" he asked thickly.

She looked momentarily puzzled. "I am?"

"This," he said and dipped his head and gave her a searing kiss.

Once again, Danielle found herself drowning in the sight, smell and touch of him. She never wanted this high to end.

Pulling back, he whispered, "Let's get married. Today. This morning. Doesn't that sound like heaven?"

"Like heaven," she echoed into his mouth. Now, she thought, now he would tell her what she longed to hear, that he would give up his dangerous job, find work here in Texas, never leave her and Ann alone again.

"But we won't be able to leave right away. There's so much we have to take care of before we can go back to D.C."

The sudden businesslike tone of his voice sent a cold

chill of foreboding through her. She raised her head to look at him. "Leave?"

"Of course." He rushed on. "We'll stay here until we can find a suitable buyer for the store, and Jusie—well, if she wants to go with us, I . . ."

Pushing him away, she lunged to her feet. "What?" Then before he could answer her she went on, shaking her head in bewilderment. "Leave? But why? I . . . I thought . . . I mean," she stammered, suddenly feeling as though she were foundering alone in the middle of the ocean in a life raft that had sprung a leak. Then abruptly she turned to go to Ann, needing to get away from him, to think. But before she could take a few steps, Keir had closed the distance between them, his hard fingers circling her waist.

"Danielle, honey, what's wrong?" he asked, taking in her pale features. "I don't understand."

"Well, apparently neither do I," she whispered. "It's . . . it's just that I thought now that you wouldn't be working for the government any longer, we wouldn't have to leave." Her voice had dwindled almost to nothing.

"Where did you get that idea?" His fingers tightened on her wrist; she could feel the heightened tension in his body.

The silence that fell over the room was formidable.

Danielle's stomach was churning, and the tears were dangerously close as her gaze dropped pointedly to his clenched fingers. "Let me go," she said dully.

"Answer me," he demanded, trying to ignore the rising heat at the base of his throat, the sense of panic festering in his gut.

"I . . . I just assumed this time . . . you would give up working for the government . . . knowing that I'm still against it," she said, swinging back around to look at him, catching the tail end of the expression that passed briefly over his face. Distracted by her own heightened emotions, she did not want to name the ones flickering across his face. Pain? Disappointment? Frustration?

"I'm sorry if I gave you that impression," he said coldly, "but I have no plans to give up my work."

Danielle could not believe that she had heard him correctly. But she had. His hard features were a testimony to his words. She should have known that it was too good to be true, she lamented. His work still came first. They were from two different worlds, with different values. Love, it seemed, was still not enough. She stood silent, her heart breaking.

The silence stretched endlessly.

"Danielle," Keir said at last, "nothing's going to happen to me. Do you think that I'd take any unnecessary chances knowing that I have you to come home to?"

She ignored that odd, almost desperate sound in his voice, hardening her heart. "No," she uttered on a strangled whisper, "but . . ."

Keir's narrowing lids failed to conceal the anger flaring in his eyes at her persistent stubbornness. "But what?"

"I . . . I haven't changed, Keir," she said, unchecked tears beginning to trickle down her hollow cheeks. "I still want . . . a real home, white picket fence and all for me . . . for Ann. And a husband who will always be there, not one who's constantly chasing danger."

"Correct me if I'm wrong, but this conversation sounds awfully familiar to me." Keir's tone showed evidence of the strain on his control.

"I won't deny that," she lashed out at him. "But my God, Keir, after what we've just been through, what do you expect?" A shudder tore through her body as she walked to the cabinet. With trembling fingers, she poured herself a cup of coffee before turning back around to face him. "I thought once you found out about . . . Ann you'd be eager to give up your dangerous globe-trotting to settle down. I . . . I thought we'd be a real family." She choked back a sob.

He cursed, raising his arm to tunnel his fingers through his thick, tousled hair. Watching his movement, her eyes were drawn to the muscles tightening on his exposed chest, before dipping lower, taking delight in the shadowed dent in his stomach, to the bold outline of his masculinity heightened by his close-fitting jeans. She averted her gaze, hot coffee sloshing on her hand. She winced.

"Danielle, honey, turn around," he ordered gently. Like a puppet on a string, she responded to his command. "Don't you understand that we *will* be a family. All of us together. Me. You. Ann. For the rest of our lives."

Danielle couldn't stop her lower lip from trembling. "But if you're gone all the time, that's not being a family," she wailed.

He wanted to touch her so badly he could taste it, but something held him back. Something he couldn't name. Suddenly she seemed untouchable. His heart skipped a fearful beat.

"In the first place I won't be gone all the time," he reasoned. "And in the second place nothing is going to happen to me. You've got to believe that." His tone was pleading now. "Anyway, I have responsibilities, obligations to people other than myself. They depend on me. Right now, they're waiting on me to head an undercover operation that, if successful, could keep the Russians from walking off with any more of our technological secrets. I can't just back away from that."

"No. I guess you can't," she said bitterly. *But you can sure as hell walk away from your responsibilities toward me.* "And I'd never have a minute's peace of mind. I'd worry about you night and day, wondering if you'd come home shot up, maimed or dead."

"Dammit, that's a cop-out and you know it. As far as that goes, I could walk out the door and get run over by a truck. I love you and want to marry you. Isn't that enough?"

"How can you say that," she cried, "after what you just went through protecting me?" She was choking on the hot throbbing ache that was growing within her. "I love you, but I can't . . . I won't live with the shadow of fear. Not . . . not anymore. I've told you what I want." She paused. "I refuse to . . . to settle for less."

He felt sick on the inside, sick that he was losing her. *Oh, God, not again*, he cried silently.

"Danielle," he reasoned patiently. "I know you've been through a living hell the last three years as well as the past few weeks, but that's all over now, behind you. We have a wonderful future in front of us. Don't throw it away. Let go of the fear, once and for all. Lean on me—trust me."

No. Her mouth formed the word, but it never got past her lips. Was she being unreasonable? Was she afraid? Afraid to venture beyond the world she had made for herself, for Ann? No, of course she wasn't. She loved him. Oh, how she loved him. Hadn't she paid her dues? Hadn't she earned the right to live in peace?

Yet, perhaps there was some truth in what he said. Maybe his work was not the real problem. Maybe it was something inside her that she could not change. She just knew that she had to have security and roots. For her it was synonymous with love.

"Keir . . . please . . ."

"You're going to do it again, aren't you? Just like before. You're going to walk out on me?" Keir asked, rage etching the lines of his face. "Because you're still afraid to get involved, to take a chance, right?" He was towering over her now. "I want to know now if you're coming with me."

She answered him with silence, turning her back.

"All right, Danielle, you win. I won't fight you anymore. If living in a vacuum will make you happy, then so be it. But don't expect my daughter to do the same thing, because I won't allow it."

If he had physically slapped her, she couldn't have been more stunned. She was trying to recover from the verbal blow and find her voice as he crossed the room to the door. There he paused.

"My lawyer will be in touch. See you in court."

The door slammed shut behind him, shattering her heart into tiny pieces. She crumpled to the floor, too numb to cry.

Chapter 13

THE DAYS CREPT SLOWLY BY, AND WITH EACH ONE THAT passed, Danielle's despair deepened. She was at a loss as to how to deal with the fear and pain that haunted her relentlessly. Fear that she would lose her child and the pain of having lost Keir again.

Yet she was determined to pick up the pieces of her life and go on as though Keir had never become a part of it again. But that was easier said than done.

Since he had walked away without a backward glance over three weeks ago, she had tried to exorcise him from both her heart and mind, but thoughts of their parting and his bitter words continued to torment her soul. She had worked like a Trojan in the bookstore, cleaning, rearranging, moving books and shelving until she was exhausted.

But it was those hours after she closed the store that were the hardest to endure. She tried to fill her evenings with Ann, reading to her, coloring with her, or simply holding her, but oftentimes Ann would fall asleep in her arms and have to be put to bed early, leaving her to face the remainder of the evening alone, staring at the four walls.

Although Jusie tried repeatedly to cheer her up, Danielle could not be consoled. She refused to contact any of her friends, choosing instead to be with her daughter and work, her panacea for making it through the days.

The only word she'd had concerning Keir was from Luke Cassidy. He had called her shortly after Keir left. Both the call and the conversation had further upset her. She remembered every word that had passed between them. The phone had rung just before closing time. . . .

"Hello," she'd said softly.

"Ms. Davis, is that you?" a deep voice had asked.

"Yes," she said with a sinking feeling, recognizing Luke Cassidy's voice immediately.

"How are you?"

"I'm fine," she answered politely.

"Well, I won't keep you long. I'm calling to let you know both Letsukov and Zoya survived their wounds and that as soon as it's convenient for you, we'd like to make arrangements for you to fly to Washington to give your deposition and make a final identification of Letsukov. Then, we hope you'll never hear from us again."

"It doesn't matter, Marshal Cassidy. I'll come whenever you want me to." She hated the thought of going back to Washington, but she had given her word.

"Fine. I'll have my office contact you with the final arrangements."

Danielle hesitated a moment. "Before you hang up," she said, "I'd like to thank you again for taking care of me all this time. I . . . I don't think I've ever stopped long enough to let you know that in spite of all that's transpired, I am grateful to you and your office for saving my life."

"It's our job, Ms. Davis, but it's nice to be thanked anyway," he said brusquely.

A short silence fell between them.

"Was that all you wanted, Mr. Cassidy?" Danielle asked at last.

This time he hesitated. "Well, actually it's not. Have you by any chance seen or talked to Keir McBride lately?"

Danielle's breath caught in her throat. Had something happened to Keir? "Why . . . why do you want to know?"

"Well, uh," he paused and coughed, "he's sort of disappeared. What I mean is, no one's seen him for about a week now, and we need to get in touch with him, and the last thing I heard him say was that he was going to Texas to see you."

Another silence.

"I . . . don't know where he is." She paused and wet her dry lips. "He . . . came, but he's gone now, and I don't know where he is."

"I see. Well, thanks, anyway. We'll be in touch. Good-bye, Ms. Davis."

Now as she stood peering out the window of the bookstore waiting until closing time, looking out at the slow winter drizzle, she was consumed with pain. She kept asking herself what would happen if Keir would burst into the store and present a solution to all their problems.

Absurd! Telling herself that merely plunged her deeper into despair. But her mind betrayed her with images of him; his face, his smile, his gentle arms.

Fate had sent him to her, and she had sent him away. But what choices had she been given? She simply could not live with the fear of waiting for him to come home only to be told he never would.

Even knowing that he was not willing to give up his work, to make a sacrifice for her or their child, that she would never come first in his life, she still loved him and ached for his touch. Madness.

With a deep sigh, Danielle turned and focused her eyes on the clock, noticing that it was now after six o'clock. It was closing time, with nothing to look forward to but another long, empty evening in front of her. She cringed at the thought. Even Ann seemed to be impatient with herself the last few days. Nothing seemed to please her either. Maybe she was getting sick again, Danielle thought, mechanically reaching behind the counter and grabbing the key. After dragging her weary body to the front door and inserting the key, she flipped the sign to "Closed."

Leaving a portion of the inside lights on, she began making her way toward the back and the stairs leading up to her apartment. Suddenly she stopped and gasped aloud. Catching her reflection in the antique mirror that dominated the wall above a slew of racks, she was horrified. She looked ghastly. Pausing a moment longer, she looked down at the slenderness of her limbs; the bones were revealed through her thin wool pants and cowl neck sweater.

But she had known and had only been fooling herself. She had climbed on the scales in the bathroom yesterday morning. Until now, however, she was able to convince herself that the loss of weight was a figment of her imagination, but now she knew this was not so. The reason her clothes, even tight-fitting jeans, were hanging on her was because she had lost over five pounds, five pounds she could not afford to lose.

Nevertheless, while the mind was capable of absorbing a certain amount of pain, the body was less resilient.

Dammit, if she didn't know better, she would say she was pining away. But how could she be such a fool to pine over a man who threatened to take her child away from her?

With an exclamation of self-disgust, Danielle made her way out of the store, and up the stairs into the apartment. After dropping her black order book on the nearest table she went into the kitchen. She heard her daughter chattering nonstop to Jusie.

"Mommie!" Ann clamored the second Danielle stepped into the brightly lighted room.

"Hello, darling," Danielle said, stooping down to lift her daughter into her arms, giving her a quick hug. "How's my best girl been today?"

Ann's tiny mouth spread into a grin as she fingered the gold chain around her mother's neck. "Me good. Played with Lisa."

"Oh, that's right. Mommie forgot Jusie was taking you to play with Melissa today."

After giving Ann a kiss on the cheek, Danielle lowered her to the floor and turned her attention to Jusie. However, before she could say anything, her daughter yanked on her hand.

"Yes, moppet," Danielle inquired absently, her eyes following her housekeeper as she added tomatoes to a bowl of fresh green lettuce. For the first time in days, Danielle felt her stomach rumble with hunger pains.

Suddenly the yank became harder. Danielle looked down.

"Mommie, why don't I have a daddy like Lisa?" Ann asked. "I want that man, Keir, to be my daddy. Can he?"

For a moment—or was it eons?—the room began to spin. Danielle blindly reached for the back of the nearest chair and clamped her hand down onto it to keep from falling.

"Danielle, are you all right?" It was Jusie's voice, but it seemed to be coming from far away, although Jusie's hands as they touched her arm were real and secure.

Without protesting Danielle let Jusie gently push her trembling body down into the chair.

"Mommie, what's wrong? You sick?" Ann's face was puckered in a frown, her eyes wide with fright as she stared at her mother.

Danielle took several deep breaths, struggling for control. Shortly the room and her daughter's face once again became a stationary object. And Jusie's face swam back into focus. But nothing, nothing short of a miracle could help the pain around her heart. Ann's words had hit their mark. Oh, God, was she wrong in depriving her child of her father? She had tried so hard to be both mother and father to Ann, but it seemed as though her best hadn't been good enough.

Keir's sudden reappearance had obviously changed all that. He had disturbed once again her well-ordered life, and nothing had been the same since.

Danielle forced a smile to her stiff lips and gazed down into Ann's trusting, upturned face. "Don't . . . don't worry, moppet," she said in a reassuring tone, "Mommie's all right. Just a little dizzy, that's all. Why don't you go play with your toys for a minute, then we'll eat."

"Me go play." Satisfied, Ann took off eagerly toward the den and the small toybox that occupied one corner.

The second Ann was out of hearing distance, Jusie sat down in front of Danielle, her kind face lined with both concern and disapproval. "You can't keep on like this much longer, you know."

"I . . . know," Danielle responded softly, tears glistening in her eyes.

"Do you love him?"

That softly phrased question caused Danielle to jerk up her head. "Yes," she whispered, sounding as if that three letter word was torn from the depths of her soul.

"Well, then, why are you punishing yourself like this?"

For a long moment Danielle sat silent, her forehead knitted, her fingers lacing and interlacing. "It's just not that simple," she wailed, wanting desperately for Jusie to understand. "I want roots, stability for Ann, for myself, and he . . . he can't, won't, guarantee that."

Jusie did not understand. Her next words proved it. "Oh, Danielle, Danielle, how can you be so blind? If only you could see that love and being loved is the most important thing in the world. Look at me, for heaven's sake, a woman who was never lucky enough to find a man to love her." She paused and took Danielle's soft hands between her warm, rough ones and squeezed gently. "Please, I beg you, don't throw the love of your life away because you're afraid to take a chance. Haven't you learned by now, my precious, that life offers no guarantees to any of us? Don't do this to yourself, to Ann."

Danielle sat staring mutely at Jusie, oblivious to the tears that flowed down her cheeks in a steady stream. Was Jusie right? And Keir? He had accused her of the same thing. Yes, of course, they were right.

Suddenly it dawned upon her that a home, family, roots were meaningless without Keir. He was her roots. Without him life had no meaning. To be completely fulfilled she needed Keir. Even though she dearly loved Ann, she could not replace Keir in her life. Nor could she deprive Keir from being a father to her child. She knew that now. Sharing Ann would be her ultimate sacrifice.

She realized, too, that it no longer mattered what he did for a living. He could be a government agent for the rest of his life if that would make him happy. It was no longer important. But accepting him and loving him for what he was, was the important thing. She had made a grave error in trying to change him; she could see that now. That was what Keir had been trying to tell her, but she had been blinded by her own selfish needs.

Did he still love her? Or was it Ann he wanted now and not her? Was it too late to salvage the mess she had made of her life? Would Keir, would life, give her another chance? Dare she try?

Jumping up, a brilliant smile changing her features, Danielle scooted around the table and flung her arms around Jusie, holding her in a tight clench for a long, thankful moment.

Then she cried jubilantly, "Washington, D.C., here I come!"

The phone was ringing off the wall when Keir walked into the den of his plush Washington townhouse.

"Dammit!" he swore aloud, reaching for it; then he changed his mind. He decided to ignore it. He knew that it was Cassidy trying to track him down, but he was the last person Keir wanted to talk to right now. He still wanted to be left alone, alone with his punishing, torturous thoughts.

The moment he had returned to Washington from Danielle's, he went to work, or went through the routine of his work, he should say. He wanted to contact her. He invented explanations inside his head. He silently recited the speech to her dozens of times while he worked. Yet he was continuously distracted; nothing was holding together for him.

His conduct was apparent to everyone, and his colleagues were alarmed, especially Cassidy. But Cassidy dared not say a word. Keir would not welcome his interference, and the office knew it.

Was it possible to die from a broken heart? he wondered as he strode impatiently over to the desk that dominated the corner of the large room. Looking down, he suddenly recoiled as though having been struck by a snake. He felt the blood drain from his face. Occupying the middle of his desk was a bulging envelope bearing the name of a well-known group of attorneys who specialized in child custody cases. His stomach rebelled. With a muttered oath he turned away.

Could he go through with it? Could he take his child away from her mother? No. He could die easier than he could do that. His threat had been just that—a threat and nothing more. But he hadn't known that when he'd contacted the lawyers three weeks ago, before he'd decided to go to the house in Virginia to be alone, to think, hoping to sort out the mess he'd made of his life.

He had been miserable at the cabin. It was haunted with the memories of Danielle, her presence, her laughter, her soft spoken voice. But at least there he had come to the soul-searching conclusion that he could not take Ann away from her. Brokenhearted, he had returned home.

But now he must come to terms with the fact that it was over. Finished. She would never come to him again. But oh, God, how was he going to survive without her?

Then he knew. He wasn't going to survive without her. He was not going to let her go. Not this time. He knew what he had to do. But first he had to see Cassidy. Now.

Danielle was nervous. So nervous that she was not sure she could get out of the taxi now that it had pulled up alongside the curb in front of Keir's Washington townhouse.

Had she taken leave of her senses coming here unannounced like this? She chewed nervously at her lower lip. What if he wasn't home? Hadn't Cassidy said he'd disappeared without telling anyone where he was going? On the other hand what if he was home, but refused to see her or talk to her? Well, all those were possibilities, but she had known that when she had thrown a few necessary articles in an overnight bag and caught the first available flight out of Houston that morning.

Now, having come this far, she was not about to back off. Realizing how much she loved Keir was all the incentive she needed.

"Lady, you going to get out or what?"

Shaking herself, Danielle took a deep breath and began rummaging through her purse for money. Dry-mouthed and visibly shaken, she handed the driver the money as she got out of the car and managed to stammer, "Thank . . . thank you."

"You're welcome, lady, and good luck."

Was it that obvious she was upset? Drawing on strength she did not know she possessed, she made her way up the walk to the front door, fighting back the memories of the wonderful, loving times they had shared here.

Somehow she reached the door and pushed the bell. Nothing.

Please, oh, please, be home, she cried silently.

The door opened, but it wasn't Keir who stood on the threshold, but a strange woman with a coat and purse draped over her arm.

"May I help you?" the woman asked formally.

Danielle circled her lips with her tongue. "Yes . . . uh . . . is Keir . . . Mr. McBride here?"

The woman—housekeeper more than likely, Danielle thought—raised her hand to push back a stray silver curl. "No, he isn't, not at the moment."

"When . . . when do you expect him back?"

"Not sure, ma'am."

"Would it be all right if I came in and waited for him? You see, I'm from out of town and I came especially to see him."

The woman looked both skeptical and uneasy. "I don't know, ma'am, I'm just leaving and I don't . . ."

"Oh, please," Danielle rushed on, a desperate note

in her voice. "I'm a . . . friend. The name's Danielle Davis, and I've traveled a long way. I . . . I must see him."

The woman's kindly wrinkled face was showing signs of weakening.

"Please," Danielle pressed, stopping short of begging.

The woman shrugged and stepped back, opening the door wider, obviously deciding that Danielle appeared sincere and harmless. "Oh, all right," she acquiesced, "come in. Mr. McBride has mentioned you. I guess you're involved in some legal dealings. But be sure you tell Mr. McBride that you talked me into this." She smiled, taking in Danielle's pale, drawn features. "By the way my name is Hannah, Hannah Robbins."

Danielle held out her hand. "Hi, good to know you."

"Nice meeting you." She paused and looked at her watch. "I have to go now. Have to pick up my grandbaby at the nursery. There's a bar in the den if you want something to drink and there's a cozy fire in the fireplace. Make yourself comfortable."

Danielle forced herself to smile again. "I'll be fine, Hannah. Don't worry and thank you."

"You're welcome."

Finally alone, Danielle, familiar with her surroundings made her way into the den. After shedding her leather coat, she went to stand by the fire. But she didn't tarry there long. Jumpy as a cat on a hot tin roof, she began pacing the floor.

What made her pause at the desk, she guessed she would never know for sure. Maybe it was the way the papers were strewn across the top that caught her attention. Or maybe it was the lawyers' names on one of the pages. Then before she realized what she was doing, her hand reached out and latched onto the top sheet. Her eyes began scanning the page, more for something to keep her mind occupied than anything else.

Suddenly, her face whitened as though she'd seen a ghost. "Oh, no!" she cried aloud, stunned, sinking trembling limbs into the nearest chair, still clutching the paper in her hand. *No, it can't be,* she told herself. Hannah Robbins had mentioned some legal dealings, but surely not this. Yet it was. It was there in black and white. Keir was going to try and take Ann away from her, after all. She had waited too long. Her stubbornness had killed his love. Surely, if he still loved her, he would not be doing this to her, to Ann.

Fool! You should have known. Life doesn't give third chances.

Frantically, she tried to stand. She had to leave, to get out of there before he came home. But her legs refused to cooperate. They were threatening to buckle beneath her. Trying again, she finally made it to her feet.

Then just as she took a tentative step forward, she heard the front door open and close. She stood helpless, unable to move, unable to speak.

"Danielle!"

He stepped closer as though he, too, had seen a ghost.

"Are you real?" he whispered. If possible, his eyes deepened in their sockets as his eyes dipped to the paper in her hand and the panicked expression on her face. "No," he groaned as though in agony, "it's not what you think. I'll admit I went so far as to contact a lawyer, but I never meant to go through with it," he added thickly. "I was planning to leave tonight for Texas to tell you that and to tell you . . ." He paused on a ragged note. "And to tell you that I can't live without you, no matter what."

Still Danielle could not say a word, but her mind was reeling. Had she really held this haggard-looking man in her arms? Had she really felt the walls of her heart ready to burst with the flood of love for him? She had tried to negotiate with the person in charge of the universe—plead if necessary—to get Keir back. And now she was hearing the words she had longed to hear. For a moment, she was afraid her heart would burst with happiness.

Looking at him now, with darkened eyes, she understood completely and forgave. Keir, she wanted to say, but her throat would not utter the sound. It was clogged with unshed tears.

Keir stared back at her, his face tormented. Then he put his arms around her, tightly, as though he would never let her go.

"Don't, my darling, don't," he whispered gently, lowering his cheek to her tumbled curls. "I'm . . . I'm so sorry," he moaned, kissing her neck.

She did not want to reason anymore. He was in her arms, and she was content to stand and hold him and hear his heart beating in her ears. No other emotion could equal her love.

"Love me," she whispered, meeting his eyes, touching the gaunt shadows in his face as if to prove to herself that he wasn't a mirage.

"I would never have tried to take Ann from you. Please . . . please believe me," he said brokenly, his mouth hovering above hers.

"I'm sorry, too, for so much," she whispered.

He closed his eyes, his mouth shaking. "Oh, God, Danielle, darling, I love you so much and want you so much. For a while there I didn't trust my ability to stay sane."

"Oh, Keir," she said, "I felt the same way. Nothing seemed to matter if I couldn't have you."

His hold tightened. "I know we need to talk, but I don't think I can." He groaned. "Right now, all I can think about is loving you, body and soul."

"Me too," she sighed, her lips probing his ear. "It's been too long."

She moved and he released her, watching her covetously.

With shaking hands, he began unzipping her dress. When she was standing in front of him in naked splendor, Keir did not move. His eyes roamed over her.

Then he began discarding his clothing. When he was naked at last, Danielle went sweetly into his arms and began kissing his face, his shoulders, his throat, moaning at the feel of his cool scented skin under her mouth.

Her soft hair spilled over the carpet as he lowered her gently onto it, his hands wooing a breast, meeting her mouth wildly, her arms wrapped around his neck, pulling him toward her.

"You are," he whispered into her mouth, "perfectly beautiful." Then his lips seared hers before moving lower to close over a nipple. Her fingers clutched at his hair while his bold lips and tongue paid homage to her swollen breasts.

Slipping away from him, she urged him onto his back and murmured, "Let me . . . love you." Her hand dipped down over his stomach to close around him.

"Oh, yes, yes," he said hoarsely, shutting his eyes, feeling the breath rush from his lungs in one sharp exhalation as she continued the gentle assault, her hands skimming down the length of his inner thigh. Hands pressed into her shoulder blades, but she was scarcely aware of his fingers digging into her flesh while her mouth, a moist flower, opened over him.

Because she was making him happy, she felt happy, incredibly happy. This was one time when there was no outside interference; there was only the two of them, heart to heart, skin against skin. And it was pure magic.

Keir could stand no more. He reached for her, cupping her chin, and kissed her mouth slowly, warmly. He gazed at her for a long moment, adoring the sight of her face, stretching to the limit the sweet pain churning inside him.

"Oh, God, Danielle, this is so right, so good," he whispered, effortlessly lifting and easing her gently onto him. "The feel of you when I'm inside you, the way you respond—it's perfect."

"My darling," she said incoherently, dying to know all of him, urging him in one desperate drive as far into her as it was possible for him to be.

Suddenly everything inside her was melting, drowning, giving way. She answered his throaty cry, racing headlong through glass walls that shattered one after the other as she reached that final, awesome, breath-taking splendor, drawing him with her into that perfect center.

"I love you. I love you." Her voice was a dazed whisper emerging from the depths of tranquility.

". . . I love you," she heard him say as she closed her eyes and with him still joined to her, fell into pure white silence.

"Wake up, sleepyhead," a voice murmured in the delicate folds of her ear. "Are you going to sleep all day?"

Languorously, Danielle stretched, then her eyes flew open. She looked around the room, realizing that she was in a bed, Keir's bed. Then, instantly, she remembered being carried to bed in his strong arms. She relaxed against him, snuggling against his body.

Keir moved heavily, stretching, then his eyes stared down into her flushed face. "My darling, my love," he said deeply.

As she watched his beloved face, a silence fell between them, while Danielle sought the words to tell him what was weighing heavily on her heart. "I . . . I just want you to know that it no longer matters to me what you do for a living," she said. "I'll support you one hundred percent, even if you're gone five days out of seven, or even if it means becoming a senator's wife," she added with a smile.

"Oh, my darling, you're priceless," he said, peering

down at her, worshiping her with his eyes. "And you don't know how much your saying that means to me. But I too have a confession to make. I had just come back from Cassidy's office, having told him I wanted a desk job, effective immediately."

Danielle gasped, causing him to pause with a sweet smile.

"That's right, my darling, I'm through trotting the globe, as you so aptly put it. I'm a changed man. Can you ever forgive me for being such a headstrong and selfish bastard, demanding you give up everything, but not willing to make any sacrifices myself? Life wasn't worth living without you."

"We're so lucky," she whispered, "to have been given a third chance."

"Marry me."

"Whatever you say."

Suddenly his face clouded again. "Would you mind very much living in D.C. part of the year, since my office is here? Maybe you could open up a bookstore here. I know how much your work means to you."

"We'll see, my love," she said. "But right now all I want is to be with you, no matter where it is."

Before he could say another word, Danielle locked her arms around his neck and kissed him, her lips filled with love and promise.

A long silence followed.

Giddy and drunk on love, they pulled apart. Danielle was the first to speak, wanting to be rid of any and all ghosts that lurked in their past.

"You have your daughter to thank for my being here, you know."

"Oh, really. Well, I can tell you that I was never so shocked in my life as when I walked into the room and there you were. But I didn't care why or how, only that you were and that I'd get another chance."

"Ann wanted to know why you couldn't be her

daddy," Danielle said soberly. "It was then that I realized what I was doing to Ann, to you, and to myself."

For a moment, Keir was speechless as tears gathered on his thick lashes. "Remind me . . ."—he paused and cleared his throat—"to thank my daughter properly when we get home."

"Home," Danielle murmured, her lips against his neck, his arms around her. "That's the most beautiful word in the English language."

"Home, my darling, is where the heart is," he pledged softly, "and my heart is yours forever."

Silhouette
Intimate Moments

more romance, more excitement

───────────── **$2.25 each** ─────────────

Silhouette
Intimate 🖤 _Moments_

more romance, more excitement

SILHOUETTE INTIMATE MOMENTS, Department IM/5
1230 Avenue of the Americas, New York, NY 10020

Please send me the books I have checked above. I am enclosing
$_____ (please add 75¢ to cover postage and handling. NYS and
NYC residents please add appropriate sales tax). Send check or money
order—no cash or C.O.D.'s please. Allow six weeks for delivery.

NAME _____

ADDRESS _____

CITY _____ STATE/ZIP _____

Silhouette Intimate Moments

Coming Next Month

SPINSTER'S SONG
by Parris Afton Bonds

•

THE SWEET RUSH OF APRIL
by Linda Shaw

•

GYPSY WIND
by Lisa Jackson

•

VARIATION ON A THEME
by Billie Douglass